the art of not breathing

sarah alexander

USBORNE

D

I need to talk to you about what happened that day.
I'll be at the Point tomorrow at 6. Please come.

Part One

ELSIE: *Why did the lobster* blush?

EDDIE: *I don't know.*

ELSIE: *Because the* seaweed!

One

THE THING I HATE MOST about my father is that he hates me.

And he has good reason to.

It's something we don't talk about.

He has pale blue, cold eyes that are one minute full of hate, the next full of so much sadness that I pity him. And I can't stand to feel sorry for him. When I look at him I get this sensation in my throat that feels as though maggots are crawling about in there. The only way to get rid of the itching is to hold my breath and swallow until I almost pass out. The best thing to do is not look at his face or eyes, or better still not look at him at all.

Fortunately, he's hardly ever home. He's either out running so that the village women can drool over his "chiselled jaw", or he's at the bank where he works in Inverness, or travelling about Scotland selling loans. You'd think he loved his job, the amount of time he spends doing it, but he grumbles that his clients only care about cars or TVs and not about the terrible wars and disasters that happen around the world. "Never mind the rain on the Black Isle," he says. "What about remote villages that flood every year?" Or, "Thousands of people die *every day* from mosquito bites in some countries." He says this one a lot when it's midge season here and I'm complaining about them. (The midges love my blood.)

My mum tells him, "Do let us know when you've found a cure for malaria, Colin. In the meantime, your son needs study books for his exams and your daughter has grown out of another school uniform." I wish she didn't use my weight as a way of getting his attention. Why can't she say the gas bill needs paying or the damp in my room wants sorting?

In the drawer by his bed is an atlas covered in ink; the blue dots places he's been to, the red ones places he's desperate to go. There's a massive red dot on Australia – he pressed the pen so hard there's ink on the next page, right in the middle of the Pacific Ocean. He nearly made it to Australia once, when he was twenty and had a job as a singer on a cruise ship. When we kids were small he told us bedtime stories about his travels, his voice smooth and soft like melted chocolate. His favourite story was the one about the port in Jakarta. The weather was thundery and the cruise ship had just left the port, next stop Australia, when he received the call to say that Dillon, my older brother, had been born. He used to say, "I was so surprised, I nearly fell overboard, but then I jumped off anyway and swam to shore."

Mum says this isn't true, that he wanted to stay on the ship. I often wonder what life would be like if he had stayed on that ship. Or if he'd actually fallen overboard.

I've picked up a few snippets about my parents' life before I was born, mostly from Granny before she died (and before she fell out with Mum). My parents moved into our house on McKellen Drive, the cheapest house in Fortrose – and probably on the whole of the Black Isle – when Dillon was a few months old. It was cheap because the walls were crumbling and it backed onto a cemetery. My father wanted to work on the ship for a few more months so they could afford to move to Inverness, but Mum wouldn't let him go away again. She didn't think he'd come back.

Instead, he tried to make money by singing in pubs around Inverness. The house never got fixed and the bills never got paid.

When yet another FINAL WARNING arrived in the post and Mum was hormonal and pregnant again, she marched my father to the nearest bank and made him fill in an application form to be a bank clerk. (This is how *he* describes it.) When he'd finally made enough money, we packed up ready to move to the city. We kids had a box each with our names on, full of our clothes and toys. But then everything changed.

My brother disappeared.

"How can I leave all these people," Mum said, staring out of my bedroom window at the headstones in the cemetery on the day we were supposed to move, "when my son is one of them?"

It wasn't strictly true – there's a headstone with his name on it but my brother isn't buried anywhere.

We didn't unpack his box. Mum taped it up good and proper so nothing could fall out. I think about his toys in the loft sometimes: a grey furry dolphin called Gordon that my father bought for him after he'd had a tantrum at the Dolphin and Seal Centre; a wooden xylophone; an Etch-a-Sketch with his name on it in wonky black lines – he would cry if it got scrubbed off; handfuls of pine needles that he'd collected (the dead ones because they were softer than the spiky green ones – they've probably turned into compost now). I try not to think of his clothes, all folded up, damp and creased. It just reminds me that he's not in them.

Instead, I imagine my own clothes all folded up. One day, I suppose someone else will have to try not to think about that.

Two

ON SUNDAY MORNING, DILLON IS hogging the bathroom. The tap's running but I can still hear the disgusting noises. He's always been a bathroom-hogger, but he spends even more time in there now he's got a girlfriend.

I pound on the door and give it a kick for good measure.

"Just a minute," he yells.

He sounds as though he's holding a boiled sweet inside his cheek, his voice strained and muffled.

"Hurry up, Dillon. I need to pee!" I shout through the door.

Mum leans on the banister at the end of the landing, glancing down the stairs, watching out for my father coming home from yet another "work trip".

She asks me if I've done my homework and I lie and say I did it all yesterday. She raises one eyebrow at me and scratches her head.

If I don't do my homework, she often tells me, I won't pass my exams and I'll end up being a receptionist like her. But I wouldn't mind being a receptionist because you just sit all day.

"Think of your exams, Elsie," she says. "Dillon will get all As for his Advanced Highers."

Dillon's got two years on me and he's a complete brainbox, so it's not really fair to compare us. I'm already a school year behind because of my Laryngitis Year and I'm only taking half the exams I'm meant to be taking – the school thought I "needed more time". Dillon's a year behind too because he also lost his voice, but he's making up for it by taking extra exams. He likes to be the best at everything, whereas I take pride in being the worst.

Dillon eventually emerges from the bathroom with bloodshot eyes.

"What were you doing in there?" I hiss.

He ignores me and disappears into his bedroom.

There's something that looks like a piece of spaghetti in the toilet. Mum calls to Dillon but he doesn't answer. I flush the toilet to drown out his silence, then turn to the mirror.

Unfortunately, my father didn't pass his good looks onto me. I got my mother's dark, wild curly hair and green eyes, which I don't mind too much, but I didn't get her petite figure, dainty nose or perfect skin. My face is blotchy and my double chin grows by the day. I tried losing weight once but the more my mum commented on what I was eating, the more I wanted to eat. I'm hungry just thinking about it.

Ruby Red is the colour of my lipstick today – stolen from Superdrug along with a packet of condoms, which I might put in Dillon's pocket as a joke, and some hairspray. The lipstick feels silky smooth on my lips as I apply it and it glues the chapped bits of skin back down. I don't blot with a tissue like Mum does. I like it when the red comes off on my cigarettes.

When I come out of the bathroom, Mum is sitting halfway down the stairs with her chin in her hands. I prod her shoulder and she slowly turns around as though she has no idea who might be behind her.

"Your father is on his way. As soon as he's back we're all going to the supermarket."

She doesn't move so I climb over her to get downstairs.

No matter how carefully and quietly I try to open the fridge, it always makes a loud suction sound.

"Elsie!"

"I'm just getting a drink," I call back, reaching for a Coke. I take a few slices of ham and throw them into my mouth before anyone comes in, careful not to wipe my lipstick off. Mum says I eat her out of house and home but this isn't true because my father pays for the food and Dillon eats like a baby sparrow, so I'm entitled to his share. Anyway, I do most of the cooking, so it's fair payment.

"A watched door never opens," I say as I climb back over her.

But then we hear the keys jangling. Neither of us goes to open the door so my father is surprised to find us staring at him from the stairs. He looks as though he's been up for days.

"I'm back," he says, as if for some reason we couldn't see this.

Three

THE SUPERMARKET IS COLD AND I've got my arms inside
my orange raincoat so that the sleeves hang lifelessly by my
side. Dillon trails behind me with his hands in his pockets,
looking embarrassed to be seen with us. I get an urge to do
my zombie impression. Twisting at the waist, making the
sleeves swish about, I stagger towards him with my mouth
open and eyes rolling around in my head.

Dillon raises his eyebrows and shuffles close enough to
whisper, "What are you doing? You look like you should be
in a mental hospital."

"You should see yourself," I reply, slipping my arms back
into the sleeves.

"Have you forgotten why we're here? You're going to really piss them off."

It's impossible to forget. Especially because it's my fault we have to go through this.

"Course not. But zombies don't like miseries. If you don't cheer up they'll get you." I roll my eyes back again and hang my tongue out. As I lurch into him, a very convincing zombie-like groan escapes from my mouth.

Dillon smiles. A tiny sideways smile, but it's there.

Then my father picks up some chocolate fingers and Mum freaks out.

"He hates those, Colin," she says, loud enough that people turn and stare at us. I look at Dillon. He shakes his head and pretends to read a label on the shelf behind.

"Well, he won't have to eat them," my father mutters.

"That's not the point!"

When my father puts the biscuits in the trolley anyway, Mum whimpers and pulls her hair, her fingers working through her curls like hungry little worms.

"Why are you being so insensitive?" she says, spitting the words out.

My father stands quietly, looking around, shaking his head. I'm not going to help him out; he *is* being insensitive. He steps back as Mum starts hurling packets of biscuits at his feet. We seem to have taken over the snacks aisle and there's a crowd of people at one end watching us. Two of them I recognize from school so I hide behind a trolley filled with Jaffa Cakes. I think about doing my zombie impression to distract them from my parents' argument but I'm stuck to the floor with shame. Dillon is still reading the label on the shelf but it's obvious he's pretending because even from here I can see it says OUT OF STOCK in big red letters.

Mum starts on the pink wafers.

"Celia," my father cries, jumping out of the way, "we're going home."

He slams the trolley against the shelf and walks off. The shelf wobbles and packets of Bourbons tumble into the trolley. When everyone else has run after my father, I unzip my jacket a little way and slide one of the packets inside so it sits neatly under my arm. Then I scoot to the next aisle where the party bits are and grab some candles. They're the flimsy ones that go in cakes, but they'll do. At least we'll have something for tomorrow.

The wait is like listening to a ticking bomb. The closer the day gets, the louder the ticking; the louder the ticking, the more my parents shout; the more my parents shout, the more I want to get in a car and run my father over.

I catch up with them as they're leaving the supermarket. Dillon walks by Dad's side and brushes Mum away when she goes to him. He always defends my father – sucking up, is the term I'd use. I don't know why, because Dad's so hard on him. He goes on at Dillon all the time about getting good grades and makes him sit in the kitchen revising if he gets a low mark. I get shouted at and banned from going out, but my father never actually makes me do my homework – he knows I'm a lost cause. For that, at least, I'm grateful.

I start on the Bourbons before we've even left the car park. No one says anything. Eventually I offer them around.

"Did you pay for those?" my father asks. In the rear-view mirror I see his nostrils flare.

I shake my head.

"For Christ's sake, Elsie. Do you want to end up in a detention centre? Because you're going the right way about it. They've got CCTV, you know?"

I do know this because I've been dragged into a back office and shown footage of myself trying to get a packet of noodles into my coat pocket. I don't know why noodles. At the time it seemed like something that might be useful.

"You can go back and pay for them if you're that worried."

My father accelerates, and when we get home he grabs the packet from me and chucks it in the dustbin. Mum doesn't defend me like she usually does. She's distracted with everything else. With tomorrow.

Four

APRIL 11TH. MONDAY. MY BIRTHDAY. School starts again today after the Easter break, but I'm not going in. Today I am exempt from school.

The sky is still a smoky black when I get dressed. I think I'm the first up but then I hear the sounds of the others – my parents moving around their bedroom, the wardrobe door sliding open and closed, my mother's hairdryer, my father's electric razor. The squirt of an aerosol, one long spray followed by two short ones, then a gap and another short one. I hear the groan of the electric shower in the bathroom as it starts up and then the running water which lulls every now and then because the pressure is bad. A dry cough from Dillon's room. There are no voices. I wonder how loud it might be if we could all hear each other's thoughts. It would be unbearable, I decide.

One hour until we leave. It zooms by, like a time-lapse video – the black outside turns to blue-grey, to violet-grey, pinky-grey and finally it's just grey, like pencil lead. I use a pocket mirror to apply my Ruby Red (it is, after all, a "special day"!), then climb back under my duvet and wait. In the mirror, I watch my lips whisper the words, "Eddie. Do you miss me? I miss you!"

My father finally knocks on my door and opens it slightly. Half a face appears, and then his whole body slides into my room.

"Are you ready?"

His voice is even, like he's bored. I nod without looking at him. I can't bear to see his eyes. Not today. He turns and leaves.

I chew a Wrigley's Extra because if I clean my teeth I'll mess up the lipstick.

Downstairs I find Dillon pacing up and down in the living room.

"What are you doing?"

"Nothing," he says, hugging his arms around his waif-like body. "Just waiting."

We pace in opposite directions, meeting in the middle on each length, occasionally brushing shoulders. My father waits in the hallway with his arms hanging slack by his sides. The silence continues, aside from the gurgling fridge, and my rumbling stomach.

Mum is the last to appear. She always wears the same outfit on this day: white jeans and a tight white T-shirt with nothing over the top, as though it were the middle of summer. She moves like a ghost through the hallway to the front door. In one fluid movement she takes the car keys from the hall table, passes them to my father, opens the front door and drapes her blue raincoat over her shoulders. We all follow in single file to the car, the glass in the front door rattling as we close it behind us. We drive in deafening silence to Chanonry Point. The drive is only five minutes – we could walk, but we never do. I think it's so we can make a quick getaway.

No one says "Happy birthday, Elsie". I say it to myself instead and picture a birthday sometime in the future when I get cards, presents and cake made of doughnuts.

Five

THE BLACK ISLE ISN'T REALLY an island – it's a peninsula that sticks out from Inverness into the North Sea. It's called the Black Isle because when the rest of Scotland is coated in snow, it remains uncovered, someone once told me. We seem to have our own weather system, which mostly involves bitterly cold winds, rain and fog. We do have the occasional blizzard, though. Chanonry Point is a spit of land on the east of the Isle which extends even further out into the choppy water. Sometimes it feels as though we're on the edge of the world.

We park up and tumble out of the car like lemmings going over a cliff. The sky is a hazy white now and the cold wind pushes the clouds out over the North Sea. As we navigate our way around the lighthouse and along the shingle beach, patches of pale blue sky appear for a few seconds at a time before disappearing again. Mum's faded blue jacket clashes with my father's brown woolly jumper as they walk side by side, stepping in unison, having forgiven each other for the biscuit episode. Mum leans into my father as though she couldn't walk without him.

Dillon and I walk a few paces behind them, Dillon's arm around my shoulders. I feel him shivering beside me and think about squeezing his hand or wrapping an arm around him but I don't. I have to take three steps for every two of Dillon's and we collide awkwardly against each other but neither of us does anything about it. His head is turned to the shore, towards the dolphins splashing about in the froth. They leap high into the air and glide back down into the water effortlessly. Watching them makes my heart expand in my chest.

Eddie loved the dolphins. He called them *fins* and even though I could say the word properly I used to call them *fins* too. I don't mind dolphins but I prefer otters because they're not as common. They're secretive creatures and I read that even though the males and females have their own territories in the water, those territories sometimes overlap. Dillon and I are like otters. We have our own spaces – I like to think of them as sandy coves – but on the edge of mine and on the edge of his, there's a little patch where we can be together and everything is okay. It's a place where we don't fight or pretend not to know each other. I worry that our patch is getting smaller though, like the tide is coming in, or maybe there are more rocks now taking over the sandy bits. I suppose otters need rocks to hide amongst.

We head up from the beach onto the grassy bank. Halfway up the slope, there's a wooden cross in the ground. My father ties a white ribbon around the cross – yanking the ends to make sure it's secure. There should be five, one for every year that's passed, but one must have flown off because I only count four. My father runs his hand over the wood and brushes sand and dirt from the engraving. I read it, even though I know what it says. My nose is streaming from the bitter wind. It's weird reading a memorial with my own birthday on it.

EDWARD MAIN
11TH APRIL 2000 – 11TH APRIL 2011

Today, we are sixteen. Happy birthday, Eddie.

It still doesn't feel real. To me, he's not gone. My twin lives inside my head and is part of me. The other day, when I wondered whether I should have a second helping of tatties, he popped up and said, *You can never have too many tatties. Finish the bowl!* Sometimes, my hands and feet get extremely cold and I know it's not me feeling cold, it's Eddie, so I wrap myself up in a blanket to make sure he's okay. I give him cocoa before bed and toast with Marmite, even though I can't stand Marmite. I suppose I eat for two.

Last week after I'd wrapped us up together on the sofa, Mum looked worried and took my temperature.

"You're burning up," she said, frowning.

"He's cold," I said by mistake.

"What?"

"I'm cold."

I got away with it because she was distracted by something in the kitchen.

I haven't told anyone that Eddie is inside me.

I'm pretty good at keeping secrets.

Mum sinks slowly into the grass and hugs her knees to her chest, burying her head between them. I'm not sure if she's shivering or crying. Dad strokes her back but looks at me and his eyes are small and droopy. Dillon tries to light a candle then gives up and pushes it down into the earth. I can barely feel my toes and have to jiggle to warm up. I run the ribbons through my fingers, feeling the smooth side and then the rough side until my father tells me to stop.

"Please don't do that, Elsie. Stop fidgeting."

I stop and take a deep breath and look at the cross. Now for the words I practised.

"Hey, bro!" I say, loudly. "Let's play chase. Bet you canny catch me!" I throw my arm out ready to high-five him. But even before I feel Eddie reach out to smack my hand, I know I have made an error. Mum pulls her head out from between her knees and stares at me open-mouthed. My father's eyebrows move up and down as though they don't know where on his face they should be. His arm shoots out towards me but then he snaps it back. He was about to slap me, I'm sure of it.

"What on earth are you doing?" he shouts.

Dillon takes my hand and I try to remember the words but my mind is blank.

"I thought he might like to play a game," I stammer.

My father leans towards me. "Are you not taking this seriously? Are you on drugs or something?"

"I just thought we could be happy today," I continue, even though I know I should stop now.

I look to Mum for help. Mascara runs down her cheeks, little black snakes edging towards her lips. My father turns to Dillon.

"Has she taken something?"

Dillon shakes his head. I will him to defend me. But he says nothing.

"I meant that we should celebrate his life. He doesn't like it when we cry."

Another slip-up. I need to be more careful. It's difficult

because Eddie's been with me a lot more recently and he shows up without warning. Ever since Granny died a few months ago. I think he's worried that I'm going to disappear too.

"Elsie, that's enough," my father says, his eyebrows now settled in a frown.

Mum remains silent. All vacant and starey. She's been like this even more than usual since Granny died. I try not to imagine what it would be like if *my* mum died.

"I want to remember when he was…" I want to say "alive" but that's not right because to me, he still is. "When he was…Eddie." The real Eddie. My twin brother.

"I said that's enough. You're upsetting your mother. This is meant to be a quiet time, so we can take a few minutes and remember him. It's about being respectful."

Mum rocks slowly back and forth, watching, crying.

"I am being respectful," I say. "I don't need to take a few minutes to remember him, because *I* haven't forgotten him."

It's out before I can stop myself. And worse than that, it might not be true. There are no pictures at home, they're all in the loft. So there are things that I *am* forgetting, like which side of his head had the curl that went the wrong way, or whether he ate everything green on his plate first or everything red. The memories are slipping away. Eddie might be right – we're sliding further apart from each other. I'm sixteen now, nearly an adult, and Eddie will always be a small, eleven-year-old boy.

"If you can't be sensible, go to the car," my father says.

I fight the urge to run away, because I know that's what they want. It would make today easier for everyone if I weren't here. But I'm not going. Why should I make it easy for them when it's so hard for me?

"I'm staying," I say, and now my tears come.

We sit in silence, apart from a few loud sobs from me. Dillon watches the dolphins and my father leans over the candle and manages to light it. The flame flickers a golden yellow for a few seconds, then dies. The smoke instantly vanishes in the wind.

The ground below us vibrates and I turn to the beach where a digger rearranges the pebbles, pushing them back up away from the shoreline, creating a steep slope.

Suddenly the scene in front of me jolts and blurs, the ground zooms up towards me and I grab the grass for balance. There's a roaring in my ears, and I get fragments of images: frothing white water; an orange high-vis jacket in the distance; Mum draped over the shoulder of a policeman; my father running towards me – brown shoes slipping on the stones. Then my father disappears, and I'm completely alone on the beach. More fragments. Dillon's face – red and angry; Mum's white top; my father holding something blue – a bit of material that flaps in the wind. The roar gets louder, like a gust of wind wrapping itself around my head; I choke as I try to get air into my lungs. Everything goes hazy and blue. I taste salt, then my body runs out of oxygen.

"Elsie."

My father's voice filters through the roar.

"Elsie, let's go, it's getting a bit gusty."

I open my eyes, gasping. I'm back on the grass and the images have gone. No one seems to have noticed the roaring or my choking. Dillon is already on his feet, moving towards my father.

"Sleep tight, Edward," my father says. Mum says it too but I only hear the first word, and then her lips move silently.

But Eddie is not asleep. He is stomping about on the grass, chasing after me, trying to slap my hands but missing. I let him have one for free and he jumps into the air and squeals before tripping over.

It's not that I can see him, exactly. I just feel him.

Two dolphins glide past. I can't see which ones they are from here, but I like to think they're Mischief and Sundance – Eddie's favourites, because he got to stroke them once.

I try to get Dillon's attention but he's looking at the water. I wonder if he's thinking the same as me: if only he hadn't left me with Eddie. If only I had looked after Eddie like I was supposed to.

"The fins are out today, Eddie," I whisper.

* * *

Later, Mum comes into my room to wish me happy birthday.

"I'm sorry we didn't do a big thing with presents. I tried but I don't even know what he's into any more. He's probably outgrown Lego by now."

"Really?" I ask. Maybe she felt him earlier too. Excitement bubbles up under my skin. "He still loves Lego," I whisper. "Especially boats."

Mum gasps and her arms twitch. I think she's about to hug me, but then she stiffens and shakes her head.

She strokes my hair instead and says, "We shouldn't do this. We shouldn't pretend he's still here."

I shiver as she continues to stroke my hair. I'm not sure what she means by pretending. Just because we can't see him doesn't mean we shouldn't talk about him, or think about what he likes. We can't simply forget he ever existed.

"I forget sometimes," she says quietly. "Like, first thing in the morning, or when I'm out food shopping. Then it really hurts when I remember."

"But do you *feel* him?" I ask.

"Yes, of course," she replies. "Sometimes." She frowns and looks around the room, uncertain. "Elsie, you don't believe in ghosts, do you?"

"No."

33

She doesn't seem to get what I mean about feeling him. It must be a twin thing. Something I'm not meant to share with anyone else.

"Well, good," she says. "Anyway, how about we celebrate your birthday next week? We could go out for a meal, the four of us. I saved some money especially."

"Sure," I say, disappointed that she doesn't want to talk about Eddie any longer. And I'm not holding out any hope for the supposed birthday meal – she says the same thing every year and it never happens.

"I did get you something small but don't tell your dad. You know what he's like."

She hands me a parcel wrapped in recycled Christmas paper. I can already tell it's clothes.

"I'll leave you to open it," she says. "And there's a card from Dillon, too."

She pulls an envelope from her back pocket. I guess Dillon's too scared to give it to me personally because he knows he should have stuck up for me when we were down at the Point.

When Mum's gone, I open the envelope first. On the front of the card is a chocolate cake with sixteen brightly-coloured candles. It's signed from Dillon and Eddie. Dillon's even tried to mimic Eddie's straggly writing. Dillon does this pretending thing, too. Sometimes I feel like we're in a parallel world where Eddie is still here, but at the flick of a switch we can be back in reality and he's gone. Those days are the worst.

The present from Mum is a teeny, lacy, black crop top. I'd be lucky to get it over my head, and even if I could I'd then struggle to fit my arms through the flimsy sleeves. I'm about to put it in the bin, but then remember Mum will want to borrow it one day. Last year's present was clip-on hair extensions – as if I needed any more hair. I got Dillon to give them to the sister of one of his friends.

Eddie would have worn the crop top and the hair extensions just to make Mum laugh. My ribcage shudders. It feels like Eddie is trying to get out.

Six

EDDIE LOVED BEING BURIED ALMOST as much as he loved dolphins. The doctors told Mum and Dad that physical activity would help his development. They encouraged us to let him touch everything, show him all the different textures. He always wanted to dig holes or build things. Mum used to collect cardboard boxes and plastic tubs from deliveries at work and bring them home for him to play with.

When we were about seven, Mum came home with a really big box and some red paint. Eddie actually wet himself when he saw the box. He wanted to get into it straight away.

Dad told us a story about the miners who live underground in the Australian outback.

"It's so hot there that you can cook sausages on the ground in just a few seconds. It's too hot to live in normal houses so you have to live underground. When it's hot, you have to say, 'It's a real sizzler.'"

"Wow!" Eddie squealed. "I want to be underground in 'Straya."

We painted the box an earthy red and while we waited for it to dry Dillon taught Eddie how to do an Australian accent.

"That's a bonzer steak you got on the barbie," Dillon said as he flipped the plastic burgers from Eddie's toy barbecue set.

"Bonzer," Eddie said, as he stamped on one of the burgers and split it open.

Dad and I glued it back together with some old UHU glue we found in the kitchen drawer. Dad loved fixing all the small things – maybe it was his way of making up for not fixing our falling-apart house.

When the box was dry, Eddie climbed underneath it, but even though there was room for me too, he wouldn't let me in.

"You're 'llowed to go to proper school," he said. "All I have is my underground house in 'Straya."

I was mad with him and called him a selfish shellfish.

"I hate you," he whispered through the air hole that Dad had made on one side. He stayed under the box for hours. I think he must've fallen asleep because later he yelled for me.

"Ellie, let me out!" he cried. "Ellie, I can't breathe."

I picture Eddie at sixteen, still calling me "Ellie", still small, still clumsy. He's at the school gate getting bullied. The younger boys, who are bigger than him, push him and steal his lunch money and I rush to save him. I thump one of them in the face and give him a nosebleed, then take Eddie home as he cries.

Shame washes over me. If he were here, and that happened, would I really save him?

Seven

I MEET DILLON ON THE stairs in the morning as we get ready for our first day back at school. His newly short blond hair is gelled at the front and spiked up – a style he's been experimenting with since he got together with Lara, this girl in my year. I used to quite like Lara – she once shared all of her stationery with me when my school bag went missing (I found it later shoved behind the bike sheds). But this year she's become friends with the handbag girls, and more importantly, she's got particularly close to my nemesis – Ailsa Fitzgerald. Dillon knows all of this, but he doesn't seem to care that I don't approve of his choice.

The spiked-up style doesn't suit him. I liked it better

when his hair was long and floppy and hung over his eyes a bit. He's wearing a light blue shirt, even though the S6s don't have to be smart. I feel slightly ashamed of the way I look. My trousers are too tight around my backside, my socks are always on show, the button across my chest is about to pop off. I don't think my uniform will last another week, let alone another year – I wish S4s didn't have to wear uniforms.

"Thanks for the card, Dil."

I try to sound chipper even though it made me feel really sad and I spent the whole night pressing the knot in my stomach.

He shrugs. "Hurry up. We'll be late."

He's always grumpy in the morning.

"You can go ahead without me," I say.

Dillon thinks life is a race but I don't see the need for getting anywhere on time. It just means spending more time in places you don't want to be. If life does turn out to be a race, I'm way behind, especially when it comes to school.

He waits though, looking at his watch anxiously. When I'm at the top of the stairs I turn around and catch him frowning in the hall mirror. He pulls his shoulders back and sucks in his non-existent stomach. He is so vain about his looks. He gets it from Mum.

Mum hands us each our packed lunch as we leave.

"Be good," she says.

I wonder whether I should stay home with her but my feet are carrying me out the door.

When we're far enough away, Dillon takes his foil-wrapped sandwich and chucks it in the hedge.

"Why did you do that?"

"Because they're disgusting," he says and pretends to heave. "I hate tomatoes."

"Why do you lie so much? Don't you feel bad about throwing them away?"

"Why do you ask so many questions?"

Dillon never answers my questions. I don't expect him to any more.

"Want one?" I say, holding out my packet of cigarettes while I scrabble in my pocket for a lighter.

"Where'd you get those? Dad'll kill you if he finds out."

"Screw Dad! He'd be more annoyed about you wasting food when there are so many starving children."

Dillon doesn't reply but he helps himself to a cigarette and waits for the lighter.

"Where do you think he goes?" Dillon asks. "You know, when he leaves the house in the evenings and doesn't come back for ages. There's no way that he could run for four or five hours."

"I know *exactly* where he goes." I take Dillon's cigarette

from him and light mine and his at the same time, like I've been doing it for years, then pass his back. Smoking is my new hobby.

Dillon turns to me, holding his burning cigarette away from himself. "Where does he go, then?"

I notice a snag in my trousers and it turns into a hole when I inspect it, revealing my pale knee underneath.

"Nowhere. He just sits on a bench near the woods – by the duck pond."

"Do you spy on everyone?"

"Aye."

Dillon chokes on the smoke and pretends that he needed to cough anyway.

"You shouldn't provoke him," he says.

"Why do you always stick up for him? Are you scared of him or something?"

"No. I just think you could cut him some slack."

"He could cut me some slack, especially on my birthday. Moping isn't going to help Eddie, is it?"

Dillon flinches. We talk about most things but we never talk about Eddie in public.

"Did you think about it yesterday?" I ask quietly.

"Think about what?"

"You know. That day."

Dillon goes quiet and I use the pause to smoke as much as I can.

"I thought about the day he chased after that dog," he says eventually.

The memory makes me smile. The dog bolting out of the hedge with Eddie still hanging onto the lead and the owner going nuts.

"See? That's a happy memory. You should've told that story yesterday. That's what we should do from now on. We should tell funny Eddie stories. Like that time he got a pea stuck up each nostril."

"That was your fault. He was copying you."

"I know. But it was a hoot, though. At least until we had to go to hospital."

We both giggle, but the image of Eddie with peas up his nose suddenly becomes too sad to bear.

"Dil, can I ask you a serious question?"

"Okay. But I might not answer. Especially if you're going to ask me if I'm sad, because I'm fine."

Dillon never admits when he feels sad. He always says he's "fine".

"No, a different question." I lower my voice in case anyone is listening. "Have you ever had a flashback?"

"A what?"

"A flashback," I repeat, louder. A bunch of S1s knock us out of the way to get past.

Dillon's mouth hangs open for a second, the same way Mum's does when she doesn't want to answer.

"I don't know what you—"

"Hey, knobhead!"

Dillon's friends are across the road, waving like lunatics. Even though Dillon's a brainbox he's still in with the popular crowd. He has tons of friends at school. I don't even know most of their names because they call each other by weird nicknames, or insults like *bender* or *knobhead*.

The boy calling him is very tall with spiked-up black hair. He always wears white Adidas trainers, even though no one is supposed to wear trainers to school.

"Dilmeister! Come on," the boy shouts.

"I'll see you later, okay?" Dillon says to me.

He waits for a car to pass then runs across the road. The boy with the Adidas trainers waves at me. I think Dillon must've told them to be nice to me. I wave back then shove my hand in my pocket and look at the ground.

Now I'm alone, I'm at the mercy of the handbag girls. These are the girls who carry handbags to school instead of rucksacks. I don't know where they put their books. When I'm with Dillon they don't pester me, but when I'm on my own they close in, commenting on the way my hair hangs or the tightness of my trousers. The leader of the handbag girls is Ailsa Fitzgerald. Ailsa is mean to nearly everyone but I'm her favourite target, ever since the day we first met and a boy from another class pushed her into the school pond. I wanted to help, I tried to, but I was afraid of falling in and being sucked under. I couldn't even speak because of my Laryngitis. I ran to get a teacher instead but, by the time I returned, half the school had seen her covered in pond slime. She's been punishing me ever since, mocking my cowardice and silence that day.

Ailsa slams into me, nearly knocking me into the road.

"Ergh, you're still here. We all hoped you'd died over the holidays," she says.

I walk on. Sometimes I do wish I were dead but then who would look after Eddie?

Eight

FORTROSE IS THE BIGGEST TOWN on the Black Isle, but it's still small. It doesn't even have a cinema or a bowling alley. The high street wiggles through the middle of it with poky shops crammed next to each other, selling buckets and spades in the summer and umbrellas in the winter. The only useful shops are Superdrug, Co-op and the bakery.

The people here like to know everything about everyone. Nearly everyone in Fortrose knows who I am.

"You're Elsie Main, right?" they ask. "You're Colin's wee one."

My father knows a lot of people, women mostly.

Sometimes I lie and tell them they must be mistaken

but they just tilt their heads in sympathy.

Despite being poky and full of busybodies, Fortrose does have plenty of places to hide. On one side of the town is Rosemarkie beach, where jagged rocks line the coast, and the otters hang out. On the other side, there's a small harbour hidden from the main road, where a handful of fishing boats are moored. Dillon and I aren't supposed to go near the water unsupervised – at least, we never used to be allowed. Sometimes I think the rule doesn't stand any more because Mum and Dad don't say much, but then every now and then one of them will freak out if we're home late and accuse us of going swimming. It's an insane rule anyway, because how can we not go near the water – we're surrounded by it. I have my own rule: it's okay to go near the water; just don't go in it.

Dillon goes off with Lara after school, probably to avoid my questions, so I head straight to the harbour – and the boathouse. Set back against the trees that shade the narrow pebble beach, the boathouse is a tall wooden structure with big arched red-painted doors and a corrugated iron roof. Right next to the boathouse is a rickety old clubhouse on wooden stilts that used to belong to the sailing club. The sailing club moved to the shiny new harbour in Inverness a few years ago, so now the clubhouse is all boarded up and the boathouse is no longer in use. This is my secret hiding place.

As I walk along the beach a seagull nearly flies into me, making me turn towards the water.

That's when I see the boat.

It's a small one with a loud jittery engine, which chucks out a plume of black smoke as the boat pulls up to the harbour wall alongside the other fishing boats. There are four boys in it, joking around, shoving each other. They're older than me, maybe seventeen or eighteen. I sit on a bench and pretend to gaze out to sea. Three of the boys are wearing what I first think are leggings, but then notice are actually wetsuits with the arms dangling down like extra legs. One of the boys is bare-chested and even from here I can see he's muscly. Two are wearing T-shirts and a fourth boy is dressed in black from head to toe; black jeans, a thick hoody and sunglasses. They all seem to be experiencing different weather conditions. They clamber up onto the stone jetty via a rusty ladder bolted to the wall. The boy at the front, in the hoody, carries a heavy-looking bag over his shoulder, and two pairs of flippers. Their laughter carries out into the dusky evening and I feel sad that I don't have a group of friends to hang out with. Hoody boy looks in my direction, and I turn away. When they have their backs to me, I crouch down under the clubhouse and crawl across litter and pebbles to the loose panel in the side of the boathouse. It's just big enough for me to squeeze through.

Inside the boathouse, there's one boat – a mouldy kayak that must have been orange once but is now a peachy-white colour. The kayak sits near the arched doors as though it can't wait to get back in the water. The rest of the boathouse is empty, with wooden beams across the walls and ceiling where I suppose other kayaks used to hang.

It's dark inside today but the afternoon light pushes through the cracks in the front door, making pale triangles of yellow on the floor. It smells musty too, like old wood and moss, but over the last couple of months I've made it quite homely – with blankets on the floor and one to wrap around me when it's cold like today. There's a small cupboard that I found discarded on the beach one day and managed to drag inside. This is where I keep my stash – Coke, sweets, matches, cigarettes (if I have any), pens, paper and playing cards. I play solitaire if I'm bored, but mostly I sit and listen to the wind and rain outside. Sometimes the fog makes its way inside.

My stock needs replenishing. I unwrap the last Mars bar and eat it as slowly as possible, trying to remember the details of the flashing images I saw at the Point, wondering if they contain any new information about what happened the day Eddie disappeared.

It's not that I don't know what happened; I remember the whole day – it's just that there are a few black spots in my memory. I can't remember what Eddie and I were talking about right before he disappeared – our last conversation together; his last conversation ever. And the moments after I realized he was gone are hazy. During the Laryngitis Year, I tried to work it all out – I even drew maps of the Point, and tried to place everyone, but I ended up more confused. I don't know why my brain wants to remember now, but I think it must be something to do with Eddie being around so much.

I make a list of the facts.

Things I know about that day:

1. Dillon was swimming with the dolphins.
2. Eddie and I were paddling close to shore.
3. One minute Eddie was there, and then he
was gone.
4. Dad was on the beach but I couldn't see him.
5. Mum was at home, baking. She arrived later after
the police called her.
6. I collapsed and Dad came to get me.
7. All my memories are tinged with a blue haze.

I remember the morning. We opened our birthday presents after breakfast. Eddie had a remote control helicopter which he crashed within a couple of minutes, and I had a new football, a real leather one. It was drizzly and windy outside so we dribbled it around the living room until Eddie smashed a glass on the coffee table, and Mum got *really* cross. Eddie had a tantrum because he didn't want to wear the blue T-shirt. Blue wasn't his favourite colour any more, but his red T-shirt had a big rip in it. And then Mum told Dad to take us to Rosemarkie beach to get us all out of her hair.

Rosemarkie is the village next to Fortrose – it's beautiful and old and has the best beach and the best ice cream on the Black Isle. But Eddie really wanted to go to Chanonry Point to see the dolphins. Dillon was on Eddie's side because he liked swimming around the Point – the strong currents were good practice apparently, and he had a gala coming up that he was determined to win. Dillon was already the Black Isle 1km open-water champion – he wanted to be the Highlands champion, too.

We were just leaving when the phone rang. Dad answered it and it was my friend Emily's mum saying Emily was too sick to come to our party later. I got in the car in a sulk, and no longer cared about the ice cream. It was too cold anyway.

After a little while of sitting and remembering, I wonder if anyone at home has noticed that I'm not there. Sometimes I feel invisible, like a wisp of air that tickles the back of someone's neck before they close the window to block the draught.

I'm about to head home when the panel door creaks open. I hold my breath and move back into the corner. It'd better not be my dad.

"Hello?" a voice calls from outside.

The voice is young.

"Someone in here?"

Then a face appears. A boy with floppy brown hair and a bit of stubble. He has an unlit rollie hanging from his mouth.

"Ah, I knew there was someone in here." He climbs through the panel and walks towards me. My pulse races as I start to gather my things.

"Don't leave on my account," he says, and sits beside me, stretching his long legs out along the concrete floor. The bottoms of his black jeans are scuffed and when I see the sunglasses in his hand, I realize he's the boy in the hoody from the boat.

"Who are you?" I ask, hoping the quiver in my voice isn't too obvious.

He lights up, and it's not just a cigarette. The space between us fills with a fog and the fumes get in the back of my throat, sickly and sweet.

"Tavey McKenzie," he says as he exhales. "Call me Tay. You like to smoke?" He holds the joint out to me, smiling. His arm presses against mine and my raincoat rustles. I wish I'd taken it off earlier, I'm suddenly really hot and now I can't seem to move.

I've never smoked a joint before but the other S4s smoke behind the school field all the time. They are much nicer to me in the afternoon, patting me on the shoulder, smiling and sometimes even offering me a cigarette. I never take one, though. I don't want to owe anyone.

"Yeah, of course," I say and reach for the joint. I think about how I'm going to get out of here.

He doesn't look like the boys at my school. Where they have styled and gelled hair, this boy's hair is messy and long, and hangs down over his ears. Where they have smooth round faces, this boy has a rectangular face with dark stubble. I wouldn't describe him as good-looking but he does have nice brown eyes and really long eyelashes that I can't help but stare at. He reminds me of a boy I saw on a documentary about youth prisons a few months ago. Even though the boy in the prison had been in a fight that ended badly (really badly), I remember feeling sorry for him because I knew he'd been misunderstood. I recognized the furrowed brow of the prison boy – the same furrow I see every morning in the mirror. Tay has this look too, like the world just doesn't get him.

I suck on the joint and get a faint taste of strawberries. Strawberry lip balm. I wonder if he's just been kissing his girlfriend. My throat tightens and I try not to choke.

Discreetly, I shuffle away from him so we're no longer touching but watch him out of the corner of my eye. I want to show him I'm not afraid, and that I meet people like him all the time.

"Who are you, then?" he asks, turning to me. I stare at his shiny lips, wondering who his girlfriend is, praying that it's not Ailsa Fitzgerald and that she's sent him to torment me.

"I'm Elsie. Are you a friend of Dillon's?" I ask hopefully.

The boy blinks. "Who?"

"Never mind. What's your name again?"

"Tay," he says slowly. "You've got a bad memory."

"Like the river?" I ask. "Did you know that an earthquake once reversed the flow of the Mississippi?" I know a lot about rivers thanks to the encyclopaedias that Granny gave Dillon one year. When I was younger I used to read about all the underground rivers around the world and wonder if that's where Eddie had gone.

"Yeah, like the river," Tay says, seemingly amused. "And no, I didn't know that. Thank you for educating me. So you must be the mystery squatter. It's quite the set-up you've got here."

"Have you touched my stuff? This is my spot, you know." Even though he seems okay, and is named after a river, this is *my* secret place. The joint makes me feel light-headed so I pass it back. I quite like the taste of it, though.

Tay tilts his head back and blows smoke rings, which float up and last for ages. I stare at them until my neck aches.

"I think you'll find this was my spot before yours," he says when the rings have dispersed. "I've just been away for a while."

"Really? Where've you been then?"

"Just away."

"You must've been away at least a year," I reply. There was no sign that anyone had been here before me when I discovered this place.

"Over five years. I moved away when I was twelve," he says.

Five years. Prison. I bet. I wonder what he did. Although twelve is pretty young to go to prison, even a youth one. Maybe it was some kind of boarding school. This is actually good news, though, because it's likely that he won't know about Eddie.

"I have to admit," Tay says, "I thought a small child had moved into my hideout." He holds up an empty sweet bag as evidence.

"I don't just keep sweets." I point to the packet of B&H cigarettes on the floor by our feet. Tay seems to find this amusing.

"Nothing wrong with sweets," he says and flicks the empty bag behind him. "So, you go to school in Fortrose?"

"Yeah, but I hate it. There are these girls that are always horrible to me."

"I hated school. Girls were horrible to me too, so I gave it up," he says, laughing. "I go to the school of life now."

"Is there a school of death?"

Tay sits forward and grins at me. His long eyelashes flutter and somehow soften his angular face. His teeth are shiny white and his lips look smooth. I wish I could apply another coat of lipstick.

"School of death? So you can learn to die?"

He seems amused. I hope he can't see how red my cheeks are. "Maybe," I mumble, trying to think of something else to say.

"You're very interesting, Elsie."

We smoke for a bit. I watch the way he manoeuvres the joint to his lips and back down to the floor. I watch him cross and uncross his legs, and play with a torn bit of leather on his shoe. He tells me that he once ran all around the Black Isle in a day, and got attacked by farm dogs. I tell him that I once hid in a bus shelter during cross-country at school and only joined in for the last lap. He commends me on my initiative, but says I should practise running in case farm dogs come after me. I tell him I'm not scared of dogs. I don't tell him what I am afraid of. When the joint's finished, he says he has to go.

"We should hang out again soon," he says. "I'll swing by."

He slides gracefully through the panel and I suddenly wish I hadn't moved away from him before. I lie down on my back and smoke with my eyes closed, breathing in the tobacco, the cannabis fumes and the lingering smell of Tay's aftershave. I no longer care about Ailsa Fitzgerald or that scummy school, or even the flashing images. Eddie is deep inside me, laughing. I remember one of his favourite jokes.

"Why are there fish at the bottom of the sea?" I ask him.

"Because they dropped out of school," he replies.

Nine

EDDIE AND I GOT JOKE books for Christmas when we were eight. Mine was red, Eddie's was blue – his favourite colour at the time – "The colour of the ocean!" Eddie loved the water even more than I did. I liked looking at it from the shore because I was afraid of getting tangled in the seaweed, but Eddie always wanted to be in it, have the waves break over his head. He was fearless when it came to the waves.

That Christmas day we sat on the sofa together to open our presents. I was uncomfortable because Eddie was sitting on my leg but he was so excited about Christmas I didn't want to upset him. So I sat still and let him cover me in ribbons and tinsel. Mum gave us the presents from Granny and we tore off the wrapping paper together. A joke book each. On the front they said *Jokes for eight-year-olds.* I had to read the title to Eddie because he couldn't read.

"It's full of sea creeeeeeeatures," he exclaimed as he flipped through it wide-eyed, looking for dolphins. "Look, look!"

He pointed to every page and illustration and held the book right up to my face so I could see. I remember feeling the shiny paper on my nose and the weight of it when he dropped it on my foot.

We hadn't seen Granny for a while. She lived somewhere near Loch Lomond on the west coast and apparently we went there lots when we were small but I don't remember. Most of the time she came to us, but the visits were becoming less frequent because she was getting too old to travel. The last time we saw her she visited us here on the Black Isle for Christmas, when Eddie and I were nine. On her last night, she and Mum had a fight. I never knew what it was about but from the cupboard Eddie and I hid in, I heard Granny say to her, "I didn't know I'd raised a wee liar." On her way out, she hugged Dad and told him to visit and bring us kids. He never did, though. She died in January this year, and Mum hasn't spoken about her since.

The best thing about Granny was that she treated me and Eddie the same, even though we weren't. I was normal.

Normal height, normal(ish) weight, and about average at school. Eddie wasn't. He was small. He walked like his legs were broken and fell over all the time. He wasn't "clever enough" to go to my normal school. Sometimes it wasn't always for the best that Granny treated us as twins because she'd buy clothes that were too big for Eddie or books that were too difficult for him, but Eddie didn't seem to mind that much.

"I'm the same as you, Ellie," he'd say, grinning, wearing a jumper that went down to his knees. Or, "If you read the words first, I'll read them when I'm ready." He got that from Granny. She told him that he'd be able to do stuff when he was ready, and she never lied about how old we were either. She didn't pretend that I was eight and he was six like Mum did.

"Ellie, what's your joke book about?" Eddie asked when he'd finished showing me his.

I pulled my book out from under the cushion and showed it to him. My foot was tingling.

"Horsies!" he exclaimed. Then he looked at my face and reached out for my hand. "Oh. I am sorry to hear that. You can share mine."

From across the room, my father guffawed.

"Celia, come in here, quick!" he called to Mum, who was in the kitchen cooking something that smelled like gone-off cheese.

She came running through, with oil splattered across her apron. "What is it?"

"Say it again, Eddie," my father said, clasping his hands.

Eddie looked at me, confused.

"Can you remember what you said about my book?"

"Horsies!"

"No, after that," I say.

Eddie grinned. "Oh, I *am* sorry to hear that," he said again, this time sounding even more like Mum when she's on the phone to friends who've "had a terrible time".

Mum clamped her hand across her mouth and doubled over at the waist.

"Oh, shit," she cried. "Is that really what I sound like? Colin, why didn't you tell me I sound so insincere? Shit."

"Don't swear, Mum," said Dillon from behind his encyclopaedia. "Mum, did you know that black holes can have a mass of a hundred billion suns?"

Mum didn't respond to Dillon's astronomy test and instead asked Eddie about the joke book.

"Jokes for eight-year-olds," she read out. "Wow, aren't you grown-up?"

"It's about sea creatures," he said. "But I can't find any fins in it."

"Well never mind, there are plenty of other beautiful sea creatures. Why don't you tell me a joke?" She wiped the

61

grease from her hands on her apron and leaned on the wall, waiting.

Eddie passed me the book.

"Why did the lobster blush?" I read out.

"I don't know!" Eddie shouted.

"Because the seaweed."

He didn't get it. He started wriggling like he always did when he didn't understand something.

"Eddie, listen again. The sea weed," I said, splitting the words.

While Eddie bounced about and poked my knee, I saw Mum take off her apron and slide onto my father's lap. Dillon held his encyclopaedia in front of his eyes when they started kissing. I covered Eddie's eyes but he didn't seem bothered by it. He just wanted to kiss me.

Eddie knew exactly what I thought about my book without me even saying anything. No one else understood me the way he did. I hadn't told anyone I was scared of horses, but he knew.

Ten

THE WATER IS GREY TODAY, the same colour as the sky, and the waves crash about inside the harbour, battering the fishing boats that line the wall. At least it's not raining. I clear my throat before I enter the boathouse so that I'm ready to speak if Tay's inside, and put more Ruby Red on to smooth my lips in case he wants to kiss me.

The boathouse is empty and just as I left it yesterday, except now it feels miserable and gloomy. I'm barely settled under a blanket when a clatter from outside startles me. Then I hear music. Slowly, I creep back through the panel onto the pebbles and realize its coming from the clubhouse above me. I crawl out from under the clubhouse and climb the rickety steps up onto the veranda. One of the boards has been taken down from the clubhouse's windows and I can see inside. A man wearing glasses moves chairs around. In the far corner, a large flat-screen TV shows a woman floating on her back in the sea with a bright red sun behind her. She sinks down under the water, her silver wetsuit making her look like a giant fish. The camera follows her as she drops through the water, going deeper and deeper, until she disappears into the abyss. I feel breathless and queasy. I'm watching my dream play out right before me, only I'm wide awake. The music is loud but sounds tinny through the glass and I feel like I'm the wrong way up. My legs start to give way just as the man turns around.

I run before he sees me.

It's a mile from the harbour to our house on McKellen Drive. The quickest way is straight down the high street and through the cemetery but I never take that short cut. I used to try – I'd stand at the cemetery gate, but my feet would never take me in.

Instead, I turn left just past the police station and take the long route round the back of all the houses. The roads weave in and out of the new housing estates – great big houses with shiny garages and neat little bay windows. Our house is more like one of the old crumbly ones in Rosemarkie. There aren't many like this left on our road.

My father opens the door as I come up the path, tripping

over the weeds, breathless and hot in the face.

"Where have you been?" he yells.

"School," I say, and squeeze past him into the house.

"Don't lie to me."

I try to ignore him but he pulls me back. His face is taut. There are new creases around his eyes.

"School finished an hour ago. What have you been doing?" He breathes noisily through his nose.

"Nothing, just walking," I say. "I'm *allowed* to walk."

His arm pushes down on my shoulder as he searches my face. "You weren't at the beach?"

"No," I say, focusing on a mole on his neck. He doesn't specifically ask about the harbour.

"Are you sure you're not taking any drugs? Because if you are—"

"You're hurting me," I whine, and wriggle out of his grip.

He looks down the path, confused, and I resist the urge to ask if he's the one taking drugs.

It's been months since I last had the dream, maybe even a year. I used to wake up feeling seasick. I would crawl into my parents' room and slide between them. Mum never asked me what was wrong but in her sleep she stroked my hair and whispered that I was safe.

When I turned twelve my father sent me back to my room.

"You're too old to sleep with us, Elsie," he said, rising naked from the bed. "Turn the light on if you're scared, but go back to your room."

He thought I was afraid of the dark. It never seemed to occur to him that I longed for the dark.

Eleven

ON THURSDAYS, MUM GOES TO see a therapist called Paul. Her appointments are in the afternoon and she gets back just before we come home from school. We're not allowed to disturb her. Usually by the time my father gets home from work, she has got up and redone her make-up. Over dinner, she says things like, "Oh, silly old me, crying again," but later, after I've gone to bed, I hear her shouting at my father – telling him that he's insensitive and that he should know by now that she doesn't mean it when she says she's okay after a session.

Today, I leave it an hour before I take a cup of tea up to her. She is lying splayed out on the bed like a rag doll, holding a scruffy teddy that used to be mine. She doesn't acknowledge me, so I leave the tea next to her. She never drinks the tea. Usually the mug is still full and cold when I pour it out the window later onto the overgrown garden below. There are a few smashed mugs down there too and I didn't put them there.

Dillon and my father are not as patient with Mum as I am. She says that they don't get as sad about Eddie as she does, although I don't know if this is true. It could be a bit true. I read in one of her books about coping with grief that the mother always suffers the most because she carried the child. The book didn't say anything about twins, though. I asked Dillon about this once and he said that I probably had the strongest bond with Eddie but he also said it was a bad idea to read books about coping with grief. He said instead of reading, Mum should go back to work full-time and look after her family properly. She works three days a week as a receptionist at a dental surgery, a job that she discovered while she was still at school. Instead of finishing school she stayed in the job to save up for a pair of knee-high boots. Whenever I ask for pocket money, she tells me that those boots were the last thing she ever bought for herself.

There's a knack to leaving the house quietly. I have to push the glass into the frame as I open the front door and then push it again from the other side so it doesn't rattle.

No one knows I've gone. It's not a conscious decision to go to the harbour. I start walking and then my brain fills with thoughts of Tay, and the way he smokes – so delicately. If it weren't for the smoke, you wouldn't even notice what he was doing. And then I think about the man I saw inside the old clubhouse, and the woman in the silver wetsuit.

It's dark when I get to the harbour. I climb the steps onto the veranda and they creak. I have to press my face right up to the window to see into the clubhouse. The man with glasses leans on the bar, reading a newspaper. His hair's not quite grey but it's light and wispy and the skin on his face is loose. He licks his fingers to turn the pages and pushes his glasses back up his nose every now and again. Eventually he looks up. I duck down under the window ledge but a second too late.

The door opens. "Freezing out here," he says, smiling down at me. "Come in if you want."

"I'm okay here."

He holds a hand out to pull me up and I take it because I don't know what else to do.

"I was making tea."

He goes behind the bar and pours water from a kettle into two cups. He smiles the whole time and moves his head and shoulders as though he's listening to some music I can't hear. The bar stool I perch on is slippery. I hook my feet around the legs but still feel like I'm sliding off.

"Are you the owner?" I ask him when he passes the tea across.

"I am now," he says proudly. His teeth are so white I think he could be a Hollywood actor. "My son and I are going to do it up and turn it into a diving club. It'll be open to the public – anyone can come in and have something to eat or drink, but we'll also rent out snorkel and diving gear, run dive trips and eventually hire out boats. I've got big ideas for this wee place. See those boats out there? I've bought a few of them – they're almost rotten but I'll replace some of the timber and they'll be as good as new. We should be ready for business in about a month."

"Oh," I say. I stare into my cup at the black tea, wondering if Tay is his son.

"I'm Mick." He shakes my hand. "What's your name?" he asks. And then I smile because he doesn't already know.

"Elsie." I pronounce it carefully, as though I'm saying it for the first time. I slide myself back on the stool and sit up straight. "Elsie Main."

"What you doing out here on a Thursday night?" he asks. "Have you lost your friends?"

"I don't have any friends," I tell him. "I just have a brother, but I don't know where he is."

He tells me he lives in Munlochy. "A quiet wee place."

Munlochy is a few villages away, back down towards

Inverness. That's where Paul the therapist lives too. There's nothing there, not even a Co-op.

Behind the bar, there's a poster of a pale-skinned woman underwater. She's smiling and tiny bubbles trail out of the side of her mouth. Her black hair fans out into the water like a silk scarf and her body is long and curvy in a shiny wetsuit. Her arms are lifted away from her body, like a bird's wings just before take-off.

Mick sees what I'm looking at. "That's Lila Sinclair. She's the under-21 National Freediving Champion. Scotland's deepest girl." He winks and says quietly, "I taught her myself."

"She's pretty," I say, wishing I had a body like hers.

"It was her in the video you were watching from outside the other day."

When I don't reply he winks at me again. I can't help but smile. I take a gulp of my tea and liquid burns my mouth and throat. I know that later the skin on the roof of my mouth will feel rough and I can play with the loose bits with my tongue.

"Can you swim, Elsie?"

"I used to." I hope he can't hear the tremor in my voice.

"If you can swim, then you can dive. The only difference is you hold your breath and stick your head under."

The thought makes me feel light-headed. I thank him for the tea and tell him I have to go.

"Come whenever you want," he says. "I do a great hot chocolate, too."

As I slide off the stool, I think that I'm not going to make it home without peeing myself. I look around but I can't see a sign.

"Erm, is there a toilet here?"

I'm so embarrassed when he takes me behind the bar and through a door that leads to steps down into a storage room.

"We've not got the main ones up and working yet," he says apologetically.

The storage room is cold and it takes me ages to go. I think about the video of Lila Sinclair and I feel a mixture of excitement and fear. It's not that I want to go into the water but I can't help but wonder what it would be like to be down there and not feel as though I'm drowning. Goosebumps appear on my legs as I sit on the toilet. Maybe I'll just stay for a hot chocolate to warm up.

When I head back up the stairs I hear voices and panic that it might be my father. I'm sure he follows me sometimes, because I know he doesn't trust me. I look to see if there is another way out but there isn't. I am doomed. I step through the door ready to face the music.

There are four boys, all in various states of undress, and Tay is one of them.

"You'll never beat me!" he says to a boy with extremely

curly hair, and then he sees me and goes quiet. His Adam's apple rises up and down and he gazes at the floor. His wetsuit is rolled down to his waist, revealing a blue shiny running top, and his feet are bare. He throws a cigarette into his mouth and runs his fingers through his slicked-back wet hair, spraying water everywhere. I wish there were a hole to fall through. I look away from him and my eyes fall on the tallest boy. He has blond hair like Dillon's and is bare from the waist up, with muscles so defined I want to run my fingers over them. He puts a dripping-wet net bag on the table and slaps Mick on the shoulder.

"Alright, Dad?"

"This is my son, Danny," Mick says proudly. "Boys, this is Elsie. Elsie, this is Danny, Rex, Joey and Tavey."

"Elsie," Danny repeats, looking from me to Mick and back to me, suspiciously. His eyes are strikingly blue, the same colour as my mum's Bombay Sapphire.

"Bit young to be a barmaid, aren't you?" he asks.

I blush and come out from behind the bar.

"That's your job," Mick says to Danny. "There's a delivery in the storeroom that wants sorting."

From a shelf behind the bar, Danny grabs a dry T-shirt and slips it over his head. He gives Mick a little head wiggle that I'm sure means *get her out of here*. Then he disappears through the swing doors. I've seen his type before. He's the kind of guy who thinks he's better than everyone else.

73

The kind of guy who looks through people like me.

The other boys introduce themselves. Rex is the one with extremely curly hair – it's out of control like mine, but his is sandy not dark. He's odd-looking, with a torso that's too long for the rest of his body and one arm covered in moles. I can tell he thinks he's the funny one of the group when he goes to hug me. I duck under his arms. Joey is the smallest out of the four – he also looks like the kindest, with long hair down to his chin, and enormous brown eyes. He's the only one still wearing his full wetsuit. "Hi," he says, shyly.

Mick puts an arm around Tay.

"Tay's my best diver," he says. "He could be Scotland's deepest boy if he put his mind to it. I'm training him to be an instructor."

Tay shrugs Mick off and steps forward. "Hello, Elsie. Nice to meet you."

He's smirking, like he's sharing a private joke with someone. My mouth dries out. Even though he's a couple of metres away, I feel like I'm right up against him and I need air. "Excuse me," I mutter and push past him and the two other boys to get to the door.

Outside on the veranda I lick my chapped lips, which are salty from the spray. I wonder if I dreamed our previous meeting in the boathouse. I jump when someone touches me lightly on the shoulder.

"Want one?" Tay is next to me, holding a pack of Marlboro Gold. I fumble, trying to grip one of the cigarettes. In the end he takes one and lights it for me. The tiny hairs above his knuckles brush my hand as he passes me the cigarette, and I get goosebumps on my neck.

"I was just leaving," I manage to say eventually.

"Me too. I'll walk with you." He points to the path and walks down the steps and away before I can answer.

"Aren't you cold? Where are your shoes?" I ask when I catch up with him. I'm almost running to keep up with his long strides.

He looks down at his feet. "Nah, shoes are for losers," he says. "You give up school yet?"

So I didn't dream it.

"I'm working on it," I say, still practically running, wondering if he's aware that I can't keep up.

When we reach the grassy strip at the top of the harbour by the road, he suddenly stops and I crash into him. He holds my arms to steady me and he's so close I feel his breath. All I can do is stare up at him.

"Sorry," I say.

"Your cigarette's gone out," he whispers.

He takes it from my mouth and lights it again. Then he steps away and looks out across the harbour. The lights on the bridge to Inverness twinkle across the night sky. I look around; we're alone.

"Erm, can I ask you a question?" I want to draw him close again.

"That was a question," he says, still with his back to me.

I'm stumped for a second. This guy is not very good at communicating.

"Why did you pretend that you didn't know me? Are you embarrassed?"

Tay turns back to me and inhales and exhales, slowly. The whole time, I stand there wondering if he heard me or if I should repeat the question.

"Don't want anyone to know about our secret place, do we?" he eventually says, with the same smirk that he had inside the clubhouse. Either he's embarrassed to be seen with me in front of the boat boys, or he's hiding something. Maybe he's on probation after leaving prison. Maybe he's not supposed to be out on his own. I picture him sitting in a cell, scratching his name on the floor.

"Hey, Mick said you were asking him about diving and stuff," he says.

"No," I reply. "He was *telling me* about diving. Freediving or whatever you call it."

"You got a wetsuit? You should come out on the boat with us – I'll have a word with Danny, I'm sure he won't mind. You don't have to dive or anything, just watch. It'll be fun, the water's pretty cold this time of year, but once you're under it's well worth the pain."

He talks really fast like he's nervous or something. I'm so busy thinking about myself in a wetsuit, thighs and backside wobbling, and thinking that Danny probably *would* mind because he clearly already hates me, that I miss something – because the next thing Tay says is, "See you tomorrow, then?"

"Huh?"

"Come out on the boat with us tomorrow. We've got a boat. It's called *The Half Way*."

"I've got school tomorrow."

He laughs, showing me his perfectly straight teeth. "Well, anytime. We're always about. Saturday maybe. Unless you're too afraid?"

A car horn makes us both jump.

"I have to go," he says quietly and suddenly all serious.

I look at the car. The driver stares straight ahead, his hands firmly holding the wheel.

"Is that your dad?"

Tay nods. "That's him." He stamps his cigarette into the ground then jogs soundlessly over to the car. All I can hear is my own heart thudding. The car squeals away even before the passenger door is closed.

My brain says his name over and over again. Tavey McKenzie. Tay McKenzie. Tay. McKenzie. Elsie McK— I stop myself just in time.

Twelve

ALONE IN THE SCHOOL LIBRARY at lunch, I google "freediving". I discover that it's also called breath-hold or apnea diving. There are so many sites I don't even know where to start. It's amazing the stuff you can find on the internet – a few days ago I'd never even heard of freediving, and now I know that there are several different types, depending on whether you go down deep or stay just below the surface, if you have flippers, and if you use weights to get down and balloons to get back up. There are forums too. I scroll through the comments:

scubasam69: Hey, I really wanna try freediving! Is it safe?

Freer-diver1: Depends on what you mean by safe. It's safe if the person doing it isn't a complete moron. Don't post stupid comments on this forum. Do some research and then ask proper questions if you're really interested. Happy to help. Freer-diver.

Poseidon_Seagod: Hey Scubasam69! It's totes safe, man. I tried for the first time last year and now I can go to about 50 metres. Never blacked out.

Pixie2Pink: Don't do it! Freediving is NOT safe. I urge you, do not do this dangerous sport. People die every year. EVERY year. You people are so stupid. Can't you just think of the poor ones who have to go and get your body from the bottom of the friggin' sea!

Freer-diver1: Pixie2pink, get your facts straight. Freediving is no more dangerous than football or rugby. It's less dangerous than cycling or mountaineering – if you are measuring by deaths. Freediving is as safe as you make it, like any other sport or activity. Follow the rules, know what you're doing. Never dive alone. Freer-diver.

scubasam69: Thanks Freer-diver1 and Poseidon_Seagod. None of my mates are up for doing it so I don't have much choice about not going alone. I reckon I can practise in my local pool though. The lifeguards will save me! Haha! Happy diving.

Free-diver1: Scubasam69. Don't make me swear on a public forum. Read the link. <u>Rules.</u>Thanks, Freer-diver.

I don't click on the link – rules are for losers, like shoes. I think of Tay's bare feet in the cold, the way the pebbles must have dug into his soles.

Eddie wriggles about inside me. His vibrations are gentle at first but they become heavier and louder until it feels like he's pounding on the inside of my skin for me to let him out.

I close everything down. Not now, Eddie, I plead with him silently. He is under the table, grabbing my legs, begging me to play hide-and-seek with him. But he doesn't want me to find him, he wants me to hide too. No one will find us in here, he says.

Even though lunch is over, I stay for a while until the librarian finds me and gives me a detention for missing my English class.

Thirteen

"HOW'S YOUR GIRLFRIEND?" I ASK Dillon when he sits down at the kitchen table that night. I'm cooking dinner, and we're alone – a rarity lately. Instead of waiting for me after school, he wandered off with Lara and left me to deal with Ailsa and her sidekicks, who spat at me and called me poodle face. It's not fair that Dillon gets to go and have fun without me.

Dillon looks sulky and picks at a stain on the table.

"Spending a lot of time with her these days, aren't you?"

My father comes in and interrupts us.

"You'll burn the sauce," he says to me as he scoops a bit

of macaroni from the pan to test it. He sits down next to Dillon, fanning his mouth.

"You're not wasting your study time, are you, pal? I know you're an adult and you can do what you want, but you don't want to throw your life away on a wee lass."

Dillon looks up at him apologetically. It makes my blood boil. Dillon should just tell him where to stick it.

"She helps me study," Dillon says. "She's more mature than other girls in her year," he goes on, looking right at me. Lara is actually nearly a year younger than me due to me repeating a year. I roll my eyes, probably entirely proving his point but I don't care.

"Well, as long as you keep on top of your schoolwork. I trust you," my father says.

He says it in that way which means, *I'm saying I trust you, so you must obey me.*

Time to play a game. I want to wind Dillon up, but I'm also testing the water for myself.

"Where do you go with Lara? To her house? Doesn't she live right on Rosemarkie beach?"

Dillon glares at me. My plan works. My father gets all jumpy.

"But you stay inside the house, right? You don't go to the beach, eh?" he asks.

"Yes, Dad. Don't worry. I don't go to the beach."

"Okay, good." He scratches his ear. "I mean, it's okay,

that stretch of beach, but the water there can still be treacherous. Not quite as bad as Chanonry Point, I guess."

He winces when he says "Chanonry Point". There's a short but very deep pause before Dillon replies.

"Dad, I haven't been swimming for years."

"Yes, I know," he says. "Right. Where's that macaroni, Elsie?"

I place the macaroni on the table as Mum comes in, and my father dishes up. Dillon hardly eats anything, stirring the macaroni and scraping the sauce off it onto the plate. It's not actually burned so I don't know what his problem is. He can't seem to take a joke these days. It's not like I would have actually told our parents that he goes to the beach. The message from my father is clear, though. Rosemarkie beach is okay, as long as we don't go in the water. And if Rosemarkie is fine, then the harbour must be too. And aside from that, what he doesn't know won't kill him.

Fourteen

THE DAY AFTER EDDIE DISAPPEARED, Dillon and I went down to the Point to look for him. Dillon told me to wait on the beach but I followed him into the water. He swam so fast I couldn't keep up with him and I struggled against the tide. I was afraid of how deep it was further out too, but I didn't want to stop until we found Eddie.

"Can you see anything?" I kept calling to Dillon, but he was too far away to hear me, and the rain was creating a mist on the surface of the water, making it even harder to see.

Every time I got out to the big waves they dragged me

back and I had to start again. My hands were numb and useless at pulling me through the water, and I became so exhausted I couldn't keep my head up. Large bits of kelp drifted around my neck and every time I brushed a piece away, another would attach itself to my skin. The water closed in around me and it was so cold, I felt like my head was being crushed. For a few seconds, I thought I'd never come back up and I thought to myself, *I deserve this.* But then the water pushed me up and I tumbled onto the beach. When I looked up I saw my father running towards me, shouting, his face raging with anger. He grabbed me around my neck and pulled me back onto the beach. My fingers were blue.

"He might be down there," I croaked.

"What did you do?" my father screamed.

Then Dillon was there too, screaming for Dad to let go. The three of us were drenched from the sea and the rain and we howled together for what seemed like for ever. I remember the greyness of my father's face when he looked at me that day – it was like the colour had been washed out.

"You're not to come back here on your own, either of you. Do you hear? You're not to come here again."

"I just want to find him," I cried as my father dragged me up the beach to the car park. "I need to say goodbye."

From the warmth of the car, I watched Dillon run back

down onto the pebbles. He scrabbled around on the stones like a dog searching for a bone until our father wrestled him back to the car too.

Later, the police came around. Dillon and I hid in the cupboard under the stairs, listening to our parents talking to them. We caught only a few words: "called off" and "too dangerous". Then I heard my name and more murmuring. I opened the cupboard door slightly to hear the rest and Dillon put his hand over my mouth.

"No, I'm sorry you can't talk to them. They're too upset," my father said. His voice was high-pitched. "We've told you everything. It happened so quickly, there was no time…"

Dillon pulled the door closed and everything was muffled again.

"Aren't they looking for him any more?" I asked Dillon.

"Shhh."

"He'll be so scared."

"He won't be scared now," Dillon replied.

"He will."

Dillon put his hand over my mouth again and said that we couldn't let them hear us. Then he whispered very quietly that an angel would guide Eddie back to us. After a few minutes I said, "Dillon, I'm not four. I know there aren't any angels. And Eddie knows it too. He also knows that there is no Santa or tooth fairy."

"You told him?"

I shrugged even though it was dark and Dillon couldn't see.

"Dillon?"

"What?"

"I couldn't see Dad anywhere."

"Shhh."

"Dillon, where did he go?"

"He was there. You looked in the wrong place."

A cloud of dust made me choke but Dillon wouldn't let me get out of the cupboard, even though I needed the loo as well and was really hungry. We hadn't eaten since breakfast the day before.

"Dillon?"

"What?"

"It's my fault. I was the one who lost him."

"No." Dillon shook my shoulders so hard I almost cried out. "This wasn't your fault. You mustn't ever say anything like that to anyone. It was an accident. Promise me that you won't say a word to anyone."

I promised and drew an imaginary zip across my lips. I didn't know then that our silence would last for a year. I followed Dillon's lead – he would let me know when it was safe to talk again. When, after a few months, we still refused to speak, Mum started telling everyone that we had chronic laryngitis. We drank a lot of cough medicine that year, and had frequent trips to see doctors who kept asking us how we felt.

After the police had gone, we crawled out of the cupboard but our parents were still talking.

"Why him?" my father said. "Why did it have to be *him*?"

Fifteen

ON SATURDAY, I HEAD STRAIGHT to the harbour. I hear the boat boys before I see them. Their voices rise and fall with the waves, a clash of different tones, all trying to be the loudest. When I turn into the harbour I see one of them – Rex, I think, judging by the amount of hair – dive off the harbour wall. His legs fly straight up into a V as he tucks his head down. He seems suspended for a second, a black star shape against the white puffy sky. Then he falls down with a soft splash and there's a dull whoop from the others. Someone shouts, "Me next!"

The sky is so bright I have to squint, but I see two more people on the wall. Tay is definitely one of them –

I recognize the slope of his shoulders – and the other one looks like Joey. Danny, the mean one, isn't there, thank God, unless he's already in the water. I bury my chin in my jacket to shield my face from the wind and follow the mud path down towards them. I glance over at the clubhouse but the door is closed and I can't see in.

"Elsie!" Tay shouts as I climb the steps up onto the harbour wall. His wetsuit is shiny, his cheeks are flushed. "Watch this." He flicks his cigarette away and launches himself into the air. I hold my breath as he twists and turns, spinning again and again before disappearing down into the water.

Joey is next. He steps off and dive-bombs straight down, sending a flurry of waves crashing into the side of the sea wall. "Bell-end," I hear Tay call. They climb up the ladder, and their rubber booties make wet footprints on the wall.

"You can be our judge, Elsie. Whose jump was best?" Tay sprawls out on the wall and lights up.

I take one of his cigarettes and sit next to him.

"Help yourself," he says sarcastically, shaking the water from his head. His hair puffs up and I try not to laugh.

"Are you not going out on the boat?" I ask, wondering which boat is theirs.

"In a wee while. We're waiting on Danny to finish in the cellar," Tay says.

Damn, that's bad news. I bet as soon as he sees me he'll tell me to get lost.

"You gotta judge on who made the biggest splash," Joey says, stretching. "I think I'm the winner."

"Eejit," Tay says.

"Twat face," Joey responds.

I suck my cigarette, playing for time as they rib each other.

"I'm not sure. You'll have to do it again," I say.

As they line up, Danny emerges from the clubhouse wearing a white T-shirt and heads towards us. I pretend not to see him. Rex goes first again, leaping into a star jump and tucking himself into a ball at the last minute.

"Fuck, yeah!" he shouts when he eventually resurfaces. Joey and Tay go together in a synchronized back somersault, landing almost at the same time, Joey with a loud splash and Tay hardly making a sound at all.

Rex shoots water from his mouth. "Your turn," he shouts up to me.

It's okay to go near the water; just don't go in it. I shake my head. "No fucking way," I yell, but my words get swallowed by the wind.

"Chicken!" Tay calls. "Come on, it's fine. I'll catch you."

I take a step closer to the edge and watch the white foam swilling around the base of the wall. The drop must be three metres. I imagine myself falling, bellyflopping. I try not to think about all the seaweed down there – it's kelp, the worst kind, thick and slithery.

"Come on, Elsie! Don't be such a girl." Rex makes chicken noises and flaps his arms so the sea froths up around him.

"Well she *is* a girl. What do you expect?" Tay shouts back and then holds his arms out as if to catch me.

Danny is climbing the steps up to the wall. I'm sure he's going to stop me.

"Don't even think about it, Elsie," he calls. "It'll hurt."

What does he know about pain? The others keep calling me into the water, hollering and clucking. They don't think I can do it. *Loser*, I hear in my head. *Loser*. Danny is up on the wall, his footsteps getting closer. It's now or never.

"Alright! Move out the way then." I can't believe I'm doing this. My hands shake as I unzip my jacket and kick my trainers off. I leave my socks on, hoping they'll protect my feet from the cold. Below, they are cheering – Tay the loudest.

"Don't…" I hear Danny call from behind. But it's too late, I'm already running to the end of the wall and then I'm flying, falling, the surface rushing towards me.

The cold rides up my body as I go down, piercing through my bones like a thousand glass splinters. The liquid swarms around my head, pushing me down and down, the cold chilling my brain. My eyes feel as though they are being pulled from their sockets and the salt stings. The water looks black in every direction as I fall head first into the immense space below. I kick and try to pull myself up with my arms but the water slides through my fingers. It's like crawling through iced gel. My ribcage heaves and shudders, my whole body goes into spasm. I'm dying. *Let me breathe. Let this be over.*

Then there's a silence in my head, a quiet that seems to grow and grow, and I let the current take me. My body wavers gently like a stray piece of seaweed floating out into the unknown.

There's a flash like a light bulb exploding. And boom, I'm back there on the day Eddie went missing, searching for him, the icy water nearly up to my waist. Dillon's frantically swimming back towards the shore. Then he gets to his feet and wades in my direction, his cheeks bright red with exertion as he fights against the current. But then I see he's not looking at me. He's looking over to his left, past the lighthouse.

"Dillon," I call. My words are tiny in the huge mass of water.

"Dillon, he's over here, this way." I point to the water, right where Eddie was standing.

"Not now, Els," he calls back. He pushes hard against the breaking waves with his thighs. What can he see? Is Eddie over there?

"Can you see him?" I shout, moving towards Dillon. The waves knock me about.

"I've got to find her. Did you see her?"

"What? Dillon, is Eddie there?" I ask again.

Dillon turns to me, breathing hard. He stops and scans the water. Then he scans the beach.

"Where's Eddie?" he asks urgently.

I point to the water and the colour drains from his cheeks. He dives straight towards me and thrashes about. Our arms and legs tangle as we both plunge down, trying to find Eddie. I can't stay down for long. When I come up for air, I'm alone. I search the surface of the water and then I search the beach. Dad isn't where we left him. There are a few people clustered near the lighthouse looking out at the dolphins, but he isn't one of them. I call for him. I call for help.

"Drag her in," I hear. It's Danny's voice. And Tay is saying, "It's okay, we've got you." There's an arm around me, someone's cheek against mine, their breath in my ear.

Another flash of an image – my father running towards me, something blue in his hands.

I open my eyes, and see only the sky.

"My legs," I murmur. I can't feel them. The pebbles rotate underneath my spine as the boys drag me up onto the beach. Dried, spiky seaweed digs into my head when they lay me on the ground. I shiver violently.

I'm on fire.

Sixteen

INSIDE THE CLUBHOUSE, WE SIT around the table by the fire. My skin is hot but I keep shivering. Mick brings a blanket and drapes it across my shoulders. A steaming cup of hot chocolate is on the table just in front of me but I'm too tired to reach for it. The boys are quiet, muttering amongst themselves, glancing at me.

"How long was I under for?" I ask, looking at no one.

It's Tay who answers. He coughs first. "Not long. Maybe ten, fifteen seconds. We got to you quite quickly."

I look at him and he's frowning. I'm taken aback by his answer – it felt like so much longer. Just like when Eddie went down and the seconds seemed to slow to minutes, and the minutes felt like hours.

Danny pokes a white contraption in my ear and it makes a beeping sound. I flinch.

"Relax," he says briskly. "I'm just taking your temperature."

Tay watches me the whole time.

"You'll be okay." Danny scrapes his chair back and the noise makes my teeth tingle. "You haven't got hypothermia. Where do you live? I'll drive you home."

My mouth is still not working; my jaw feels numb and I can't form the words.

"McKellen Drive," Mick says. "The house by the cemetery."

My body slumps down in the chair and a feeling of dread passes over me. I have been stupid to think that Mick doesn't know who I am. Everyone knows who the Mains are. Our house was on the local news during the search for Eddie. My face, too – my parents gave the police the first photo of Eddie they could find. It was a slightly out-of-focus picture of the two of us on the beach, my arm around his, Eddie holding a pebble out to the camera, grinning with his wonky smile, his face ghostly white in the overexposure. At first they showed the full picture on the news but after a few days they cut me out. All that was left of me were my fingers, pressed tightly into Eddie's arm.

I see a flicker of fear in Danny's eyes. He storms over to the bar and rubs his face, as though he's trying to work out what to do. I'm confused. Most people go quiet when they realize who I am, but then they're immediately nice to me, as though I might break if they raise their voices. They don't usually seem afraid or angry.

I want to close my eyes and disappear, but I can't help glancing at Tay. His mouth is slightly open, like he's thinking too hard. He can't possibly know. He wasn't even here when it happened. Or was he? Danny marches back over to us and grabs my arm. It hurts but I don't say anything. I guess that he's just annoyed that he's got to deal with me.

"Come on, Elsie," Danny says. "I'll drive you home."

"I'll come with you." Tay stands and moves around the table but Danny pushes his palm firmly into Tay's chest.

"You've done enough damage."

"Sorry, Elsie," Tay says. "Get home and warm up, eh?" He smiles and I feel a hot rush of blood. Already, I forgive him.

Danny drives smoothly and slowly, both hands on the steering wheel. He's like an older, stronger version of Dillon, with a long neck and blond stubble on his chin. He even sounds like Dillon as he lectures me.

"You could've got yourself into some serious trouble."

"I'm fine."

"Look. I don't think you should come back to the harbour. I'm guessing your parents wouldn't be too happy if they knew you were jumping into the sea."

"Well, they don't have to know about it, do they?" I say.

He purses his lips. "It's hard to keep secrets around here."

It sounds like a threat. I run my hand through my frizzing-up hair in a way that I hope shows him I'm not bothered. It's not like he would have the guts to turn up at my house and tell my parents that he let me jump off the harbour wall into ice-cold, life-sucking water, right?

"Why have I not seen you around before?" I ask.

"I don't know," he replies. "Maybe you just weren't looking."

"You didn't go to school here?"

"Inverness. I lived with my mum before, but spent most weekends here. Only moved to the Black Isle when my dad decided to open the diving club."

When we pull up outside the house, he stares at our front gate for a while. Then he unbuckles my seat belt for me and reaches right over me to open the car door. It makes me feel claustrophobic. He stares at me as I gather the strength to move.

"Stay away from the harbour, okay? I don't want you to get hurt."

My eyes feel heavy and I fight sleep. I don't tell him that for a few seconds down there, for the first time in five years, I stopped feeling any pain at all.

Part Two

COLIN: What did one *tide* say to the other *tide*?

CELIA: I don't know, what did one tide say to the other?

COLIN: Nothing. It just *waved*.

One

I PAINT MY MOTHER'S NAILS Mocha to match mine. We sit at the kitchen table, both glancing at the window, waiting for my father to come home from his Saturday "meeting". Lots of people want to discuss loans on Saturdays, but I'm pretty sure most banks close at two p.m. and it's already nearly five. Beads of sweat break out on Mum's forehead every now and then. I'm still feeling hot and cold after idiotically hurling myself into the North Sea.

"Who was that guy?" Mum asks, staring at the spot where Danny's car had been earlier. "Your boyfriend?"

"Just a friend."

She snaps her head to me. "I don't think you should

hang around with him, he's too old for you. It's odd that he would want to hang around with someone your age – I don't trust him."

"He's eighteen, same as Dillon."

But she's right. There's something suspicious about him and he knows too much. My throat feels itchy just thinking about him.

Mum blows on her fingers and then reaches under the sink for the bottle of Bombay Sapphire. It's half empty and I know she only bought it two days ago. She glugs it straight from the bottle and when she finally puts it back down her eyes water, but there is a serene look on her face.

"Go on, have some," she says. "You seem as miserable as me sometimes. Let's not let those boys get to us." She takes another gulp and slams the bottle on the table in front of me.

"I thought everything was okay with you and Dad."

"Never assume," she says. "Never think that everything's okay."

The gin makes me retch after the first sip. She throws her head back laughing and says, "It's a bit of an acquired taste."

I want to acquire the taste. I get a glass and pour some into it.

We stay there, at the table, and as the light fades our bodies form long, wavering shadows over the kitchen surfaces.

She glugs from the bottle and I take tiny sips from my glass, getting used to the burning in my throat. She doesn't stop me when I pour myself some more.

"I miss her," she suddenly says.

At first I wonder who she's talking about, but then I work it out. I sometimes forget that Granny isn't around any more – she stopped visiting when Eddie and I were nine so it's been a long time since I saw her. Dad says she visited once after Eddie had gone but I must have been at school that day.

"Yeah, I miss her too. It's hard to believe she's gone."

Mum looks wistful, like she's remembering something nice. She never talks about her childhood, except to say that when she was really small, it had been good.

"Why did Granny leave the Black Isle?" I ask, thinking it's a good way in and maybe Mum will open up to me. She seems to be in a sharing mood.

"It was the bridge," she says, as if that's all the explanation needed.

"The bridge? Why? What happened?"

"It got built."

I find it strange that a bridge could make someone leave their home town. Before the bridge was built, you had to drive all the way to the bottom of the peninsular and then back along the estuary to get to Inverness. The bridge has always been there for me so I don't know any different.

It's not even like we go across it much any more, but knowing that we could makes this place seem less forgotten.

"Wasn't the bridge a good thing?"

"Granny didn't think so. For her, the bridge meant more people. Tourists, city locals. Strangers. She didn't like it at all. She'd moved to the Black Isle to get away from all the people. She liked the isolation."

"Didn't you feel cut off?"

Mum takes another sip of gin and looks up at the ceiling.

"We used to play on the mud banks. That was what we did at weekends. I'd look across at the mainland, and I used to feel proud of being on this side. Like I was something special. My mum stayed a year or two after it was built but she couldn't cope. She wanted a quiet life."

I can't imagine a quieter life than living here. And these days I'm glad about the tourists. I can hide amongst them. They don't know who I am.

"Mum, why didn't you and Granny speak any more?"

I sip my drink and wait for the answer.

"I screwed up, Elsie. I made a terrible mistake and I have to live with that."

"What mistake?" I whisper, leaning in close.

She moves away from me and sits back in her chair.

"Let me tell you something. Don't ever let anyone in your life die without them being able to forgive you. And, Elsie, don't make my mistakes."

"What mistakes?" I ask again but she changes the subject.

She tells me again the story of how my father was on the other side of the world when she was giving birth to Dillon.

"I kept calling the ship. That's men for you, always last minute," she slurs. "And here I am, eighteen years on, still wondering if he's coming home."

"Is he going to leave us?"

She looks at me. "Me, yes. But he'd never leave you."

She starts laughing then, and when I try to take the gin away she clamps her hands around the bottle and tells me that she is a bad person and everyone thinks so. I'm scared of her when she's like this – when she starts to sway and I wonder whether she'll topple right over and crack her head. But she's like one of those wobbly clowns with the ball inside – just when I think she's going down she springs back up with those fixed eyes and that cherry-red grin.

"I miss Eddie," I say, hoping that she'll want to talk about him.

"Shhh," she replies. "Eddie's asleep."

Eddie is not asleep. He is sitting in the kitchen sink, staring out of the window at the stars. "There's the bear," he says to himself. Then he turns to me and whispers, "Ellie, we never see shooting stars any more. How are we supposed to make wishes?"

It's gone midnight when my father comes in. Mum is asleep with her head on the table and her arms dangling by her sides. I try to look at my father but the kitchen tips back and forth. When I attempt to stand up, I slide straight to the floor and bile rides up my throat. His polished shoes catch the moonlight just before I vomit all over them.

Two

THE JACKDAWS CACKLE AND SCREECH outside and in the distance the church bells chime for Sunday mass. My head hurts too much for me to get out of bed, and the smell of cooking bacon downstairs makes me feel queasy. I wonder if Mum realized how much I drank. Perhaps she thought it was water in my glass. I reach for the notepad by my bed and make a new list.

New things I remember about that day:

1. Dillon wasn't swimming back to look for Eddie. He was looking for someone else. Find out who.

2. My father definitely wasn't on the beach when Eddie disappeared. Find out where he went.
3. My father was holding something blue when he ran to me after I collapsed. Find out what.

I haven't got much to go on but I know two things for sure. Dillon and my father are hiding something, and I'm capable of remembering more – I just have to be under the water for it to happen. I remember my first flashback, at the Point on dry land – but that was only fragments. The real memories are lurking beneath the surface, I'm sure.

My father knocks on the door and I shove the notebook under the covers.

"Breakfast is ready," he says, barely looking at me.

"I'm not hungry."

"Neither is your mother," he replies. "At least you got most of it out of your system."

He looks at his shoes. He doesn't tell me off, and I wonder why. Perhaps the bacon is the punishment. For me and Mum.

He wanders over to the window next to my bed.

"There's a cold draught in here," he murmurs. He tries to pull the window closer to the frame and cement dust falls on his hand. "This place is falling apart."

I slide back under the covers. As he leaves, he says, "By the way, you're grounded for a week."

I hate him.

Another question spins around my mind. Does Tay know about Eddie? Would it be so bad if he did know? *Yes,* I answer myself. Because if Tay knows about Eddie, he'll always be wondering about the bit of me that's missing.

Three

THE WEEK PASSES SLOWLY. MUM cries a lot but she doesn't offer me any more gin. Dillon leaves the house before I'm even up so he can walk all the way to Lara's and walk her to school. He doesn't even come home for dinner. I'm not allowed out because of the gin, but my father works late and has no idea that I go to the harbour after school every day.

I wait for Tay in the boathouse but he never shows up. I know he's been there, though, because I find a pair of goggles and diving boots and a smelly towel on top of my cupboard. I'm sure that by now Danny has told him everything and he doesn't want anything to do with me. It's always the same. No one wants to be friends with the girl whose brother died. What if she cries? What if she wants to talk about it? What if she's all weird and morbid? I long to be in the water again, to remember more, to recreate that moment where nothing hurt.

On Friday, Mum goes to work and I skip school to avoid a maths test. In the morning I get supplies for Mum from Superdrug and pile up the goodies on her bed when I get home. Mocha lipstick and several colours of nail varnish. A mascara too. I'd taken the nearest one because I was in a hurry, but it turns out to be a volumizing one, which she could do with. For lunch I eat a plastic-cheese sandwich with extra pickle and butter on both sides of the bread. I find the Veet I grabbed in my jacket pocket. My legs dangle over the bath, covered in white foam, while I smoke a cigarette. When I'm done, I wash the foam and my hair down the plughole, clean the sink, bleach the toilet and spray the room with Lemon Scent.

Next, I move to Dillon's room. Even after all these years it feels funny to be in here. I don't know how Dillon copes with it, with the big space by the window where Eddie's bed used to be.

I lie on the floor and shimmy my head and shoulders under Dillon's bed. There's old food down here, encrusted into the carpet and smeared along the wall above the skirting board. It makes my stomach turn. There are boxes of books and magazines and mouldy socks, but Dillon's old wetsuit isn't here. I try the wardrobe and it smells bad too. The top shelf is empty and thick with dust and the bottom shelf is filled with neatly lined-up shoes. I pull out the hoody he always wears and search the pockets for money. My fingers get covered in something sticky – macaroni cheese. I heave silently as the stale cheese smell wafts into my mouth. I almost cry.

But then I see it. The wetsuit hangs right in the corner and I sniff one of the arms. It smells damp, like old boots, but I run to the bathroom and yank it on. It's so tight it hurts my fingers when I try to stretch it over my hips but as I finally pull the zipper up at the back the fabric folds around my body, holding me in place and I feel warm and glad. I hold my breath. At thirty seconds, my arms start twitching and at forty-nine, I exhale loudly. I think of all the times I've held my breath when I've been upset or angry – I must have only managed about twenty seconds. I take in a few deep breaths and try again, feeling my face go red as the seconds tick by. I make it to sixty. Just. I'm too exhausted to do it again.

That evening, my parents go to the pub – they always go on Fridays because Mum feels better by then – well, better enough to talk. *A debrief,* Dad calls it, and he always sighs when he says it.

I walk past Dillon's room and hear creaking. I peer through the keyhole and see Dillon in bed with Lara.

They're mostly under the covers but Dillon is on top and I can see his shoulders and the small muscles in his back contracting and relaxing. They're very quiet. Dillon grunts a bit but the noises are mostly just breathing. When they've finished I see Lara's breasts, which aren't anywhere near as big or wobbly as mine. They're small and perfect. Dillon lies beside her with his eyes closed, breathing lightly, hardly moving. Lara takes one of Dillon's hands and places it on her breast. He smiles but doesn't open his eyes.

I wonder if this is Dillon's first time. I wonder if it's Lara's first time. If it were me, I wouldn't choose to do it in my parents' house. I would find a dark secluded place. The boathouse maybe.

The girls at school talk about sex a lot. They group together in the playground to look at magazines. I've never seen what's in them but they talk about Positions of the Month and the boys talk a lot about girls' anatomy. A few months ago a naked picture of Fifi Kent was sent to everyone in our year by her boyfriend's best friend. I didn't see it, though, because I don't have a mobile phone – it would be too depressing to have a phone that no one ever called, and anyway, I want to be left alone. Some nasty things were said about Fifi Kent and now she eats lunch alone too. Sometimes I think about sitting with her but I suspect that she wouldn't want to talk to me.

One last glance before I head downstairs. Dillon is propped up on one elbow, staring longingly at Lara, twirling a strand of her mousy hair. I shouldn't spy on people. I see things I don't want to.

Four

AS SOON AS THE WEATHER starts warming up, or even before, the Black Isle teenagers have parties down on the Point by the lighthouse. I've never actually been invited but sometimes I follow Dillon down there and hide in the shadows. Today is the first one of the year, even though it's not quite May yet, and Dillon has tried on three different shirts. He finally settles for a really ugly brown one. His hair is perfectly gelled and spiked. I hover by the door as he lies to our parents and says that he's going to Lara's house. He makes a point of saying that her parents will be there and they're all having dinner together. I wait for my parents to go back into the kitchen, then go after him.

The party is in full flow when I finally arrive, having gone the long way round to avoid the cemetery. It's mostly S5s and S6s but there are a few kids from my year too – the ones who have older boyfriends. Everyone takes their own blankets to sit on, and cooler bags full of beer and vodka. Marty Jenson, the school DJ, stands in the middle with his decks, one hand spinning records and the other fist pumping the air. A crowd of girls cluster around him, showing him their best dance moves (which are pretty crap) and he drools over them. Lara is sprawled out on a rug next to Ailsa Fitzgerald. She calls Dillon over and he sits down between them, putting his arm around Lara. Ailsa hands him a tin but Dillon shakes his head and instead takes a small bottle of something else from his pocket. Vodka, probably. Or gin. He once told me that they were the least calorific alcoholic drinks. The music gets louder.

I head up onto the bank and sit next to Eddie, my hoody zipped up so it covers my mouth and the midgies can't get me – they seem to have arrived early this year. I wish I'd poured some of Mum's gin into a water bottle. At least it would keep me warm.

If anyone looked up from the beach, they'd probably see that someone was up here, but they wouldn't know it was me. No one looks up, though. They're all too busy hugging each other and swigging their drinks. From my vantage point I can see couples getting it on in the long grass and behind the big boulders along the beach. I try not to look. Instead, I scan the crowds on the beach for familiar faces. For Tay. For Danny.

I don't have to search long. Tay is right there, walking towards me.

"Elsie Main," he says looking down at me. He pushes back his hood, and I pop my chin out so I can talk.

"How did you know it was me?" I ask, shivering. Also, how did he know my surname? Alarm bells start ringing. He *must* know.

"Just a hunch. Can I join you or are you having your own party?"

"You can if you want," I say, already feeling defensive. "But the party is down there."

Tay looks down at the beach and frowns.

"I know. I just came from there and it's the worst party I've ever been to. It stinks as far as parties go."

"What's your idea of a good party then?" I ask him.

He shrugs and sits beside me – in between me and Eddie. I think about moving away from this spot but I can't come up with a good enough excuse.

"So, what did Danny say?" I ask.

"About what?" Tay starts rolling a joint. "Smoke?"

"No, thanks. About the other day. Did he saying anything after he'd dropped me home?"

"Nah, haven't even seen him."

"Oh," I say, relieved. Danny must have decided to keep quiet about Eddie, for some reason.

"I came to the harbour a couple of times but you weren't there," I say.

"I know. Mick said he saw you sneaking around."

Damn. I should have been more careful.

"I wasn't sneaking. I've been coming to the harbour since long before you turned up."

"I know."

"Good. Glad you know."

"Fine."

"So, what have you been up to then?" I ask.

"Why?"

"Just asking. You know, making conversation, like people do."

"Not much. This and that."

I sigh. "Okay. Fine."

This isn't going well. I don't know why we're acting like we've had some kind of fight.

"If you don't want to talk to me then why did you come up here?" I ask.

"Easy," he says, putting his hand on my arm, smiling. His eyes soften and I instantly dissolve. How can this person who is so difficult to talk to make me feel like liquid inside?

"I came to see if you were okay. After your suicide mission. I would have called but I don't have your number."

"I don't have a number," I say. "I mean, I don't have a mobile phone."

"Phones are for losers," Tay says, not missing a beat. He pulls his mobile from his pocket and lobs it towards the sea; a second later it makes a small splash. I stare at him open-mouthed.

"Did you just throw away your phone?"

"Aye, got no one to call. So, are you okay?"

"Well, I'm fine, no thanks to you," I reply, pretending I'm still annoyed, but also wondering if he just threw away an expensive phone – if he did it to impress me, or whether he always does crazy stuff like this.

"I'm sorry. I didn't think you'd jump," he says.

The smoke from his joint gets in my throat. We sit in silence for a bit, and I watch Dillon and Lara. She is practically on top of him, kissing his neck. And then I notice Ailsa staring at him with a fat bottom lip. Everyone fancies Dillon. There must be something about him. Something about him that I don't have. There's a break in the music and I hear the faint shushing sound of the sea washing over the pebbles. The wind is giving me a headache and I feel a bit sleepy. I yawn loudly.

"Cold water shock," Tay says.

"What?" I feel alert again.

"You have tiny temperature receptors in your face. When your face hits cold water your heart rate slows down and your blood vessels shrink. Your body saves oxygen for your heart and brain and stops you inhaling. That's what happened when you jumped."

"Oh great. You could have told me before I jumped," I reply.

But his explanation sounds familiar. I think I've read something about this once before when I was doing some biology homework. The human body – the only interesting thing we learn about at school. I did a project about babies and how they can survive extreme conditions. Like being in cold water.

"The mammalian reflex?" I ask, impressed that the phrase has come back to me. "That's what helps otters and dolphins stay under the water for so long."

Tay grins at me as he unfolds himself and stretches his long legs out.

"Exactly," he says. "It's just that us humans aren't so good at it."

He shuffles a bit closer and then he looks at me intensely, making me nervous.

"Look, I really am sorry," he says. "There's something I should tell you."

God. Here it comes. He's about to tell me that he knows who I am and that he doesn't want anything to do with me. I feel a huge weight of disappointment roll around in my stomach. I'm going to kill Danny, if I get the chance.

"Sure, fire away," I instruct, resigned, ready to jump up and leave.

He looks at the ground while he talks.

"I shouldn't have asked you to jump," he starts. "But – and I feel really bad about this – when you jumped, I was actually quite pleased. I thought, hey, this girl's got balls."

"Balls?" I repeat, not quite sure where this is going.

"Yeah, you know, courage."

"I know what 'balls' means."

"Okay. Well, that's all I wanted to say."

What? This guy has the weirdest conversation style. Part of me wonders if it's down to the drugs. Or perhaps he just doesn't like talking. If he wanted to sit in silence, I wouldn't mind – it would stop me saying something stupid.

"I had laryngitis for a year," I say eventually, hoping that he'll interpret what I'm trying to say – that he doesn't have to talk...

"Aye?" Tay's ears twitch and he puts his hand on his throat and gently strokes it.

"I didn't speak a word to anyone except my brother for nearly twelve months."

Tay nods. He seems to understand.

"Any other medical problems I should know about?" he asks, smiling

"No, you?" I ask straight back.

He laughs loudly. "Sometimes my shoulder dislocates all by itself. But other than that, I'm a normal, healthy seventeen-year-old boy." He carries on laughing and I frown at him.

"Sorry," he says. "I don't know why I'm laughing so much. Sometimes I laugh for no reason. It's an affliction. Anyway, you never gave us your verdict the other day."

"On what? Freediving?"

"No, on the winner of the jumping competition."

I breathe a sigh of relief. If Danny had told Tay about Eddie, I'm sure Tay would've mentioned it by now. I picture Tay's perfect formations, his taut body flying through the air and the way he emerged from the water hardly breathless. My stomach quivers but I can't give him the satisfaction of telling him how great I think he is.

"Me, of course!" I proclaim. "I think I get extra points for being so dramatic." I lower my voice. "And, you just told me that you thought I had balls, so I must have impressed you."

He smiles and shakes his head and says, "Okay, I'll give you that one, but I want a rematch."

"I'm not sure about that."

"Oh, come on. You shouldn't let one bad experience put you off."

"Danny says I can't come back to the harbour."

Tay lights a long piece of grass and then puts it out with

his fingers. Then he does it again. His attention span is worse that Eddie's.

"Tay?" I prompt gently.

He snaps his head up and grins at me. I pull my hood down away from my face so I don't look so much like a boy, even though I know my hair will be wild and I won't be able to brush it after it gets tangled in the wind. I see him look at my hair briefly and then he stares into my eyes.

"Hey, don't worry about Danny. He just doesn't like being in competition with girls. He can be a bit of a twat sometimes," he says.

"If you don't like him, why are you friends?"

Tay snorts. "We're not really friends. He's my cousin, so we have to get on."

"Oh. But what if…" I trail off, remembering I can't tell Tay the real reason Danny told me to stay away. "My parents are a bit strict," I say instead. "They worry."

"So we stay out of sight then. Plenty of places we can dive, or jump, without anyone seeing us."

He winks, and leans forwards slightly, trying to look into my eyes. I feel the ground fall away from me. If he kisses me now, what do I do? I wait, bracing myself for his lips on mine, at the same time thinking that I'm crazy for imagining he would want to kiss me.

There's a screech and then hysterical giggling. We both look down the bank and see a group of people heading towards us. One of them, a girl, is struggling to get onto her feet. I recognize her long straight hair – it's Lara. Dillon holds one of her arms, and Ailsa holds the other. They drag her upright and she stumbles again. She is wasted.

Tay gets up.

"Come on, Elsie, let's get away from here."

But it's too late. Dillon has seen me, and so has Ailsa.

Dillon lets go of Lara and runs up the bank.

"Elsie, what are you doing here?" he gasps. He has to rest his hands on his knees to catch his breath. I can tell he is slightly drunk. He stares at Tay but looks like he's having trouble focusing.

Tay grabs my arm and tries to pull me up.

"Get your hands off my sister," Dillon spits.

Tay lets me go and they stare each other out. For a minute I think that Dillon is going to punch Tay, but Lara wails from down the bank and he turns around. Tay scarpers. I've never seen anyone move so fast. In a flash he has disappeared into the darkness before I can even go with him.

Dillon collapses next to me on his knees. He looks like he's about to be sick.

"Can you take Lara home?" he calls to Ailsa. "I've got to take Elsie back."

"You should have left her with her ugly weirdo boyfriend," Ailsa shouts into the night.

At least I don't fancy my best friend's boyfriend, I think. She makes my blood boil. And right now, so does Dillon.

"I don't need you to take me home. I was perfectly happy sitting here," I hiss.

Dillon pulls me to my feet, and he's surprisingly strong.

"Stay away from that boy," he says, slurring.

"Why? What's it to you?"

Dillon looks in the direction that Tay ran off in, and then drags me onto the path that leads back home via the golf course.

"Because I'm your brother and I'm looking out for you. Mum and Dad will go bonkers if they find out."

"You're not supposed to be here either," I remind him.

"Loser," Ailsa shouts. I'm not sure if it's directed at me or Dillon. I'm in the mood to go home now anyway. I could do without all these people suddenly having my best interests at heart. It's not like anyone's cared until now whether I have any friends or not. Screw them.

Dillon grips my arm firmly all the way home. Just a few months ago we were sneaking around together and now we seem to be at odds. He doesn't want anything to do with me any more. I'm sure Lara and Ailsa have been turning him against me.

Our parents are in bed when we get back, and we are wet and cold from the damp sea air.

In the kitchen, I stand by him as he drinks a pint of water.

"Who were you looking for?" I ask. "*That* day."

He frowns at me and stumbles up to bed.

I lie on the sofa and let Eddie tell me jokes until past three a.m. He gives me the wrong answers for the jokes but I don't mind. I get him.

I want to get Tay too. I just don't know how to get inside his head.

Five

WE DIDN'T KNOW WHAT WAS wrong with Eddie for a long time – in fact no one really knew for sure. He was clumsy and I was nearly a head taller than him. He didn't understand things and was always getting confused and upset.

"Boys always develop slower than girls," everyone said – my parents, busybodies in the village whenever we popped out for a walk or to the shops, the local doctors, the doctors at the hospital in Inverness.

I pretended that I wasn't very good at running and I pretended to fall over. I used to break glasses and get my words mixed up on purpose so they didn't think Eddie was different. But I couldn't keep it up for ever. And I didn't understand why things were so difficult for him. I continued to pretend at home but I didn't want other people to think that I was stupid or clumsy, so at school I started to show people I could do stuff. When I won the fifty metre race one year, I hid the gold ribbon from my parents.

It was the P2 teacher at school who finally did something about Eddie's behaviour. She called in an Occupational Therapist. Eddie and I did lots of tests. I didn't have to do them but I wanted to. We had to pick up balls and wooden blocks and put them in boxes or in holes. We had to repeat phrases and do things like jumping and skipping. I can't really remember what else but when all the tests were done my mum had a long meeting without us. Dad sat with us in the car. Eddie wanted to listen to nursery rhymes but Dad wouldn't put the CD on. He sat very quietly in the front seat while Eddie ran trucks up and down my arm. Eventually, Dad got bored and took us inside. We waited outside the door and we could hear everything.

"These things just happen, Mrs Main. It's not your fault."

"We can give him some medication to calm him down."

"Your son will always have difficulty doing everyday things, Mrs Main."

"The best you can do is try to make life a bit easier. Get him some Velcro shoes. Let him use plastic cutlery."

Eddie never had Velcro shoes or plastic cutlery. I found

the list of these suggestions in the bin the day after the appointment, torn into pieces.

That evening, after seeing the therapist, Mum gave us spaghetti hoops with mini sausages and then she went upstairs and cried. I gave Eddie all of my mini sausages. I told him to sit up straight and hold his head up. Then I got him to lie on the floor and hold onto the underneath of the sofa while I tried to stretch his legs. I stretched until he said, "You're hurting me, Ellie."

I didn't like being bigger and stronger than him. I felt like a giant. I used to say, *Eat your greens, Eddie, and then you'll be as tall as me*, and he always did what I said. I used to say, *Give me your sweets, lie on the grass, let's play a game, Eddie*. And he always listened to me.

He shouldn't have. He should have learned not to listen to me, and then I wouldn't have to feel so guilty.

Six

ON WEDNESDAYS, MR JONES OPENS the technology room at lunchtime so pupils can work on their projects. There's usually a few of us who show up every week. We're the ones who pretend it's our choice to sit alone with our sandwiches. The ones who are a bit different, whether on the surface or inside. I think I fit into both categories: different on the surface because I'm not thin and I wear boys' clothes; different inside because of my Laryngitis Year and because half of me is missing.

Technology is my favourite subject, because Mr Jones lets us get on with our projects and I don't have to speak to anyone. This term, we have to make something out of wood. I've chosen a boat because it reminds me of happy times. Dad used to take us on summer boat trips around the Black Isle to see the dolphins. Eddie loved it – he loved the spray, and getting to sit on Dad's shoulders to be the chief fin spotter. "Look, there's Mischief! And there's Sundance!" he'd shout, remembering all the names the guide had mentioned but not really knowing which dolphin was which. And he especially loved being allowed to drive the boat. I liked to sit at the back and watch the water get churned up by the motor, the noise of the engine drowning out any bad thoughts I had about Eddie being different.

Today, there's only one other person in the technology lab, a boy called Frankie who smells like sour fruit and has dandruff. He looks pretty normal, apart from the dandruff, but he's different on the inside. He talks like he's about twenty-five and he knows stuff: weird stuff about physics and engineering and books. I actually don't mind him – he's quite funny sometimes – only I don't let anyone see me talk to him. It's better to have no friends than for people to think that Frankie is my friend.

When I pull my drawer open I find that the mast for my boat has been snapped in half and the cotton sails have been torn into tiny pieces. I turn the boat over and on the bottom, written in Tipp-Ex, it says *As if you could ever get a boyfriend*. I fight the tears; I don't cry at school. Instead, I hold the two halves of the mast in my hands and clench my fists, letting the splintered pieces puncture my skin. I swing around to look at Frankie and he stutters and shakes his head.

"I couldn't stop them," he mutters, letting his wood spin out of the lathe onto the floor. "I tried, but they just mocked me." He bends down to pick up the block of wood and his goggles fall from his face, then I hear a crunch as he steps on them.

"You shouldn't have said anything," I shout at him. "It makes them worse." I keep fighting the tears and my nose tingles. While he picks up the broken plastic, I turn the lathe off before he can do any more damage, then turn my back on him.

By the end of lunchtime I have a new mast. It's not as good as the first one but I won't let them get to me. I put the mast in my bag for safe keeping. I tell myself that one day I'll have a real boat and I'll be off exploring. I don't yet know where I want to explore but maybe there are some undiscovered islands in the North Sea. Maybe I'll find another place like the Black Isle, with beaches, otters and a boathouse. The difference will be that no one will know who I am.

Next week, in class, I'll make new sails and they will be bigger, better and stronger, and they will carry me wherever I need to go.

Seven

DILLON HAS STARTED TO DO fitness circuits in the garden. He runs around the perimeter, then hangs onto the crooked branch of the apple tree to do pull-ups. His mouth stretches wide in a grimace and the veins in his forehead pop out when he does this. He manages five then falls into a heap amid the tangled roots and weeds. He lies there panting on his back before he hauls himself into press-up position and pumps up and down, grunting with every push.

I slowly walk towards him and stop at his head. It's nearly dark and the security light comes on, lighting up the sweat beads on his forehead. Dillon's arms tremble as he heaves himself up. He yelps like a girl when he sees me.

"Jeez. You really should stop spying on people," he says, collapsing again into the grass.

"I wasn't spying. Mum wants to know if you want any dinner."

Dillon shakes his head and presses his hands into his stomach.

"I had dinner at Lara's," he says.

I raise my eyebrows at him, and he raises his back.

"Speaking of you spying on me," he says, changing the subject, "why were you at the party last weekend? You shouldn't be out that late."

"Why is it okay for you to go to the party and not me?"

"Because I'm older," he says. The way he says it reminds me of how I used to say that to Eddie, as an answer for why I could do things that he couldn't, hoping he wouldn't understand that being a few minutes older wouldn't make a difference. I feel a pang of guilt. Perhaps it did make a difference, though. If Eddie had been born first, he might not have stopped breathing.

"Lara is younger than me and you took her to the party."

"That's different. I was there to look after her."

Dillon struggles to his feet and brushes the grass from his shorts. He looks scrawny and childlike. It's chilly out here and I don't like being so close to the cemetery. Just as

I'm looking at the gate that leads to it, it opens and my father wanders into the garden. He looks at us both through teary eyes, and then wanders inside.

"Do you remember what Dad was holding in his hands the day we lost Eddie? Something blue. I think he must have got it when he disappeared from the beach."

Dillon's mouth twitches. "Els, don't hang around with strange boys, okay?"

"We're just friends," I say.

"Promise me?"

I nod. I'm not going to tell him that in my pocket is a note from Tay that I found at the boathouse. It says *Meet me at the harbour at 6 a.m. Thursday*. Tomorrow. There was a wetsuit with the note but it looked too small so I left it.

I don't need Dillon to answer my questions because the answers are in the water.

My first ever secret rendezvous with a boy. I make sure I find my waterproof mascara before I go to bed. I stay awake for most of the night, feeling the butterflies in my stomach.

At about three in the morning, I hear Dillon having a nightmare. I stand in his doorway watching him thrash about, like he's trying to grab something above his head.

"You let him go," he cries in his sleep.

The butterflies are going crazy, and so are the maggots in my throat. Dillon is screaming at me in his dream. I watch him until he stops, then crawl back to bed and wait for morning.

Eight

"WHAT THE HELL IS THAT?" Tay asks when he sees me in Dillon's wetsuit.

We stand on the harbour wall at six a.m., getting soaked in the drizzle and morning fog. It gets light early in the mornings now, but even though it's daylight everything is dark grey. The Black Isle has no colour today. The only sign that it's the beginning of summer is the swarm of midgies around my head. They love the damp weather and there's no breeze to shoo them away.

As rain pours from my nose and eyelashes, Tay kneels in front of me and pulls at the worn fabric, trying to hitch it up my legs.

"It's full of fuckin' holes, Elsie. Where did you get it from?"

"It's my brother Dillon's. He doesn't use it any more."

"Ah." He lets go of me and stands up. He looks towards the road and shivers.

"You okay?"

He continues to look over my shoulder. "Does Dillon know you're here? He looked the protective type."

I'm not sure about that. Dillon is thin and gentle. I don't think anyone would describe him as "protective". Not in a physical way, anyway.

"Is that why you ran away? You were scared of him?" I joke.

Tay does a nervous laugh and then places his hands on my shoulders. "Scared? Don't be ridiculous."

"Then why did you run off?" I ask, trying to keep the resentment from my voice.

"I just noticed the time, and had to go. I've got a strict dad too."

I've seen his dad and he's even scarier than mine. Not sure I'm buying his story, though.

"So Dillon doesn't know you're here?"

"God, stop stressing. He's not going to beat you up. He was drunk, that's all. He doesn't really care who I'm with." Although that might not be true.

Tay wipes the rain from his face and ushers me towards the edge of the wall.

"Come on, let's get in the water." He looks at my worried face. "It's okay, we're not jumping."

We climb down the metal ladder attached to the side of the wall, Tay first and me hoping he doesn't look up and see my enormous backside. I hear a light splash and look down to see him already in the water.

"Come on, slowcoach," he shouts to me. "Not afraid, are you?"

Now is not a good time to be ridiculing me. It makes me want to turn around and go home. When my foot reaches the last rung, I slip and fall into the water. It's so cold that when I try to swear, I discover I have no breath. Tay grabs me and pulls me upright. The water is only waist-deep here but it is freezing.

"Got you, now just crouch down, like me."

He pulls off his wetsuit hood that was around his neck and tells me to put it on. I'm too cold to argue. I'm too cold, too afraid, to do anything but follow his instructions. We swim a few metres out to a buoy, and I hold onto it, shivering while Tay does a test dive to make sure everything's okay. I hold my hand above the water and feel the rain bouncing up. Rain falling on water doesn't make as much noise as rain on the roof of our house, and because I'm already wet I hardly notice it. Out here, I feel like I'm in another world.

The mist blocks my view of the mainland and there is

no one in the harbour. Other than Tay below me, I am the only soul around. No one is yelling or crying. It's magical. I'm enjoying it so much I'm slightly disappointed when Tay comes back to the surface.

"Are you ready for your first freedive?" He fist-bumps me, and places a heavy rock in my left hand. "To help you get down. Hang onto it until we come back."

"Okay. I'm ready," I say. Even though I'm not ready.

"Three deep breaths on the surface, slowly, then on the fourth one we go down. Hold the rope – it's two metres to the bottom. We'll kneel there until you give the thumbs up sign to say you want to go up."

I pull my mask onto my face and after three breaths we go down. The pressure quickly builds in my ears. I swallow. My ears pop. It takes only a couple of seconds to hit the bottom and the sand is soft. Tay gives me the okay sign, a circle made with his thumb and forefinger, and settles on his knees with his arms folded and his eyes fixed on me. He has no hood, no mask and no booties. He is definitely hard core. With my right hand gripping the rope, I shiver gently and focus on counting instead of the cold water. At thirty, I finally look around and discover I can see quite far. The visibility down here is actually better than on the surface. A small fish swims past and then turns and swims back again. I let go of the rope and draw patterns in the sand. Tay shakes his head and places my hand back on the rope. My chest is pulsating now. I try to hold on for another twenty counts and take in my surroundings. I want to remember this for ever. This is the coolest moment of my life so far. If only I hadn't waited sixteen years to try it. It's totally amazing.

To my left there is an anchor covered in green slime. And something white. It looks like a shoe, half wedged into the muddy bottom; a shoe – and one that looks very familiar. A scuffed white trainer.

Boom. I'm back there again.

Eddie's hand squeezes mine as he steadies himself on the rocks. He nearly takes me down with him. We stand ankle deep in the water and today we celebrate our eleventh birthdays.

"Just stand still, Eddie," I snap. "The fins won't come if you're splashing about."

He whimpers. I look over to where Dillon is far out in the water beyond the Point, and wave my arm, beckoning him back. I shout too but he doesn't even look over.

"I want the fins," Eddie says again and stomps his feet. This time he yanks his hand out of mine and I'm not quick enough to catch him as he splashes into the water. The cold spray hits me in the face. The wind is picking up and the waves are getting bigger. It's too cold to be paddling – at least Dillon has his wetsuit on.

"Get up," I shout to Eddie. "Come on we're going back."

I hold my hand out but he refuses to take it. It's so typical that this day is only about what he wants. I look to see where Dad is so he can come and take Eddie in. I can't see him anywhere. He's not sitting down where we left him. Eddie's trainers are on the beach but Dad is not. I'm so cold that my hands have gone blue. I breathe on them but it's not enough.

"Hurry up, Dillon," I say under my breath.

"Where are the fins? Where's Mischief? Where's Sundance?" Eddie asks, still sitting in the water as the waves break around him.

"Come on. We need to get you dry."

"No. I want Dillon."

"Well, Dillon's over there. He's probably with all the dolphins because he's not splashing about making a racket. Get up."

Eddie doesn't move. I reach down and take his hand. It's even colder than mine.

"I want fins!" he shouts at me.

Then everything goes blurry.

I toss the rock and bolt.

Tay is right behind me as I surface.

"Hey, you're supposed to give me the signal," he says, oblivious to my panic. "But, nice one, how did it feel?

You did pretty well." He checks his watch. "Fifty seconds – nearly a whole minute."

I'm not even listening to him. I've got to know what I just saw on the bottom. As soon as I've got my breath back I'm swimming towards the boat attached to that anchor, towards the shoe.

"Elsie, wait! What's wrong?"

He catches up with me and even though I've only swum a couple of metres I'm exhausted.

"There's something down there," I gasp.

"Like what?" He looks alarmed.

"I don't know. It's probably just some rubbish."

Tay doesn't laugh or say I'm crazy. He tells me to swim to the wall and wait by the ladder.

"Off to do my environmental bit," he says and dives down.

He takes for ever to come back up. The rain has lessened a bit but the sky is still thick and low. I keep telling myself that it wasn't a shoe and even if it was, it wouldn't be Eddie's. Why would Eddie's shoe be in the harbour?

Tay bursts through the water.

"One mouldy trainer." He holds it up by the laces for me to see.

My eyes adjust. A white trainer.

But it isn't Eddie's, it's far too big. I see that now. The

leather tongue is green from the scum at the bottom. Some kind of shelled creature falls out and I feel bad that I've destroyed its home.

I want to ask if he saw anything else down there but my teeth are chattering and I just want to be warm. My arms feel weak as I climb the ladder but Tay is behind me pushing me up, and I don't even care that he's touching my backside.

"Come on, in the boathouse, let's warm up."

"I want to go home." My voice shakes with cold.

"You know fifty seconds isn't bad for your first attempt. Well, it's kind of your second attempt." He slips an arm loosely around my shoulder and does a sort of mini stroke of my arm before pulling away.

Only fifty seconds? Time is playing tricks on my mind again. Those memories of Eddie struggling against me seemed to last for ever.

"Are you okay?" he asks, finally noticing that I might not be.

For one crazy moment, I want to tell him everything. But if I do, he might not take me back in the water, and I can't stop now. Even though the things I'm remembering about that day aren't good, at least I'm remembering. Now I know that Eddie and I were arguing before he disappeared.

"I have to get to school," I say.

"Skip school, spend the day with me."

"Another time," I shout back as I start for home – my thoughts racing. *Tay wants to spend the day with me.*

The house is empty when I get back. In the shower, I lather myself in lime and tea-tree oil shower gel, and let the cool water cleanse every part of me. I shake the new memory from my head and instead concentrate on how good the water felt before I saw the shoe. I pretend I'm falling down a waterfall, imagining my hair fanning out the way Lila Sinclair's does in that poster at the clubhouse. I imagine Tay's arms around me as I lean back into him. I think about the water on his eyelashes, and the way he shakes his hair off his face. By the time I get out of the shower my fingers are wrinkly but my skin is glowing and tingling.

Nine

IT'S NOT UNTIL I HEAR the entire English class sniggering that I realize I've been asked a question by Mrs McIntyre. There's no way I can fake the answer; I switched off as soon as we entered the classroom. I decide to be honest. I use my mother's technique.

"Sorry, I was miles away. Can you say that again?" I wave my hand from side to side as an apology and give a little smile.

There's more cackling and someone to my left slides a piece of paper in front of me with something scribbled on it. I scrunch it up and shove it in my pocket. McIntyre isn't amused. I get my second detention of the week for not listening.

As I leave the classroom, Dillon's girlfriend Lara taps me on the shoulder.

"Why didn't you read my note? It had the answer on it."

Before I can respond, she's pulled away by a blonde frizzy-haired girl, another one of Ailsa Fitzgerald's sidekicks. "Don't bother trying to help her," whispers the sidekick. "She's *such* a loser." The girl steps towards me and I feel a sharp jab in my side. She flashes her compass at me as she strides off, dragging Lara with her. Blood oozes through my white school shirt and makes a dark stain on the inside of my blazer. I press the wound with my thumb to stop the sting and the flow of blood. On the way home, I'll swing by the Co-op to get some stain remover, but I'll have to wait until that busybody Mrs Harys has finished her shift. She watches too closely, and she does the head tilting thing and says my name loudly in front of all the customers, which results in more head tilting.

I feel for the screwed-up paper ball in my pocket and open it up. *Soliloquy*, it says in Lara's neat, round writing. I drop it on the floor and remind myself that apart from a few revision classes, lessons are nearly over for the summer term. Just exams to get through now, and at least compasses are banned in most exams.

At lunchtime, I walk to the back of the school field so I can smoke. Lara is sitting down in my space, cross-legged on her coat, which has a red satin lining. I start to move away to find a new spot but she calls me over.

"I don't know where Dillon is," I say.

"He's in the library."

"Oh. Then what do you want?'

I wonder if Dillon has dumped her but she doesn't look upset. I can't help looking at her chest – her blouse is open enough for me to see the curve of her perfect cleavage. She folds her arms.

"Can I have a fag?" she asks. It sounds odd, like she's saying the word for the first time.

"Sure," I say. I suddenly feel cool, more grown-up than her.

She makes space for me on her coat but I lay my own out and sit next to her, leaving a sliver of grass between us. As we smoke, I pluck strands of grass from the ground and sprinkle the little green pieces on my coat. She does the same but hers are in neat little piles and mine are spread everywhere.

"I know you watch us," she says. She stares straight ahead.

"I don't know what you mean," I say, feeling my palms sweat.

She turns to me. "I don't mind. You can watch if you want."

I think about Dillon's shallow breathing. I think about how I watched them at the party.

"You know there're places you can go if you're into that sort of thing," I say, lifting my head slowly.

"I'm not!"

"Yeah, loads of places, Dillon told me about them, I'm surprised he hasn't taken you there yet. He takes all his girlfriends to the woods on the other side." I smile to myself as she squirms beside me.

She asks me if I've been to the other side and I tell her no. She asks if I've ever had sex and I tell her yes.

Lara hugs me, pushing her small perfect breasts against me. When she lets go she says she won't tell anyone. About what? I want to ask.

Ten

"I LOVE THE RAIN," TAY says, breathing out smoke.

"I wish it would stop raining," I say, reaching for the joint. "Then we could go out on the boat."

"Soon," he says. "Maybe tomorrow."

He rolls over and props himself up on his elbow, his face centimetres from mine. He holds his cigarette out to the side so as not to cloud me in smoke.

"Were you okay after our dive in the harbour? It was only when I got home and thought about it that I realized you'd bolted when you saw that shoe. Why did it freak you out?"

Part of me still wants to tell him everything. About

Eddie, about Dillon, about my father. But then I imagine myself talking and it sounds ridiculous. How do you just come out with something like that? *Oh, I thought it was my dead twin brother's shoe, and I think my dad and my older brother are hiding something about the day he died.*

What if I cry in front of him? And anyway, I don't want to share Eddie – it would be like giving a part of me away.

"I wasn't freaked out," I reply. "I just wondered what it was."

Tay flicks ash onto the floor, then rolls onto his back. I watch him smoke. He watches me.

"There's so much rubbish in the sea," he says. "It's careless, some of the things that people lose."

I'm one of those careless people.

"I've found all sorts," Tay continues. "Wallets, dolls, keys…mobile phones." He stops to give me a wink. "Cushions, laptops. Even a hairbrush once, covered in hair. I mean, how do you accidentally drop your hairbrush in the water?"

"I dropped my Barbie in the water when I was a kid."

Tay smirks. "I didn't think you were a Barbie kind of girl."

"I'm not," I say, reaching for the joint. "That's why I threw it off the bridge. My mum went nuts."

My turn to interrogate.

"Tay, can I ask you a question?"

"You don't always have to ask me if you can ask me something."

I play-punch him on the arm and it feels nice to touch him.

"I do, because you don't always answer. And I'm just being polite."

He rolls in close to me again and licks his lips. It takes every effort for me not to grab him and pull his face to mine, but I have no idea if he wants me to.

"Why did you leave the Black Isle? Where did you go?"

It's the wrong thing to ask. His smile disappears and he sits up.

"Can't we just be in the moment?" he grunts. "Why do we have to talk about the past?"

He fumbles for his cigarettes, and when the lighter doesn't work he throws it across the floor.

"Sorry," I say. My cheeks get hot. "I wasn't prying. You don't have to tell me anything." I say this even though I want him to tell me everything.

"No, it's fine." His eyes lighten up a bit and he seems to accept my apology. "It's just not that interesting, that's all."

I wish I had just kissed him instead of talking. I never learn to keep my mouth shut. I give him the lighter from my pocket. He says thank you. Then he opens up.

"I didn't choose to leave. My dad didn't want me around.

He thought I was trouble and he wanted to work or hang out with his mates, not look after me."

I nod this time so I don't risk saying anything stupid. Tay keeps talking.

"I was always in trouble, little things like skipping school, getting into fights, breaking stuff around the house. Stealing. The police picked me up a couple of times – it was never serious but, you see, my dad's a cop and I was destroying his reputation. He didn't want to deal with me, so he ignored me. And then one day, he snapped and said he'd had enough. I came home from school and he had my bags packed. He drove me straight to the bus station and sent me off to my mum's. I didn't even get to say goodbye to anyone. The bastard."

"That's shit," I say. "So you were with your mum all this time?"

"Yeah, she lives in Dornie."

"Where?"

"West coast. It's pretty remote."

Tay seems small and vulnerable now and I'm responsible for making him feel sad. I put my hand on his leg to show that I care and he shocks me by taking my hand and squeezing it.

"I've stolen stuff too," I say.

He grins. "I knew you were badass. What kind of stuff?"

Hardly "badass". I blush when I think about the packet

155

of condoms I stole. "Make-up, mostly," I confess. "Hairspray, razors. Pot Noodles."

Tay lets go of my hand and slaps his thigh when I mention the noodles.

"What? What's so funny? What do you steal?"

He laughs harder.

"I don't do it now, but bikes were my thing." He can barely get the words out.

I try to ignore his hysteria. "What kind of bikes? Like, bicycles? Didn't you have your own?"

"When I was eleven I stole a moped – the idiot left the keys in the ignition and I thought I'd just take it for a ride and bring it back. But then…" He carries on laughing and it's contagious.

"I crashed it," he finally finishes. "Broke my arm. That's why my shoulder dislocates sometimes too. My dad had to pay for a new bike."

"Oh my god. So that's why he sent you away?" I ask, half shocked about the moped, half impressed.

Tay wipes his eyes and clears his throat. "Actually, no. A year after my broken arm, I stole another bike. A bicycle this time. And that was the final straw, apparently."

He looks sad now, and doesn't say anything else.

"So what made you come back?" I ask. I seem to be on a roll with the questions.

"My uncle invited me back. He said he was setting up

this dive school, and would train me to be an instructor in return for a bit of help with the club. Diving was my thing in Dornie. Nothing else to do. I really wanted to train as an instructor but the courses are so expensive and I didn't have a job. Mick's dive school was the perfect opportunity. My mum was happy to pass me back to my dad again. She's given him instructions to make sure I don't stay out all night. He even searches me and confiscates anything I shouldn't have. It's not cool having a cop as a dad. I thought that it would be good to come back, to hang out with Danny and Mick again, but this place is still a shithole. And Mick's hardly ever free to go diving."

"And Danny?"

"He's always on my back, telling me what to do, who to speak to."

"So? Ignore him. He doesn't own you," I say.

Tay smokes silently. "No, he doesn't," he finally says.

"What's wrong with this place, then? I think it's okay."

"The people. You know, small place, small minds."

"Oh, thanks." I suppose I'm one of those people.

"Apart from you, of course." He turns to face me. "Pot-Noodle girl."

And then he's kissing me and I kiss him back. He tastes like cigarettes and weed and strawberry lip balm, and his lips are soft and smooth. Our mouths work together and there's no crashing of teeth like with the last boy I kissed.

I'm living in the moment, I think to myself. And then Eddie pops up and tugs on the inside of my ribcage and he wants to play chase. *Not now, Eddie.* But he pulls me away.

"You okay?" Tay whispers.

"Yes," I whisper back, trying to lean in again. "Are you wearing strawberry lip balm?"

"Yes," he replies, moving his head back so he can look at me. "Don't you like strawberries?"

"I do. I just don't know any boys who wear fruit lip balms."

"You do now." He looks at me intensely. "Your eyes," he murmurs. "They're so green."

"Yes."

Suddenly he turns away. "It's late."

He gets up to go.

"Wait," I call. "Did I do something wrong? I was only messing around. I like the lip balm."

He shakes his head and lingers at the entrance.

"No, of course not," he says, his voice all gravelly. "I just don't want to make my dad mad."

Then he disappears. My lips tingle like he's still there, and when I close my eyes the tingles go right to my toes.

When I crawl out of the boathouse an hour later, I see Danny down on the harbour wall, staring out to sea. Giddy from the kiss and the smoke, I decide to confront him. Before I'm even halfway along the wall, he turns around.

"I thought I told you to stay away."

His hair looks shiny in the moonlight and rustles gently in the breeze. One of us is swaying slightly. I think it might be him.

"You don't get to tell me what to do. It's not really any of your business where I go or who I hang out with."

He walks closer and I smell beer on his breath.

"No, but if you had any ounce of sense you'd listen to me. Tay is not good for you to be around. He doesn't know what he wants. He's reckless, and he probably won't even be here for long."

"He's here to help you and your dad, you know."

I feel myself getting hot, but I want to have my say – someone needs to stick up for Tay.

Danny is too close. I take a step back.

"Watch out," he says sharply, grabbing me by the shoulders. For a second I think I'm going to tumble into the water, but then he pulls me to him. "You were too close to the edge," he says.

"Christ, I can look after myself," I say, releasing my arm from his grip. "My mum said you were odd – she saw you the day you dropped me home. She said you looked untrustworthy and I think she's right."

Danny snarls. "That's rich coming from her."

"Hey, what's that supposed to mean?"

I feel tears building up and quickly blink them away.

I hate it when strangers say stuff about my mum when they've never even met her. Tay's right, this is a small town.

He looks out across the bay and folds his arms. "Nothing, I'm sorry. I just know that she's had a few issues. Look, are you okay to get home? I can drive you if you want."

"No," I say. "You've been drinking."

I make my way back down the wall and across the road. When I finally turn back he's still standing on the wall. I feel a tickle in my throat and hold my breath and swallow until it eases. Tay's kiss keeps me warm on the way back, but the nice feeling is tainted by Danny's cruel words.

Eddie stays quiet all night. He doesn't want to talk to me.

Eleven

THERE'S CHEWING GUM IN MY hair. A nasty off-white colour against my black mop of curls. In the toilets, I cut it out with scissors I took from the art cupboard, along with the curl it was stuck to. The first chance I get, I spit on the gum and slip it into Ailsa Fitzgerald's bag. I get caught and have to spend lunchtime in the library under supervision.

Dillon is in the library too, doing a bit of last-minute study before his Business Studies exam. He's hunched over the desk with his head in his hands and his pens are neatly lined up beside his notebook.

"What's happened to your hair?" he says, grabbing the small tuft on top of my head.

"Ailsa and chewing gum."

"Oh, that sucks," he says.

I sit beside him. I don't tell him that his amazing girlfriend watched the whole thing and didn't do anything about it. I don't even care, because there's only one thing on my mind.

"I'm going to be a freediver," I whisper.

He looks up and stares as though I've just told him I'm going to the moon.

"I'm going to fail," he says.

I glance at his notepad. In his writing it says:

FAIL FAIL FAIL FAIL FAIL

Each FAIL on the page is underscored heavily in red and black and more red. I grab the pad, rip the page from it and screw it up. With the black pen I write on the next page, I am Dillon. I am brilliant at everything.

He tears off the part of the page I wrote on, scrunches it up, and puts it in his pocket.

After school, Dillon is himself again. His exam must have gone well, or perhaps it's just the relief of it being over.

"What are you going to do about Ailsa?" he asks. "You should've done the same back to her."

"I would've done but I didn't have any chewing gum. Anyway, I thought you were friends with her."

"Not really. She just follows me about," he says and then scratches his head. "Hmm. I might have a plan."

He disappears into his room and comes back with a bag of something really rotten.

"Fruit," he explains. "I forgot about it until there was a funny smell."

"Thanks." I step back and turn my nose from the stench. "But what do I do with it?"

I follow Dillon into the kitchen and he wraps the almost liquid fruit in several layers of foil and then puts the bundle into a plastic sandwich bag.

"Here you are. When you get near her, unwrap it and chuck it in her bag."

"Okay, thanks, Dil. I didn't know you were such a rebel."

"Never underestimate the Dilmeister." He winks at me and I catch the sparkle in his eye, something I haven't seen for a while.

I place the parcel on the table and my stomach growls.

"I wonder if Mum'll let us get a takeaway."

"She called to say she'd be late."

In the fridge I find only sausages and a half full tin of ravioli. I can't be bothered to cook the sausages so I eat the ravioli cold, standing over the sink in case it drips.

"Want some?"

"No. You really are gross."

"Thanks for the compliment," I say.

As I put the empty can in the bin, Dillon comes up behind me.

"This new hobby of yours, it hasn't got anything to do with that boy, has it? The one you were with at the party?"

"No," I lie. I'm worried that he'll tell Dad, and that Dad will ground me for the rest of my life.

I feel a slight rush at keeping something from Dillon. It's like I have power. If he can have secrets, then so can I.

Later, in the bath, I hear Dillon grunting through press-ups in one room, and my parents arguing in another.

"What should I do, Celia? Leave you in bed to rot?" The floor creaks as he paces up and down.

"It's hard for me, Colin. You don't understand how hard." Her words are slurred.

"Bullshit. How hard is it to pick up the dry-cleaning from two streets away? And how hard is it to buy a carton of milk?"

"I thought you'd get milk on your way home," she replies.

I feel bad about drinking it all now but there was nothing else.

"I need that fucking jacket for tomorrow!"

I wince when my father swears. It doesn't suit him. I reach up and turn on the cold tap. The water thunders down by the side of my head and I start to shiver. When the whole bath is freezing cold I roll onto my stomach, take a deep breath and plunge my head down. My chest spasms but I fight it and fight it, keeping myself under by pressing my hands into the side of the tub. After thirty seconds the pain subsides. There are no groans or grunts, no arguments. I'm only thinking about one thing – soaring along the seabed in a silver wetsuit.

Twelve

TAY DIVES DOWN INTO THE clear water and I watch him glide with his arms locked together out front. He looks beautiful and elegant. I feel like a cumbersome whale in the water.

We are at a place called Sandwich Cove, up the coast past Rosemarkie beach, where no one will find us. To get here, you either take a boat from Rosemarkie pier or you trek across fields and through brambles. The seabed here is made of rocks not sand, which is why the water looks so clear. It has a reddish tint when you look into it.

"You make it look so easy," I say when he resurfaces.

"That's because it is easy."

I put my mask on and try again. I struggle against the current for a few seconds then bob back to the surface.

"Stop fighting the water, and just go with it. You've got to let it take you."

"But I can't go down."

"Who says anything about going down? As soon as you're under, that's it."

Frustrated, I push away from him, slightly out to sea, and launch myself down to the bottom. It's not that deep but as soon as I get to the seabed I grab a rock and hold myself, belly down, on the floor. The seconds tick by. I brace myself for the memories to flood my mind. The rocks down here are jagged and dig into my hands but I grip them tight. Some of them are covered in a wispy kind of seaweed that looks like parsley, not at all like the big bits of kelp along the shore and in the harbour. The parsley swishes about in the current. There are shells too, stuck to the rocks, purple ones, black ones and white speckled ones. The images don't come and I'm annoyed but also relieved. Down here, I'm not a loser. I'm also a lot lighter. I move my head from side to side, swishing my hair about. I pop a couple of bubbles from my mouth and watch them float up.

When I burst through the surface, Tay is there, clapping.

"Two minutes. You're almost as good as me."

We swim out a bit further. I'm starting to get cold but I don't want to leave.

"What's the deepest you've gone?"

Tay tilts his head back into the water. "I don't know. Why is everyone so obsessed with how deep?"

"Isn't that what it's about?"

He lifts his head and flicks water in my face on purpose.

"No. Not at all. Come on, let's dive." He grabs my shoulder.

"How deep is it here?"

Tay sighs. "About twelve metres, but we're not going to the bottom."

From here I can see the lighthouse on the Point. I can just about make out small dots on the beach. Dolphin watchers.

"What about out there?" I ask, pointing towards the bit of water just away from the lighthouse, where Dillon used to swim, where the dolphins show off.

I feel Tay's fingers tighten around my shoulder.

"Deeper," he says. "There's a drop-off. It goes to about forty-three metres."

I shiver. "Ever been?"

"Nah, nothing to see down there. Right, enough talking, let's go under."

The drop-off. The very bottom of the bay. I picture the seabed gently sloping away from the shore and then suddenly falling away. That's where I need to go. That's where Eddie would have gone.

"Elsie, come on."

I notice I've been holding my breath. I let it out and tear my eyes away from the Point, refocusing my attention on Tay. It's not that hard. I could look at him all day.

I take three deep breaths, like Tay does, then dive down. I kick and kick but I only seem to move horizontally. Finally, I give up and wait on the surface for Tay. I watch his shadow dart about and I count three minutes, and I don't even know how long he was down before I started counting. When he surfaces, he looks like he's been on some kind of magical experience. His eyes are glazed and shiny. He puts his arms around me and kisses me on the mouth. He tastes of salt.

"Come on, El," he says into my neck. "Let's go and warm up."

I love how he just called me El – I feel so much older.

On the way back to Fortrose, I try to ask Tay for diving tips but he ignores my questions and tells me about all the different rocks that can be found on the Black Isle.

"Did you see the different coloured layers?" he says, pointing to the shoreline. "There's sandstone, black shale, limestone. Sandstone is what the Pictish people used to carve their sculptures. If you look carefully on the beach, you can sometimes find bits of their artwork. You can find fossils too."

"Why are there so many layers?" I ask, feigning interest.

Tay kicks a pebble. "The passing of time, I guess. Earthquakes causing the land to shift. Do you ever think about all the people who've walked along this beach before you?"

"Not really," I say. "Isn't that a bit morbid?"

"No. It's history. It's amazing what you can find on the beach if you look hard enough."

"And under the water?"

"Yes, but most of the interesting stuff ends up on the beach."

He bends down to pick up a small flat black rock. "See? It's a fossil."

"Why don't you like talking about diving?" I ask him. "Especially when you're so good at it."

Immediately I feel annoyed at myself for giving him a compliment but at the same time, I want to know.

"That's the beauty of it," Tay says. "I don't need to talk about it. It's just something I do, like breathing."

I grin. "You mean it's like *not* breathing."

He smiles slowly at me, like he's just realizing something.

"You're right. And I'm glad I get to not breathe with you."

Later, I lie on my bed with my palms facing out. I slowly breathe in over five seconds and hold, then breathe out over ten seconds. After five goes I feel dizzy and sleepy but it passes. I take a big breath in and count to a hundred and twenty. It was easy. I do it again, I count to a hundred and forty; I do it again, I count to one fifty; I do it again, I count to one forty; I do it again, I count to one thirty-nine. I lose count. I wonder how many seconds it would take to get to forty-three metres.

Thirteen

THE BOATHOUSE IS MY SECOND home. I meet Tay most days after school to dive or just hang out. I get away with it by telling Mum that I'm going to study club after school. Now that summer is well on its way it stays light really late, and it's hard to remember to go home. Sometimes we see Danny and I wave to show he can't get to me. He never waves back, and Tay moves me along and tells me to ignore him. Sometimes we pop in to see Mick but he's usually too busy to talk to us. He still makes the best hot chocolate though, and there's always a good selection of diving magazines to thumb through.

Every time we go into the water, I push myself to go a

little bit deeper and the thrill of it fills me with adrenaline and makes me want to go deeper still. Ten metres, then twelve, then fourteen, then sixteen and finally eighteen. Sometimes Tay comes down with me, other times he hovers near the surface and then comes down to pull me up when he thinks I'm down too long. If he can't meet me, he leaves me little notes about diving which I sit and read in the boathouse. They're amazing, full of little tips on how to increase my lung capacity, drawings (of me!) demonstrating how to do dolphin kicks and frog kicks. How to reserve my energy. What to do in an emergency – release my weights and kick for the surface. A list of things to remember: 1. Be confident. 2. Never dive alone. 3. Let your mind control your body. There aren't any tips on how to go deeper though. I don't understand why Tay isn't interested in that. Especially as Mick told me that Tay can go the deepest out of anyone.

At school, I create my own bubble to hide in. I barely listen in revision class. I hide Tay's notes inside my textbooks and re-read them instead. I haven't done any extra preparation for my exams, but I don't even care. If I fail, they might kick me out of school, and then I could dive all the time.

I'm smiling at a picture Tay has drawn of me in the lotus position with a speech bubble coming out of my mouth saying *Tay is the best teacher* when I feel something hit my ear. Then an elastic band flies past me and falls by my feet. I do my best to ignore it, but when the bell goes I am surrounded.

"What you got there?" Ailsa grabs the drawing and shows everyone, then tears it into tiny pieces.

"None of your business," I say.

Ailsa grabs my hair and one of her sidekicks stamps on my foot.

"I know you put the rotten fruit in my bag," she hisses. "Don't think you're going to get away with it."

When she pulls her hand away she takes a clump of my hair with her. It hurts so much I want to cry, but I do not cry at school. It's Lara who comes to my rescue.

"Leave her alone," she says. "Find someone else to bother."

Ailsa stares at Lara, open-mouthed, and then pushes her to the side.

"Well you would stick up for your pathetic little boyfriend's sister, wouldn't you?" And she marches off with her sidekicks in tow.

Lara doesn't move. I don't want to, but I force myself to say thank you to her because it's polite. Then I realize she only did it because she wants to talk to me about Dillon.

"I'm worried about him," she says. "He seems really distant. Is everything okay at home? I know he's got exams, but so have we."

I don't correct her to say that my exams haven't actually started yet. I'd be even more of a target if everyone knew how few subjects I'm actually taking.

"Yeah, everything's fine," I say, wondering how much Dillon has told her about Mum's drinking and Dad's disappearing acts.

"I guess you guys have a lot to deal with," she says. "If you ever want to talk…"

She looks genuinely concerned and I feel sorry for her. I hope my brother isn't the shag-then-leave-them type.

"I think Dillon is okay," I say. "He's just a bit stressed over his exams."

But she's right. Dillon is being very weird. He's having nightmares, and he never eats the food I cook, even when it's healthy. I need to take him to the beach to cheer him up and get him away from his books. I also want to ask him again who he was looking for on the beach that day. I haven't had any new memories and now that I'm comfortable in the water I'm starting to think I might not have any ever again.

Fourteen

THERE IS A HUGE SWELL and the wind churns up the water so it looks like frothed-up egg white. Tay isn't in the boathouse where we agreed to meet. After a few minutes, I hear the door to the clubhouse slam, and then voices. I crawl outside and peer around the corner.

Danny and Tay are on the veranda, having what looks like a heated discussion. The wind is too loud for me to hear properly but I catch the end of the conversation.

"You know what you need to do," Danny says.

"Fuck you," Tay replies and then jumps down the steps two at a time. I slither back into the boathouse and pretend that I've been there the whole time.

Tay is agitated when he comes inside, swearing under his breath, and kicking things about. After he discovers all the beers are gone, he slams my cupboard door so hard that the whole thing topples over.

"I can go and get more beers if you want?" I offer. I quickly work out that Mrs Harys won't be working at the Co-op. The other lady is always so engrossed in serving customers, I can easily get four or five tins in my pocket before she notices anything suspicious. Then I just run.

Tay sits down heavily and leans back against the wall. "It's fine."

I light us cigarettes and pass one to him. Even when he's angry, he smokes delicately.

There's a nasty yellow bruise on the bridge of his nose. He sees me looking and turns away, so I don't say anything but I'm guessing what I heard wasn't Tay's first fight with Danny.

"I can't do the rings," I say after a while. I take in another lungful of smoke and click my jaw like Tay has shown me but the smoke comes out in sideways clouds.

Tay puts his arm around me and tells me he thinks the sideways smoke looks better anyway. I can't help but look at the bruise – there's a small cut too that's scabbed over.

"Must have whacked myself in the face while I was asleep," he says. He touches it gently with his finger and flinches.

I frown at him. "Who were you talking to just now? Danny?"

"No one."

"Tay, I could hear you. Why did you tell him to fuck off?"

"He's just being a twat. He says I need to help more with the diving club. He thinks I shouldn't be spending all my time with you."

"So? I thought you didn't have to listen to him."

Tay brings his knees up and then stretches out again, like he can't get comfortable. "He says you're too vulnerable."

And then I know that Danny has told Tay about Eddie. I shouldn't have provoked him by waving all the time, and there's a chance he saw me having a teary moment in the water the other day.

"He's told you about Eddie, hasn't he?"

Tay is silent for a minute and just smokes. At first, I panic and think that Danny was right, Tay doesn't even care; then I wonder if he just didn't hear me.

"Tay?"

He turns to me and reaches out to stroke my hair. Then he puts his cigarette down and touches my forehead with his. Finally, he pulls back and picks up his cigarette again.

"I know about Eddie," he says. "And I'm sorry. Why didn't you talk to me about him?"

He doesn't give me the pity head tilt. Instead, what I

178

read in his face is disappointment that I didn't tell him myself. And something else. Admiration perhaps.

"I can't pretend to know how you feel," he continues. "But just so you know, you can talk about it, if you want. Or not, if you don't want to. I guess you don't want to, otherwise you would've talked to me."

I'm so relieved that he's not running away that I kiss him, on the lips, and I have to rein myself back in before I literally eat him. And he is just as hungry for me. And then, when I've kissed away all my fear and I feel Eddie getting embarrassed for me, I tell Tay everything: about the day Eddie disappeared, the police search, the flashbacks I've been having. Tay holds me against him as I talk. I can't see his face but I can tell he's listening because he breathes lightly and twirls my hair. I've never told my story to anyone before. Everyone I meet either already knows, or doesn't need to know. I tell him about how my family is falling apart, about Dillon not eating and about his nightmares.

"He wakes in the night shouting 'You let him go!' And it's completely my fault."

Tay squeezes my hand. "It's not your fault, El."

I sit up and look at him. His eyes are watery but he quickly wipes them dry.

I'm ready to tell someone my biggest secret.

"It *was* my fault," I say. "I was supposed to hold Eddie's hand the whole time we were in the water. I shouldn't have let go but I did. He's never said it to me, but I know Dillon blames me. My dad does too."

"Don't blame yourself." Tay almost shakes me. "It's not your fault. You were only small. The water out there is so unpredictable. If you get caught in a rip tide or a strong current, it's impossible to hold onto anything. Trust me, I know."

He passes me a cigarette and says he wants to hear more about Eddie. We sit and smoke while I tell him Eddie stories. Tay laughs at the story about the dog and Eddie hanging onto the lead.

"What was wrong with him?" Tay asks when I take a break from telling stories.

I flinch slightly at the question before remembering that it's a normal thing to ask.

"A few things. We don't know really, or at least Mum never told us. The doctors kept changing their minds, but it was probably to do with being starved of oxygen when he was born."

"I'm sorry," Tay says. "He sounds like a cool kid."

When it's nearly time for me to go, I feel sad. It's been a long time since I shared Eddie like this, and rather than giving part of me away I feel like I've gained a bit more of Eddie. And then the guilt comes rushing back.

"The hardest thing," I say, "is that we don't know what happened to him. Sometimes I think that we're all just waiting for him to turn up. I wish that we'd found him so we could have said goodbye properly."

Tay makes a choking noise and I feel bad for burdening him, but then I look up and he's just coughing.

"You can say goodbye in your head," he says quietly. And then he says, "Maybe it was a good thing that you didn't have to see him. Bodies that have been underwater don't look human."

My head instantly fills with nasty images of mutilated zombies. "I can't believe you just said that."

I try hard to picture Eddie underwater, alive. His dark curly hair bouncing in the current, his lips red and smiling. That's the only image I hang onto.

"Sorry," Tay replies, looking confused. "I wish I could help."

I turn to him. "There is something you can do."

"Of course, anything," Tay whispers.

"Help me get to the drop-off."

His mouth falls open.

"No way," he says defiantly.

"Yes way. I think it's where Eddie would have ended up. I want to go down there and see."

"What do you think you're going to find?" Tay's eyes are wide in horror.

"Nothing. I don't know. It's not like I think he's still down there, but I just want to go to where he died. You know, like if someone dies in a car crash, the family all go to the place where it happened to put flowers and notes there. I want to do that."

"And if someone falls into a river, the family put flowers on the bridge or by the side of the river. Not in it."

"Only because they can't go in the river. But that's the difference, Tay. I *can* go down. I know how to. It's the only way to get closure."

"That's not the way to get closure. The best way to let go is to start living your life."

"You just said you'd do anything for me."

"I would. But it's too deep. It's impossible. You'd need to hold your breath for at least four minutes."

"I just want to say goodbye."

Then he pulls me around to face him and presses his body into mine.

"Okay, here's the plan. I'll think about it. But we have to lie low for a bit, stay away from Danny and the harbour."

"I'm not giving up diving."

"I'm not saying that. I'm saying that we'll have to make sure no one sees us. We dive at night-time."

"In the dark?"

"Yeah, it's even better in the dark. That's the thing with art. You have to always look at it from a different perspective."

"You've lost me. What's art? The sea?"

"Diving. Every dive is different and two people doing the same dive will have different experiences. And if you dive in the same spot at a different time of day, it will be different. It's the same with a painting. If you look at a painting in different light, or even no light, you'll have a new perspective on it. Don't you think?"

I raise my eyebrows. "Are you crazy? The drop-off is too dangerous but diving in the dark isn't?"

But I feel a thrill bubble away inside me.

I long for the dark.

"The sea comes alive at night," Tay says. He kisses my collarbone and then he moves his hand up inside my jumper. I don't stop him. His hand is rough against my breast, and I feel slightly lopsided. I'm not sure if it's the crazy amount of nicotine racing through me or Tay massaging me that's making me dizzy, but I let him lie me down on the floor. He lifts my top right up and pulls my bra down, then his mouth is on me and he's telling me how nice I taste. I wait for Eddie to pop up and force me to stop, but he doesn't. Eventually, Tay stops of his own accord, and pulls my jumper back down. He looks worried.

"Thank you for not running off," I say.

"Why would I run off? That's crazy, I'm not going anywhere."

Tay's arms tighten around me.

"I miss him," I say. "I miss my brother."

Fifteen

THE NEXT DAY, TAY IS different. I try to snuggle into him so we can plan our night dive, but his arm is stiff and I can't get comfortable.

"What's wrong?" I ask, looking up at him.

"Nothing."

"Okay. Right, if you say the drop-off is beyond my limits then I need to practise. There must be places that I can practise going deeper, like down to thirty metres maybe."

"Elsie, stop. This isn't going to work."

"What do you mean?" I don't understand what he's saying but I know I don't like it. My breath catches and I feel hot.

"I mean I'm going to be quite busy from now on and I won't be able to see you as much."

"I'm going to be busy too, my exams start next week, but I'll still make time for you."

"No. We can't see each other."

"What's happened? Yesterday we were planning our secret night dives, and now you're *dumping* me?" I knew yesterday was too good to be true. "Is this because of everything I told you about Eddie? I'm such an idiot. I don't know why I thought you'd understand. If it is, that isn't really fair because you were the one who got me in the water in the first place and made me think about everything. And now you're going to leave because you can't handle it?"

"No, that's not true at all."

"Okay, so it must be to do with Danny then. I can't believe you're such a coward. Why do you listen to him when he clearly hates you?"

"Don't do this, El. It's nothing to do with anyone, it's just me. I don't want to hurt you."

"You already have," I say. My voice wobbles.

"I'm sorry," he mutters. "You're better off without me in your life."

Nothing makes sense. He stares at me, focused on something on my face. I feel my cheek but there's nothing there. He reaches out and strokes my cheek over and over again until I feel quite scared.

"What are you doing?" I ask.

He pulls his hand away like I've given him an electric shock. Then he kisses me really hard on the lips. So hard it actually hurts. His hands are all over my body, trying to feel every part of me. As I try to pull away I smack my head against the wall.

"Sorry," he gasps. He staggers back, then grabs his stuff and leaves.

I follow him outside but he's vanished.

For a minute, I don't move, I've got nowhere to go. But then I wander down to the water and wade in. I don't even bother to take my shoes off. I'm not sure the sea does come alive at night. The water looks black and lifeless here.

At home an hour later, I lie on my bed with my soaking wet trainers still on and cry. It's a different kind of crying to how I used to do it. Now, the tears fall silently from my face and I don't sob, because if I did, the air would be coming out.

Sixteen

DILLON IS DRYING OUT. HIS skin is all shrivelled and flaky, and stretches across his collarbone so tightly I almost expect the bones to pop out. His bulging knuckles are rough, with small dots of blood on them. It looks painful, and he rubs them and blows on them every now and then. If I didn't know better, I'd suspect he'd been in a fight.

He scrapes the sand into a pile using his bare feet. After each fresh heap he shakes the grains from his feet and starts again. It's the warmest day of the year so far, and we both wear cut-offs. The trip to the beach takes my mind off Tay and the dull ache in the back of my skull.

"What are we making?" I ask, and drag more sand onto his pile. "A mermaid?"

"What are you, twelve? But okay. You can do the tail."

"That's not fair! I should do the top part."

"No, that's a man's job."

I shove him and he falls right into his pile, squashing it flat. While he's lying there I kick sand onto his stomach, trying not to get it in his face. He's laughing and his cheeks are the pinkest I've seen them in a long time and then I'm laughing so much I'm crying and get a stitch.

"Bury me, then," he says, almost choking through his laughter.

We dig a bit of a hole and then Dillon jumps in. As I fill it up with Dillon inside, I notice frown lines on his forehead that never used to be there. I try to smooth the creases from his forehead with my fingers. He yells when the sand from my hands falls into his eyes. He has his face scrunched up like the inside of a cabbage.

"Relax," I say. "I'm just exfoliating you." I feel the grains scratch my skin as I crunch them into the creases.

When only Dillon's head is poking through the sand, I sit beside him and look out to sea. The water is calm and flat. I feel as though I could pick it up and hold it in my hands without it slipping off. It's funny how water can look and feel so different depending on what day it is. I'm starting to understand what Tay meant about different light.

"I miss our days like this. When your exams are over, can we do it more and have picnics like we used to?" I ask.

"You have exams too, remember?" Dillon says.

"I'll be fine. Everyone says it's impossible to fail technology so at least I'll pass one." I give him the biggest smile I can muster.

"Are you okay?" he asks. "You look like you've been crying."

"I will be," I say. Even though I don't think I'll ever be okay again. "So, picnic soon?"

"Sure. Without the sandwiches, though. I don't much like sand in my sandwiches."

"Dillon, you're not fat, you know," I whisper.

The sand cracks and falls away as he rises from his cocoon. "Let's go home," he replies.

Seventeen

DILLON AND I GET HOME just as Dad is leaving. He carries the last box to the car and Mum stands at the gate with mascara all over her face.

"I don't deserve this, Colin," she says between muffled sobs.

He sees me and Dillon standing in the road.

"Look after the kids, okay?" he shouts to Mum.

He slams the boot and moves to the driver's door.

Dillon runs to him. "Don't go, Dad," he says.

"It's not for ever," my father says. "Your mum and I just need a bit of space. I'll be back, alright, pal?"

Dad hugs Dillon for a really long time. I hope he notices

that Dillon is just skin and bone.

I go to Mum and put my arm around her. She's holding Dad's atlas.

"You're better off without him," I say, and she leans into me.

I wonder if part of me wants her to go through this so someone understands how I feel – so someone else knows what it's like to be deserted by the person you trusted the most. But, actually, we're all better off without him. Dillon and Mum will realize this one day.

After Dad's gone, Dillon storms past us into the house, knocking the atlas from Mum's arms so it falls into the weeds.

"You drove him away," he snarls. "You should be the one to go."

I've never seen him this furious. My father always manages to ruin the few good days Dillon and I have together.

Part Three

EDDIE: *What did the* seaweed *say when it got stuck at the* bottom *of the* sea*?*

ELSIE: *I don't know.*

EDDIE: Kelp! Kelp!

ELSIE: *That's funny, Eddie. Your best one.*

One

DAD'S BEEN GONE A WEEK and Dillon spends most of his time in the bathroom with the shower running hot to create a steam room. He won't even talk to me because if I hadn't dragged him to the beach, he might have been able to stop Dad from leaving. Dad's called every day to wish us good luck with our exams, but I've been too busy holding my breath to speak to him. I haven't seen Tay for eight days. He hasn't called at all. I've taken three exams and probably failed them all. Five more left. I can't bear to go to any more revision classes and it's too depressing to stay at home with Dillon, so I spend most of my time at the pool with the entire under-three and over-seventy population of the Black Isle. Life officially sucks.

I sit alone on the floor at the bottom of the deep end of the pool, and it feels gritty under my backside, other people's dirt digging into my skin. It's impossible to stay still because there is nothing to hold me down so I drift from side to side. I burst up to the surface, creating waves with my body and arms, and a mother with a baby throws a disgusted look in my direction and I don't even care. I bob up and down in the small swell that I've created, watching the water spill over the sides into the overflow drains.

A pair of legs covered in blond hair appears in front of me. I look up and see Danny.

Not good. Life just got even worse.

There's nowhere to hide but under the water. A minute goes by, and then another and then I need to breathe. He's crouched down when I surface, arms balanced on his knees.

"I thought it was you. Can we talk?"

"I'm busy," I reply and then go down again.

I last only a minute this time.

"I don't want to fight. I'll wait until you've finished." He points to a bench at the side of the pool.

I don't have the energy to go down again. There's no getting away from him.

"Pass me my towel, then," I say as I climb up the ladder.

The heat from his body stops me shivering as we sit on the bench.

"You told me to stay away from the harbour. You didn't say anything about the pool. Not that I have to listen to you anyway."

"We might have got off on the wrong foot."

"I haven't seen Tay, if that's what you want to know."

"I was wondering, actually. I haven't seen him either. My dad's going mad because the diving club is supposed to open next week and Tay's nowhere to be seen. We can't get through on his mobile – it's like the number doesn't exist."

Bits of towel fluff are stuck to my legs and I flick them off one by one onto the wet tiles by our feet. They soak up the water and float away. I wonder where Tay is. It doesn't make any sense, because the reason he was here was to train as an instructor for Mick's school.

"Well, you sent him away, didn't you?" I ask.

Danny scratches his neck. He has a shaving nick that looks sore.

"Look, I didn't tell him to leave. I just told him not to hurt you."

"Well, I'm sorry that you're a man down, but I can't really help you."

"Maybe you can help. I need a favour."

I almost laugh in his face. I can't imagine what he'd need help with.

"The clubhouse still needs work before we open. We need someone to help us finish decorating it, and then when we're open, we'll need help with equipment and the boat – someone to come out on the boat with us on dives and be a spotter and generally help out."

"You want me to be your minion," I say. I can't believe that he thinks I'd want to be his slave.

"No, it's not like that. It makes sense – we need someone who's interested in diving and who isn't afraid to get a bit dirty. Think of it as a kind of apprenticeship."

"So you'd pay me?"

"Not in cash, in dives. I'd give you lessons, proper ones."

"I already know how to dive, thanks. Anyway, I've got exams. I'm too busy." I stand up to go and hold the towel tight around me.

Danny stands too and towers above me. It feels strange being this close to him. I remember the first time we met at the clubhouse when he looked right through me.

"Okay," he says. "Well it's up to you of course, but don't you want to be a better diver? Go deeper, dive for longer?"

Yes! I want to say. *Yes, I do, but just not with you.*

"I'm late for dinner," I say, wringing the excess water from my hair onto Danny's dry feet.

"Well, let me know if you change your mind. Good luck with your 'revision'," he replies, nodding towards the water.

* * *

It's not that I change my mind, exactly. I go down to the harbour on the off chance that Tay might be there. The clubhouse now has deep blue walls, with swirly wave patterns running around the bar area. The boat boys are sprawled out on squashy red cushions in the middle of the floor, poring over maps, drinking Coke. Tay is not here. Coward. A lump grows in my throat.

Rex sees me first and calls me over.

"Hey, mermaid! What's new?"

Danny pats the cushion next to him and asks what I think of the place. "It's nice," I tell them as I sit down. "It's like being underwater."

For some reason they think this is hilarious.

Rex jabs a finger at the map and when I look closer it seems to be some sort of intricate plan of the sea floor. He explains there's a wreck just off Lossiemouth. It's at forty-three metres.

"We're going in a month or two. You wanna come?" Rex asks. "Danny says you might be our new spotter now that..." He trails off.

"She can dive with us," Danny says. "Tay's been teaching her, a bit. But now I'm going to show her how it's really done."

The boat boys go quiet.

I suck in my breath, the way Tay taught me, first into my belly, then into my lungs. I sit in lotus position like this for a minute, and when a minute is up, I do a little dance, pretending that my arms are dolphins, twisting, turning, diving. Even as the boat boys, Danny included, roll around in hysterics, I keep my breath inside me until my body is screaming for me to release. It feels good when I breathe out.

"Fuck me," Rex says, sighing.

"No thanks," I reply and suddenly I am a new confident me. Joey is killing himself beside me. I remember Tay's first lesson. Step one: be confident. Inside, I smile.

"So what's this place called now? Doesn't the dive school have a name?"

"Actually, that's your first job, Elsie," Danny says. "We need to paint the name on the front. *Black Isle Divers*."

"Really? That's not very exciting."

"It's fairly self-explanatory," Danny says. "We want people to know what we do."

"I get that, but it seems a bit bland. And people might think that you can only come here to dive, when really, you can come here just to hang out, watch the boats, look across at the mainland, eat."

The three boys ponder this for a moment and then Rex says, "She's right. It's a shite name."

"We can't change it, the business is already set up: the bank, the email address, everything," Danny says dismissively.

"So just change the name of the actual clubhouse then," Joey says. "How about No Limits Cafe?"

"The Dolphin," Rex says.

I hear Eddie calling out for the fins.

"How about The Black Fin?" I suggest, and immediately regret it but it's too late.

Mick appears behind the bar. "Perfect," he says. "Any more ideas, Elsie?"

Perhaps Eddie won't mind that he inspired the name of this place. I jump up and run to the back corner. "Yes, you should keep all these cushions but move them here, and move the TV screen here so that people can watch films. And Lila Sinclair should come for the opening."

Mick whistles. "I think she might be in the Bahamas, but I'll see what I can do."

I feel excited for the first time since Tay and I were planning our night dive. Eventually I ask Joey if Tay has gone back to Dornie. I feel like Tay would trust Joey the most. Joey looks at Rex, and Rex shrugs. No one seems to know. Tay does a good vanishing act.

"I reckon he'll be back," Joey says.

Whatever the reason for Tay's disappearance, the best chance I have of seeing him again is to hang around with the boat boys. He's got to come back at some point. And in the meantime, I'll learn to dive. I'll learn to dive deep.

We go back to looking at the sea chart.

"It's here," Joey says, taking my finger and placing it on a patch of darker blue. Eighteen metres is the deepest I've been. I have a long way to go to get to forty-three.

Two

AFTER A WEEK OF PAINTING and putting furniture together in between taking pointless exams, Danny finally allows me to join him and the other boat boys on a dive. I get through my maths exam, just about, although I can't answer most questions in the second half of the paper, and arrive at the harbour mid-afternoon. Joey and Rex are feeding the seagulls on the harbour wall. They're wearing new matching wetsuits that have red zippers on the back. Rex holds a piece of bread out to Joey, then whips it away and sticks it in his mouth. Joey elbows him, and then goes back to clucking at the gulls.

"We're going to Sandwich Cove," Danny explains,

appearing from nowhere. "There's an underwater cave there. Up for it?"

"Yeah, of course," I say, even though I'm afraid of caves.

Danny passes me a yellow waterproof duffel bag.

"It's a loan, just for today."

Inside, there's a diving watch and a diving suit. The wetsuit is tight but it slides on much easier than Dillon's smelly old one. The fabric feels smooth against my skin. I can't stop beaming and just manage to stop myself from throwing my arms around Danny's neck.

The Half Way is one of the smallest boats in the harbour. It just about holds the four of us. It chugs along slowly, giving me time to compose myself, and by the time we arrive in the small bay, a little way up the coast from where Tay and I used to dive, I'm still nervous but more excited. We moor up to some craggy rocks that are sheltered from the breaking waves and stay in the boat to put our gear on. I accidently elbow Rex several times as I pull on my wetsuit and he shouts loudly that I can't keep my hands off him. Joey tells me to ignore him. Danny points to where the cave is. To get to it, we have to swim back out to sea and around to the next bay.

The water is freezing but I have booties on and the swim warms me up.

When we get to the next bay, Danny stops swimming. "Wait," he says, holding me back in the water. He stares at the cliff face as though there might be a monster lurking just beneath the surface. The Loch Ness Monster perhaps. I giggle nervously.

"We can't do this today," Danny says. "There's a current, I can feel it."

I look around. The bay is as flat as a millpond. And the water around my legs is still and cold.

"Don't be a twat, Danny boy. Come on, I'll lead the way," Rex says, swimming on.

"Stay close to me, Elsie," Danny says. Then he speeds off to catch up with Rex and I can hardly breathe by the time I reach them. Danny is in charge again now. I can't help wonder if he's a little scared of caves too though. I feel a surge of warmth for him, but quickly shake it away.

"The entrance of the cave is five metres below the surface. When we get there, follow the light and keep kicking hard until you get to the far wall and then frog-kick straight to the surface," Danny says. "Watch out for bits of rock that jut out – keep one hand near the wall, and the other above you."

We dive down and Danny points to the rocky coral-covered archway which leads to the cave. I want him to go first but he motions for me to go ahead. It's dark inside the arch. I swim as fast as I can, my fins hitting the coral with every kick, but finally I see the opening and the dark water turns to a hazy green. When I get to the far side I look up and see the surface a few metres above. I start frog-kicking like crazy but the fins are getting in my way. We've been under for less than a minute but already I want to breathe. I'm just thinking about removing the fins when Danny appears next to me and he takes us up. It seems to take for ever – the clear water is deceptive and the surface is much further away than I first thought.

Finally, we break through and Danny asks if I'm okay.

"Yes, except the fins don't fit properly."

"They do fit. You just need to work on your fin kicks," he says.

"How do I improve my fin kicks?" I ask.

"Your kicks aren't very efficient."

"Yes, but how do I make them better?"

He demonstrates with his hand, pushing his fingers back and forth in invisible water. I have no idea what he means. Tay would be able to tell me how to improve. He would show me, then draw a diagram, and then let me practise as many times as I wanted.

I miss him.

Danny motions to some steps carved out of the rock. I pull off my fins in the water and heave myself up. The steps lead to a narrow ledge where there's just enough room to sit with my legs dangling over the side. The ledge looks as though it's been made by the rock shifting over time, but someone has clearly spent a long time carving out the steps and making sure they're even. Once I've got over the journey in, the sight takes my breath away. Light shines from two cracks in the ceiling and fills the cave with golden rays. Hundreds of stalactites hang down, the water on them glistening. Danny sits next to me.

Below us, the shadows of Rex and Joey shimmy up to the surface.

"The vis is the bollocks," Rex says when he comes up. "You can see right to the bottom, did you look?"

I didn't look down, I was too focused on getting up to the surface – but he's right: the water is the clearest I've ever seen, with no sand and grit that normally makes it murky.

"Welcome to the King's Grotto," Rex says, as though he owns it. "Isn't this the coolest place you've ever been?"

"It's amazing," I say, still taking it all in. The air in here tastes stale, but being in an underwater cave is mind-blowing. If I'd known about this place before, I would have chosen it for my hiding place.

"See the throne?" Rex points to a little enclave opposite the ledge where I'm sitting that actually looks like a seat. "We always bring a rock or pebble from outside for good luck. We put them up there."

Rex hauls himself out of the water and scrambles up the rock face to the throne. I notice that the ledge he's on runs all the way around the cave back to where I'm sitting.

He places his rock in the throne then somersaults off the ledge back into the water. We watch him sink to the bottom and then zoom back up like a torpedo.

Joey climbs the steps and passes me his stone to add to the collection. It's a small, heavy one. A wave of vertigo passes over me as I stand and I try not to look down. Danny grabs my hand. "Don't, it's dangerous," he says. But I shrug him off. Slowly I inch my way around to the throne, keeping one hand against the wall until the ledge widens. Finally I reach the throne and inside it coloured stones sparkle under the rays – red, green, blue. I catch a glimpse of something yellowy-gold among the darker stones towards the back. It's like stumbling on someone's treasure. I run my hands over the stones, feeling all the different textures; smooth ones, sharp ones, rough ones. As I reach further in, my finger gets caught on something. It's too dark over here to see what it is – a bit of fishing net perhaps, or some other sea rubbish. I yank my hand out of the throne and turn around to admire the view. The boat boys are all on the ledge opposite me. Danny's face is white, like he might keel over. I'm about to ask if he's okay when Rex yells for me to jump into the pool. I'm not falling for that again. Slowly, I inch my way back along the ledge and by the time I reach them, Danny looks normal again, but a little agitated.

After the thrill of the ledge I start to shiver, and Danny says we can't stay long because the air is too thin.

On the way back I take more notice of my surroundings and see that the archway is covered in molluscs, and blue soft coral that looks like hands, waving.

"Deadman's fingers," Danny explains when we're back on the boat, and I shudder.

"I'm impressed, Elsie," Rex says. "You're quite the diver. You should try jumping off the ledge next time, though. This wuss won't do it." He nods to Danny, who rolls his eyes.

"Because it's fucking dangerous," he says.

Back at The Black Fin, while we're drying off by the fire, Danny says I can keep the wetsuit and the watch.

"It's a peace offering. You can keep it here, as long as you rinse it after each dive."

It's the first new piece of clothing I've had for a year. "Thank you."

He sits next to me as I towel-dry my hair.

"I'm sorry if I seem overprotective," he says. "I can't help it, knowing what happened to your brother."

I stop drying my hair and look at the floor.

"How does your family cope?" he asks. "It must be so hard living here, reminders everywhere, water everywhere."

I wonder why he can't see that I don't want to talk about Eddie with him.

"We manage," I say. "Why are you so interested?"

He folds his arms. "I don't know. Sorry. I just remember it. How sad everyone was at the time – it was all anyone talked about for months, and it's stayed with me, I guess. And now I see you every day, I can't help thinking about it."

"I'm sorry I remind you of sad times," I say, and it sounds more sarcastic than I mean it to. "Thanks for letting me come to the cave."

"I'm glad you didn't jump off the ledge. Don't ever do that jump. Rex is an idiot."

"Is that why you looked like you'd seen a ghost? Because you thought I was going to jump?"

"What?"

"When I was standing by the throne. You looked really frightened."

Danny fiddles with a loose thread on his T-shirt. "Oh, aye. I thought you'd jump. Do me another favour, don't ever go there alone. Promise?"

I nod. I have no intention of going there on my own. I walk away feeling slightly uneasy. I'm still angry with Danny for sending Tay away and his questions felt intrusive, but at the same time he seems a bit sad and he's making an effort to be nice to me. Without warning, my brain suddenly pictures the two of us kissing. I quickly shake the image of Danny away, and think of Tay instead.

Three

THE NEXT DAY, WE PAINT the front of the clubhouse and officially christen it The Black Fin. Mick has ordered a stencil, and when it's fixed in place – a job that Mick and Danny insist is one that only they can do – I get the pleasure of painting the letters. Mick holds the ladder and keeps telling me what a great job I'm doing, even though Rex is yelling up telling me I've missed bits here and there. Afterwards, Mick lets me have half a shandy to celebrate and it immediately makes me light-headed. Without Tay around I haven't spent any time in the boathouse drinking. I still think of him every day, and wonder whether he's thinking of me, but every time I'm off in my own thoughts

Danny pulls me back. It's like he senses what I'm thinking about and gives me a job to take my mind off it. It doesn't work, though. I spend the day alternating between imagining myself diving with Tay, and kissing Danny. It must be my hormones.

"We've got a group of guys who want to go snorkelling," Mick says as I'm finishing my drink. "Our first customers. Can you make sure all the equipment is ready?"

"Is the dive club officially open for business then?"

"Against all odds, it would seem so," he says. I wonder if he's referring to Tay's disappearing act.

He hands me a sheet of paper with a list of wetsuit and fin sizes written on it. I don't want to do it, I want to sit here and think about Tay, but I can't complain because Danny's being so nice to me, with the new wetsuit and promising to take me on more dives.

"You can come if you want," Danny says when I don't move straight away.

"I can't," I say feebly. "I've still got a few more exams that I should study for."

"Oh. I forget that you still go to school," he replies, and it makes me feel very small. I wonder if he does this on purpose or if he's completely oblivious to how he makes me feel.

I scoff at myself then, because *I* don't even know how he makes me feel. One minute excited and like I'm part of something, and the next like I'm something he accidently trod in.

I go out into the back and make lots of noise as I move crates of equipment around, trying to find the right sizes. I had no idea there was so much stuff here. It all looks and smells new. Mick joins me and helps me lift the heaviest boxes.

"I don't know what we'd do without you," he says. "You know, you're like the daughter I never had."

Instantly, I feel better and he play-punches me on the arm.

"I like what you've done with the place," I say.

"Thanks, Elsie. I only wish I'd done this sooner."

"So why didn't you?"

"I wanted to make sure it was the right thing," he replies.

"So how did you know it was the right thing?"

Mick laughs as he picks up the last crate. "You ask good questions. In the end, I realized I would never know unless I tried it. If the answer doesn't come to you, go and find it." He winks at me, and I want to hug him.

"You can talk to me anytime, you know," he says. "Tay'll be back. Young love, it's tough."

"I don't love him," I say. "I don't even like him."

I want to ask Mick what happened with Danny's mum, if he loved her, if he's ever loved anyone. Something tells me he has a sad story.

"My advice to you, Elsie, is go with your heart, not your head, because your head doesn't know what it wants, it only thinks about the moral high ground. And if your heart isn't happy, when you try to share it, you'll make others unhappy too."

"Wow, Munlochy's deepest dad," I say.

He throws a wet, smelly towel in my face and then pulls me into a hug and growls in my hair.

Four

I TRY NOT TO GIGGLE as Danny demonstrates a squat. We're on a bit of the beach just down from the harbour, heading away from Fortrose. The beach is narrow and hidden from the coastal road by a thick layer of trees. Even though no one can see us, it's still embarrassing.

"I feel ridiculous," I say mid-squat.

"Are you not taking this seriously?" Danny pushes down on my shoulders and my thighs feel like they're about to shred.

The strengthening exercises are torturous. Danny has me doing lunges, squats, spotted dogs, running up and down the pebbles, lying in the water moving my legs up and down. At the end, my legs are like jelly and I can't even get up. It makes me wonder why Dillon does stuff like this for fun.

"We're going for a dive," Danny says, zipping up his wetsuit.

"Can't," I say. All I want to do is sleep.

"You can," he says softly.

He kneels by my head and moves my sweaty hair off my face. His touch sends weird impulses through me.

"The water will wake you up. Come on."

Suddenly his face is close, his lips inches from mine. Does he know that I've been thinking about him? Before he has a chance to move in I sit up, afraid of what might be happening between us. He backs off, slightly embarrassed.

After the dive, when we're heading back to rinse our suits, Danny touches my shoulder and says, "I think you're really brave."

I sidestep so his hand falls away.

"Can we go to the cave again tomorrow?" I ask, thrashing my wetsuit about in the rinsing water, trying not to look at him in case I accidently grab him and kiss him.

"No," Danny says quickly. His tone of voice makes me wonder if things are a bit awkward between us now. "The water is really choppy at the moment. It's too risky."

"How about the drop-off then?"

Danny straightens his T-shirt. I think he's about to tell

me it's too dangerous, too choppy, too risky, but he just clears his throat.

"Soon," he says.

"It's nearly the summer holidays," I remind him. "I can practise every day."

"Keep up the exercises then," he says. "You'll need steel thighs for the drop-off."

He smiles thinly, and tilts his head. I realize I completely misread his body language earlier. He doesn't have feelings for me – he just feels sorry for me.

Five

ON SUNDAY, MY SHEPHERD'S PIE bubbles over in the oven. The cheese drips down through the grills and sizzles on the bottom. Dillon is stressing over his revision at the kitchen table.

We both have our last exams tomorrow. It's biology day.

"Let me test you," I say.

He passes me his biology book. He has dark circles under his eyes and his cheekbones are jutting out.

"What's the difference between DNA and RNA?" I ask.

"DNA is double-stranded, RNA is single-stranded."

"It says more than that here."

He exhales loudly and puts his hands around his waist,

pressing into his ribs with his thumbs.

"The sugars are different. I don't know, I can't remember."

"Try," I say. "You have to know this, your exam is tomorrow."

"Pyrimidine and purine bases." He signals for me to move to the next question.

"That's the wrong answer."

He grabs the book and starts flicking through the pages.

"Your brain has shrunk," I say.

Later, after I've quickly skimmed through my own biology book and Dillon's spent an hour on the phone begging our father to come home, I follow him to the bathroom. I jam my foot in the door as he tries to close it and because I'm stronger than him now he staggers back into the sink. He's shaking.

"Please, Elsie. Leave me alone."

"No!"

I shove him and he almost loses his balance. He now has the same frame as Mum, but he's at least a foot taller than her.

"I'm not leaving." I fold my arms.

"Fine," he says and moves me out of the way so he can get to the toilet.

He bends at the waist over the toilet and my shepherd's pie shoots out of his mouth like a thick beef soup. He straightens and then leans again. I cover my mouth and my nose. My eyes water.

"Don't cry," he says, wiping his mouth. "I'm sorry about the pie."

This makes me sob loudly.

"How do you do that?" I ask, still covering my face. "Without even…"

"It just happens," he says. "It just happens when I lean over."

"God, Dillon. You need help. I'm going to speak to Mum and maybe you can talk to her therapist."

Dillon grabs my wrist and leans in close. "You tell anyone, and I'll tell them about your diving."

"Okay, calm down. I won't tell," I say, moving my head away from his mouth. "Why don't you get in the shower? You smell really bad."

While he's in the shower, I find laxatives in his bedside drawers. I take three, but nothing happens. I hide the rest under my bed along with my Superdrug stash.

I picture my life in the future. When Dillon has starved himself to death I'll have let two brothers die. Dad will be long gone and that just leaves me with Mum. Every day will be like therapy day. I wonder if I could hold my breath for a whole year. I play a game with myself: if I can hold my breath for an extra twenty seconds in the morning, I'll have one last read of my exam notes.

Six

FINALLY, EXAMS ARE OVER. BEFORE I leave the building for the summer I go to collect my boat from the technology block, but it's not in my drawer where I left it. Anger rises within me. Ailsa. I check everywhere, in all the bins, under the tables, behind the cupboards, for bits of my boat. Nothing. I ask Mr Jones and he frowns.

"Ask him," Mr Jones says, pointing to Frankie. "He's always around, he must know something."

"What have you done with my boat, Frankie?"

"Relax," he says calmly. "I rescued it from that ugly girl who's always harassing you."

He goes to his drawer and takes out his wooden box.

His box is beautiful, way better than my boat and I feel a pang of envy. It's covered in grooves forming different shapes that look like maths and physics symbols. I should have tried harder, should have spent more time on my boat instead of reading my diving notes. Frankie lifts the lid of his box and pulls out my boat. It's in one piece.

I grab it from his hands and then remember to say thank you.

"It's really good," he tells me. "The sails are in perfect proportion. If it was real it would go really fast."

"Thanks," I say again. "I like your box too."

He blushes, and then asks me if I want to go crabbing with him, just as Lara wanders into the room.

"Elsie, I've been looking for you everywhere."

She stands between me and Frankie with a hand on her hip and swishes her hair into Frankie's face. She's been searching me out a lot recently, accosting me in the corridor, begging me to tell her where Dillon is, why he isn't spending any time with her.

"I don't know where he is," I tell her. "He finished his exam an hour before the end so I guess he's gone out to celebrate."

I swallow a huge lump in my throat. He practically ran out of the exam and he didn't look in a celebratory mood. He looked like he was on his way to throw up.

"Actually, I don't even care about him any more," Lara

says. "I came to see if you wanted to hang out over the summer. Go into Inverness and stuff. You know, get drunk, find boys to kiss or whatever."

She says *whatever* as though it might mean something sordid. I try not to think of her and Dillon. Until a few weeks ago I had been wondering about doing *whatever* with Tay over the summer. I feel hot just thinking about it. And then I think of Danny and feel even hotter. Frankie jumps in and saves me.

"Elsie and I are making plans to go rock-pooling. Aren't we, Elsie?"

The appalled look on Lara's face makes me smile, and suddenly rock-pooling is exactly what I want to do. If anything, because it might cool me down.

"Yes, we are," I say, mimicking her hair flick, which doesn't really work because my hair is too curly and too heavy. "Why don't you come?"

Now Frankie's face falls but he can't have everything his own way. Either Lara comes with us, or I don't go at all. I don't want Frankie getting the wrong idea. Lara isn't too bad, really, just a bit skinny. And Frankie, well I owe him, I guess.

We make plans for the next day, because I want to get it over with, and then finally, school is out.

Seven

I WAKE UP FEELING FREE. No school. No Ailsa. This is the start of two months of nothing but diving. Before I get out of bed, I hold my breath for three minutes and ten seconds. Soon, very soon, I will make it to four minutes. I'm nearly ready for the drop-off.

I shuffle along the corridor to Dillon's bedroom and stick my head around his door. His room smells of vomit and aerosol. Dillon stirs. His feet stick out the end of his bed, twitching.

"Dil, are you awake?"

He groans and I wander over to the window where Eddie's bed used to be. The cemetery is in full view and some of the shiny headstones glint in the sun, winking at me as though they want me to go down. I turn away.

"Wakey, wakey, sleepyhead."

"Go away," Dillon growls. "I'm asleep." He kicks the duvet into the air and moves his feet back inside the bed.

"But it's the holidays."

"Exactly," he mumbles.

"I'm going rock-pooling later with Lara and Frankie. Do you want to come?"

Dillon lifts his head above the duvet and stares at me. He looks even worse than he did yesterday, with cracked lips and grey skin. I feel myself recoil slightly. He could be an extra in a zombie movie.

"It'll be fun," I say. "We're going to look for crabs."

"That sounds exciting. Why are you going with *her*?"

Because she asked; so I can pretend to be normal; because it's a decoy from what I'm really getting up to this holiday.

"Because there's nothing else to do and for some reason your girlfriend wants to be my friend."

"She's not my girlfriend." Dillon stretches and sits up in his bed. His greasy hair is stuck to his forehead.

"Well she seems to think she is. I mean, she says she doesn't care about you any more, but I don't believe her. It was only a week ago that she was obsessively looking for you all the time."

He laughs lazily, as though he's too tired to do it properly. "That girl's got issues."

"Well, if you're breaking up with her then I'm not doing your dirty work for you."

"I'm not asking you to," he replies. "Right, get out of my room so I can get dressed."

He flings a dirty sock in my direction.

As I leave, something green lodged behind the wardrobe catches my eye. An old cuddly toy of mine – Jasper the frog. I pull him loose and shake him in the hallway and the dust hovers for a moment in the landing before tumbling down the staircase.

In the kitchen after breakfast, I show Mum the finished sailing boat. It's so hot today that the heat has even made its way inside our house, warming all the surfaces. I hold the boat in the palm of my hand while she inspects it, running her fingers along the smooth wood. She blows a piece of hair off her face and wipes sweat from her forehead.

"You really made this?" The awe in her voice makes me feel proud.

The sails curve out as though the wind is pushing against them, and a tiny model of me is gazing out over the steering wheel. I show her how the sails have string so they can be cast up and down and she continues to coo over it.

"It's even waterproof," I tell her.

"You should test it out, Elsie. See if it floats!"

Her cheeks are flushed. She leans across the sink to open the windows and tries to waft air inside.

"I have an idea," I say, placing the boat on the sideboard. "The paddling pool."

She sucks in a breath and I think she's going to cry but then she smiles.

"That's a great idea," she says softly. The smile stays on her face but I notice the tiny tremble in her jaw.

The three of us drag the paddling pool into the garden. It hasn't been used for years and Dillon is convinced it's got a hole in it. He gets his bicycle repair kit and puts his head to the rubber, listening for air. Mum unravels the hose and starts filling the pool as Dillon and I take turns blowing air into the valves. It takes ages because Dillon keeps stopping to check for punctures. At least that's what he says. I keep a close eye on him, hoping that I don't have to call an ambulance at any point. I don't know how much longer I can keep his illness a secret.

Eventually, the pool is full of water and not leaking. Somehow it already has grass and dead leaves floating in it. The bottom is creased from its years of scrunched-up storage but it still looks inviting in this heat.

Mum disappears upstairs and comes back wearing her swimming costume with a pair of white denim shorts.

Her skinny legs look silky, like she's just moisturized them.

"Come on, Els, in you get."

I roll my trousers up above my knees and climb over the side, then place the boat down carefully and wait for it to settle.

"It works!" she squeals.

Even Dillon is impressed. He suggests that I put a motor on it to see how fast it can go but I tell him it wouldn't be a sailing boat then.

"It's tremendous," Mum says. She kisses me on the cheek and I see Dillon wrinkling his nose at us but I'm beaming. I don't even mind that she's wearing my lipstick. We watch the boat whirl around the pool for a while, its sails billowing gently in the hot breeze and then I take it inside to dry it off and keep it safe.

When I get back outside, Mum is lying in the pool, still wearing her shorts. She stretches her arm out and motions for me to join her. Dillon trips me up with his foot and I fall in face first, just missing her legs. I turn to her, afraid that I've hurt her, but she's laughing.

"It's beautiful, isn't it?" She lifts her head to the sun. "We should do this more often."

"Maybe we could go to Fairy Glen one day this week," I say. "And swim in the waterfall."

Mum nods and strokes my hair. "We do alright, don't we?"

Dillon lies down in the shade under the apple tree, pretending to be asleep. When Lara rings the doorbell, he jumps up.

"I'm not here," he says, running for the stairs, wheezing.

Eight

FORTROSE IS BUSY NOW IT'S holiday season. Most visitors stay near Chanonry Point to see the dolphins or play golf, so we head to Rosemarkie beach instead. We keep walking until we find an empty cove that has enough rock pools for the crabs to hide in.

Frankie runs ahead and shouts back to us when he finds a nest of crabs. Lara and I climb over the rocks slowly behind him, Lara afraid of ruining her white plimsolls and me afraid that if I twist my ankle, I won't be able to dive.

"Was Dillon hiding from me?" Lara asks as we stand high up on the rocks, looking down at the water as it splashes into the rock pools.

"No," I say, a bit too quickly.

"I thought I saw him running up the stairs as I came to the door."

"He was running to the bathroom. Hangover," I lie. "He went into town last night to celebrate finishing school." Dillon should be pleased that I'm so good at lying.

Lara scrapes the rock with her foot and it breaks away, covering her plimsolls in red dust. She tries to rub the dust from her shoe with her finger but it smudges and stains. I look around for Frankie so we can talk about something else. Even crabs and shrimps would be better than discussing Dillon.

"Maybe we should go into Inverness on Friday," Lara suggests.

"Dillon would hate that."

"No, I meant just you and me."

"Got no way of getting there," I say, coming up with a flaw in the plan. I can't think of anything worse than a crowded bar full of drunk kids from our school.

"Bus," Lara suggests.

"How would we get home?"

"Um. Taxi?"

"Haven't got any money." It's a good excuse and it's true.

"I could borrow some money from my mum," she says, twiddling her earring. "I can't wait to drive. Are you going to have lessons next year?"

"What for? I can walk everywhere."

"You're so funny. I don't mean drive around here. I mean drive into town. Go places."

"I don't want to go places," I tell her. I do want to go places, though, but not anywhere that you can take a car.

"Please, just come into town with me. Everyone goes. If you're worried about Ailsa, she won't be there. She's gone up north."

I cringe when she mentions Ailsa. I wonder if they've fallen out and that's why she wants to hang out with me. Maybe Ailsa has been nasty to her too. I wonder where Tay is. I imagine him swimming with dolphins, then I imagine him kissing another girl.

I nod towards Frankie. "Is he coming with us?"

Lara scrunches her nose up. "No offence but I'd rather it was just us. He really smells."

Frankie waves frantically at us. He's holding a large crab with several legs missing. I wave back but he shakes his head and beckons us down.

"We can see from here," I yell.

Frankie holds a finger to his lips and shushes us, then points to behind the rocks. He looks as though he's about to pee himself.

I scramble down the rock and Lara carefully follows, reaching for my arm for balance.

"Otters," Frankie whispers loudly when we get to the bottom.

My stomach flutters. I have never seen them this far up the coast. I half expect Frankie to have mistaken seals for otters but when I peer around the rock, there they are. Three of them. Two bigger ones nuzzling a smaller one. The baby's fur is slick and looks almost black. Its face is tiny and round and its whiskers are nearly as long as its body. I wish I had a camera so I could show Dillon later. We perch on the boulders and watch as the waves gently wash over them.

"Are they dangerous?" Lara whispers as she moves behind me.

"Don't be ridiculous," Frankie says. "The baby one is just like a puppy."

I feel Lara tense beside me and I pat her on the leg. I tell her that they're more scared of us than she is of them but I don't think she believes me. The baby looks in our direction with big pebble-black eyes.

After a few minutes, Frankie dips his bucket into the rock pool. I hear the clatter of something wriggling around inside it.

"Only a small one," he says, sniffing.

"You just stole their dinner," I say.

He looks into the bucket and back to the otters. "They're not eating, they're resting."

I explain to Lara how otters smash crabs against the rocks to break their shells. "They're really clever. Like humans."

The two large otters are half in and half out of the water with their front paws close to the baby's head, protecting it. Its long whiskers look golden in the sunshine.

"They can't swim, the babies," I continue. "Their mothers have to hold them underwater so they can learn how to dive."

Lara gasps. "Isn't that a bit cruel?"

Frankie looks at Lara and wrinkles his nose. "It saves their lives. I don't think this one wants to go in though." The baby struggles to keep its paws from slipping into the water.

"Still seems cruel," Lara repeats and Frankie snaps at her. "Go home then, if you don't like it."

Lara looks at me for backup but I say that we should be quiet or we'll scare the otters away. She lowers her head and tries to detach a limpet from the rock.

We keep watching, until a group of children come running up the beach behind us and scare them. The two bigger otters nudge the baby one until it plops into the water and then they swim away, the water streaming off their heads. The kids come splashing through the rock pools with their buckets and nets and Frankie is eager to show them how it's done. I watch one of the boys, the smallest one. He is so excited he doesn't know which way to run first. His older sister chases after him. "Careful, Dougie." She grabs him by the hand. "Don't fall."

I keep watching the boy's dark hair and the way his mouth hangs open, the way he hesitates before jumping across a rock pool. His sister gets annoyed when he soaks his trousers. I want to tell her not to be angry with him. To tell her that one day, she might not even have the chance to be angry with him.

"Hey, why don't we go back and get ice cream?" I say, and we retreat.

"So, how about this night out?" Lara asks again.

"Maybe," I say. "I'll think about it."

When we get to the end of the beach, Frankie releases the crabs back into the water. Some of them swim away, legs spinning round and round, and some of them are definitely no longer alive.

Nine

WHEN I GET TO THE harbour the following day, I immediately sense something is wrong. Even though it's boiling, Danny stands on the jetty with his arms folded tight across his white T-shirt as if he's freezing. Joey and Rex are climbing aboard *The Half Way*, swaying, waving their arms about. The tide is low and the boats nearer to this end of the harbour are already grounded in mud. I'm only a few minutes late. I overslept but still wanted to make time for breathing practice. Three minutes and twenty seconds.

"Hurry up," Danny snaps. "Or we won't get out of the harbour."

"What's wrong?"

Even if the boat was stuck in the mud, Danny would have us dig it out before we gave up on a dive.

"Nothing, let's go."

He grabs my arm and pulls me towards him. Rex hands us both a beer as we climb on. Danny refuses to take his one.

"They're meant to be for after," Danny says.

I put mine aside too. The last thing I want is to be drunk right now. I need to be on the ball. Danny starts the motor before I've even sat down and my neck jolts.

As the boat speeds up, I close my eyes and pretend I'm flying. For a few minutes I am alone, the wind caressing my face.

I feel a hand on my leg and when I open my eyes, Rex is grinning at me.

"Are you ready for your surprise?"

"Where are we going?" I ask, leaning away from Rex. We're heading around the Point but too far out to be aiming for the cave.

Danny speaks slowly. "We're going to the drop-off."

"Fuck yeah!" shouts Joey.

"Really?" I try not to show my nerves. This is not how it was supposed to be.

It's then that I realize I've forgotten my mask.

Danny cuts the engine. We drift.

"I'm not ready," I blurt out. "I forgot my mask."

Danny cracks a small smile. "We're not going to the bottom," he says, almost sneering. "Not anywhere near it."

I'm relieved but still feel uneasy. Why are we here if we're not going to the bottom? Joey and Rex are already clumsily pulling their fins on. Danny chucks me a mask from the bag of spares. I know it won't feel the same.

"There's a line," Danny says. He's in instructor mode now. "We're going down twenty metres. It's cold, dark and miserable down there. You won't want to go any deeper."

I wait for more instructions but he doesn't say anything else. There's a slight breeze out here and it skips across the water, making the ripples travel in a steady line further out to sea.

Rex and Joey jump off the boat on the opposite side to where the buoy is. Usually, I see which direction they travel but today I can't see anything. The water is too dark. I'm guessing they swam under the boat to find the wire.

"Where did they go?" I ask Danny, breaking the silence. He is fiddling with a weight belt. Sliding the weights on, tightening it, sliding the weights off again.

"Over there." He points a little way back towards the harbour.

"They didn't go down the wire?"

"Told you. There's nothing to see down there."

"Then why are we here? We don't have to go down today," I say. "We could go another day."

The weight belt clangs onto the floor of the boat.

"I thought this was what you wanted. To go deeper. It's good prep for the wreck dive."

It is what I want, I remind myself silently. But now I'm here it doesn't feel right. I'm not ready to see it. I'm not ready to do this without Tay. My eyes prick and I wipe them quickly before the tears come.

The boys eventually surface a few metres away and swim back, whooping and swearing about how damn good the water is. They seem more alert than when they went down, and this reassures me.

"Ready?" Danny asks. He puts his weight belt on and sits on the side of the boat with his fins in his hand. I start to fasten my weight belt, the one he was fiddling with, but my fingers are shaking too much. He reaches over and fastens it for me. His hands around my waist make my breath quicken.

"Ready?" he asks again.

My brain is still hesitating, wondering how quickly I can pull the motor cord and drive us back to the harbour but once again I find my body doing the opposite of what my brain is thinking. My body moves closer to the edge of the boat, my hands adjusting my mask and pulling on my fins. Then I sit on the side next to Danny.

"I'm ready." *I'm ready to go to the bottom and you can't stop me. No, I'm not ready. But this is my chance.*

"Let me get a head start, okay? Feet first. There's a bit of a current just below the surface. Three minutes max, okay?"

As Joey reaches the boat, Danny drops off the other side and I follow him. I cling to the buoy and wait for him to go down. My weight belt is so heavy I struggle to stay on the surface. When I can't feel Danny's movement below me any more, I fill my lungs, then stomach and let go of the buoy. In the darkness, fighting the current, I grip the wire and follow it down, desperately trying to bring my body in close to it, but my legs float out behind me. The pressure in my head builds but my ears won't pop. Danny's face is right up against mine as we descend. Every now and then he lifts one hand and motions for me to relax, slow down, stay calm. I focus on his face as the water around us gets cooler and darker, and the pressure in my head gets larger.

Finally, my legs no longer feel as though they're being pulled out. We settle our bodies so we are vertical again and I hold the wire with one hand. I dare myself to look down, following the cone of light from my torch. The water is muddy brown with white bits floating in it. A dust cloud billows below us. Small grey fish emerge and then disappear. My watch says forty-five seconds, then forty-six, then forty-seven. My ear pops with a loud bang. I groan but the water muffles the sound. The pain is excruciating for a second, but then the pressure in my head is gone.

It's now or never. Danny is turned away, shining his torch on some kind of flatfish – a flash of orange in the darkness. I let go of the wire and sink towards the dust cloud. As soon as I hit it, water seeps in through the bottom of my mask. The salt stings and I can't stop blinking. I resist the urge to swim back up and instead let my weight pull me down.

A high-pitched voice tears through the water.

"Over there!" the voice cries. The voice is mine. I'm on the beach that day, yelling to everyone to look at the spot where Eddie disappeared. I make my way to the edge of the water but fall down onto the pebbles. Shaking, murmuring, I try to work out if I'm looking at the sea or the sky. There's a loud crack of thunder and it keeps on going, vibrating through my head and then I see my father's feet moving across the pebbles towards me. In his hand he has my mother's blue coat. He throws it over me.

"Help, someone! I need help," he cries. "She's fainted."

Danny grabs my arms and pulls me up towards him. I kick as hard as I can for the surface and lactic acid burns in my thighs.

The air above the water is cold but I suck it in and wait

for the dizziness to pass. All this time, I thought the blue haze that tinged my memories might be significant in working out what happened that day, but it turns out it was just Mum's coat.

"What the fuck was that?" Danny growls. His blond hair is skewed to one side and he has red marks around his eyes where his mask was pressed against his skin. I yank my mask down so it sits around my neck.

"I slipped," I lie, trembling.

"You mean you let go on purpose. Damn, Elsie – why do you always have to take risks?" Danny's lips are pursed again. He brushes a clump of seaweed from his hand and tries to shake the water from his ears. "I nearly didn't find you," he says.

"How was it?" Joey calls from the boat, oblivious to Danny's anger.

"She let go of the wire," Danny says, glaring at me.

Rex and Joey help me out of the water and I slide over the side ungracefully, landing on the bottom of the boat with a thud.

"What happened?" Rex asks, handing us beers. Now I really want that beer. I sit up and drink nearly half of mine in one go, hoping it will stop the shakes.

"I slipped. But I didn't go very far. It's not really a big deal."

Rex smokes and looks at Danny, confused.

"How deep did you go then?"

Danny coughs and presses a button on his watch.

"Thirty-two metres," he says neutrally.

"I was just following something. A fish maybe. I didn't notice I was going deeper." I smile to show them I am fine and it works. It makes me feel at ease too. I almost believe this is the truth.

Rex and Joey laugh and pull fish faces.

"That's what happens when you go that deep. It messes with your mind," Danny says.

"Nice one, Main," Joey says.

"You're a true mermaid now," Rex says.

Thirty-two metres. I shiver because I realize then that I was only eleven metres from the bottom. If Danny hadn't grabbed me, I might have got down there.

"I bet Tay could've got to the bottom."

Even before I've finished saying his name, I know I shouldn't have. They all eyeball each other and go silent.

"What?" I ask.

"Nothing, mermaid," Rex says.

"Have you heard from him? Has something happened to him?"

"*I've* not heard anything," Joey says defiantly.

"God! Will someone please tell me what's going on? Where is he?"

There is more silence and I grab the oar and hold it out

in front of me as though I'm about to defend myself against a tribe of warriors.

"If you don't tell me, I'll jump off and I'll go to the bottom and you won't be able to stop me."

I don't know why I'm acting so crazy. Maybe the depth really has messed with my mind.

Danny flinches. Then he speaks in a whisper.

"He's back."

The oar lands on Joey's foot. He bites his lip but doesn't say anything.

"Since when?"

"A couple of days ago."

So that's why Danny is in a mood. The boys all hang their heads guiltily. Joey looks up and shrugs.

"I didn't know until this morning," he explains, thinking that it matters to me.

"Right, let's go back then."

I don't let the excitement or fear show on my face. So he's back. And he owes me an explanation. I reach over Rex and start the motor. The boys all fall to the floor, but Danny scrambles back up, and drives us back to the harbour.

I glance at the black water. I picture Eddie's body tumbling down into the drop-off and let out a sob.

"Are you okay?" Joey whispers.

I nod. These last few weeks I've imagined that Eddie might have been at peace in his last moments; the bright colours, the sense of freedom, the lightness. But the water here is cold, dark and creepy. He would have been terrified. My stomach starts cramping. For the first time, Eddie's death is starting to seem real to me. I'm even surer of my plan now. I've got to get to the bottom, to say goodbye, to tell him that I'm there, to tell him that I'm sorry.

Ten

LARA SNEEZES RIGHT AFTER I'VE put blue mascara on her so she has to wash it off and we start again. We are locked in the bathroom so my mother doesn't interrupt us. Every time a floorboard creaks in the hallway, Lara whispers, "Is that Dillon?"

"I told you, he's not here."

It's hot today and I feel horrible and sticky. I wipe my sweaty hands on a towel.

"What's the deal with him?"

"You tell me," I say. "You spend more time with him than I do."

"Not any more," she says sadly.

I feel a bit sorry for her. She obviously really likes him.

I don't want her to wear my Ruby Red, so I search through my make-up bag and find a pink one that I think will suit her better. When I've finished, she pouts in the mirror.

"He won't be able to resist me," she says, running her fingers through her perfect straight hair.

She's wearing skinny jeans and a top that she borrowed from her mum, and tries to make me change out of my combats.

"I don't have anything else. Isn't it enough that I've agreed to come with you?" I ask.

Especially when all I want to do is find Tay. I've been to the boathouse several times and there's been no sign of him.

"Your turn," Lara says, waving the mascara at me. "If you wear make-up maybe no one will notice your clothes."

"Not much you can do with this face," I say.

When I look in the mirror, though, I'm reminded of how much I've changed recently. My cheeks have thinned, and I no longer have a double chin. Danny's workout sessions are responsible for this. I'm not sure I like the way I look, though – older, more grown-up. I don't have Eddie's round baby-face any more.

The bus drops us in the centre of Inverness, and Lara leads us straight to a bar.

I suddenly have a wave of dread that we're going to

bump into my father. Even though I haven't spoken to him, I'm sure he has a way of knowing what I'm up to.

"Head up, look confident," she whispers as we join the queue.

I can't believe it when the bouncers let us in. I had my fake birthday in my head just in case.

She gives me a tenner and tells me to go to the bar while she visits the ladies' to touch up her make-up.

"I'll have what you're having," she says.

The bar is hot and sweaty, and Beyoncé is belting out from a speaker. Everyone is really dressed up and I suddenly wish I had tried to squeeze into one of Mum's sparkly tops. The girls are all in high heels and tiny skirts. But even with my new appearance I wouldn't want to get my legs out. I put flip-flops on because Lara said they would be better than trainers, but now they are stuck to the floor and my feet are covered in beer.

I finally get to the bar and order two shandies. The barman looks at me strangely. I think he's going to ask me for ID but he eventually asks, "Lager or bitter?"

"Lager," I say, and give him the tenner.

While I wait for Lara, I get jostled and spill half the drinks. I close my eyes and imagine that I am under the water and that I have all the space in the world. Tay is there, gliding beside me. And then, in my daydream, he starts to talk.

"What are you doing, Elsie?"

I open my eyes and he's right in front of me. I blink. It's weird seeing him outside the Black Isle. He looks different. His hair has grown longer, and hangs over his eyes. He's still wearing his black jeans but instead of a T-shirt or hoody, he's wearing a checked short-sleeved shirt. *Punch him or hug him?* I can't do either because I'm still holding two pints.

"Aren't you going to say hi?" he asks, as though he just saw me yesterday.

I tighten my fists around the glasses. "Danny said you were back."

This has the desired effect. Tay flinches.

I sip my pint, not knowing what to say.

"Can we talk?" he says. "Somewhere quiet?"

"I don't think there is anywhere quiet." Beyoncé has turned into Katy Perry. All I want to do is get out of here. Where the hell is Lara?

"I need to find my friend."

Tay looks around. "What does she look like?"

"Skinny, long mousy brown hair," I say, which pretty much describes most of the girls in here.

But we don't have to look for long. She's at the other end of the bar and she's not alone. She's with Dillon.

Where do all these people keep coming from? Did Lara know he was here? I honestly thought he was at home in bed.

"Shit," I say.

Tay stiffens beside me. He must recognize Dillon from the party at the Point.

"Let's get out of here," Tay says, taking the pints from my hand and placing them on the bar. He grabs my wrist and we start to walk out but it's too late.

Dillon blocks our entrance, and Lara stands next to me. She looks upset.

Before I can say anything, Dillon gets right up to Tay and punches him on the nose. Even with Katy Perry blaring out about how she kissed a girl, I hear the crack.

"Fuck," Tay says into his hands, bent over.

I'm too shocked to move. Dillon just stands there panting, holding his fist, blowing on it.

"Take the fight outside," someone yells.

"What the hell are you doing?" I shout to Dillon.

Then Tay stands up and throws a punch back. He catches Dillon under his chin, and Dillon staggers back, knocking his head against the door.

Lara goes to him. "He's bleeding," she wails. "We need an ambulance."

This is all too surreal.

"You just hit my brother," I say to Tay.

Tay's nose is bleeding all over his shirt. "He started it."

We all go outside. Lara is completely hysterical, fussing over Dillon, checking his head for cuts, and yelling for someone to call an ambulance. Tay and Dillon pace about, trying to stop their bleeds, staring each other out. The air out here isn't much cooler than the sweat box we just came out of.

"Christ, Dillon, we were only talking," I explain.

I go to him and look at the cut on his chin. It's pretty small. It could have been a lot worse. Dillon is taller but Tay definitely has the muscles.

"I'm going home," I say to all of them. "Thanks for stopping by."

"You can't leave us," Lara wails, indicating herself and Dillon.

"Elsie, wait," Dillon says. "I'll take you home."

I shake my head and walk off. My flip-flops don't make for a very dignified exit but it doesn't matter too much because before I have a chance to look back, Tay is next to me, bundling me onto a passing bus.

He drags me to the spare seats at the back, and all I can do is sit down before I fall down. I have a few tissues in my pocket, so I give them to him. He nods thank you and holds them up to his nose. He's got a black eye, too. That was some punch.

"What just happened?" I ask.

"Your crazy brother punched me in the face."

"I wasn't asking for a literal explanation. And don't call him crazy."

"Sorry."

"Seriously, what just happened?"

Tay inspects the bloody tissue and frowns. "I have no idea. One minute I was talking to you, the next I was in a fight."

I catch sight of our reflections. We look ridiculous, Tay all bloody, and me all hot and sweaty. I can't help but laugh.

"What?" Tay asks. He folds the tissue in half and puts it back to his nose.

"Great night, huh?"

He takes my hand. "One of the best."

The boathouse no longer smells of weed, just damp wood and moss. We sit in our usual corner on one of the blankets. The bleeding seems to have stopped, and Tay's face is now caked in dry blood. I try not to wince every time I look at him. His eye socket is a deep purple, and all swollen.

"Let's get one thing straight here. I'm not on your side. You hit him too. I'm only here with you because you kidnapped me."

"Did I force you to come to the boathouse?"

"Why did my brother hit you?"

Tay doesn't answer the question for a long time. He breathes deeply and picks at his face, his hand trembling. It must be the shock.

"Maybe he thought I was someone else?" he says. "Or he really doesn't want you to have a boyfriend."

"But I haven't got a boyfriend, have I?" I reply. "I'm so confused, Tay. I don't know what you want from me. You disappear and then just turn up again, and what? You want to pick up where we left off? Pretend that you didn't leave?"

"No, it's not like that, Elsie."

He's back to calling me Elsie. It feels so cold, so impersonal.

"I left because I had to. I'm messed up, I do bad things. I came back because I miss you."

"You miss me? What do you miss exactly? Having a quick grope every now and then?"

"That's not fair. I missed being with you, Pot-Noodle Girl."

He leans in and lifts my chin with his fingers. When I look into his eyes, I feel all floaty.

We kiss. It's gentle at first, and then he pulls me onto his lap and neither of us can stop. Even when I accidentally bash his nose with mine and he yelps we can't stop. He holds me tightly and all of my bad feelings disappear. We are just in the moment, with each other. Until he tries to undo my trousers.

"Stop," I gasp, still kissing him.

He pulls away.

"Sorry. I got carried away. It's okay if you're not ready."

"How do I know you're not going to leave again?"

"I won't leave," Tay says desperately. "I can't. Mick gave me my job back at the diving club. I don't want to leave again."

"I filled in for you, while you were away."

"I know," he says. "I wish I hadn't gone. We'll just have to come up with a plan. You'll have to tell Dillon that I've left again. We'll have to keep this a secret."

"For ever?" I ask, horrified.

"Not for ever. Just until we've worked it all out."

"Worked what out? Why did Dillon react like that? And what's the deal with you and Danny? Is there something you're not telling me?"

"No, El. I swear. I'll talk to them both, tell them I'm serious about you, that I won't hurt you again. Just give me some time."

Back to "El". The way he says it makes my chest burn.

"Okay," I say. "Just fix it, and fix it quickly."

Eleven

THE NEXT DAY, MUM FUSSES over Dillon. She brings out the whole first-aid kit just for one tiny cut.

"Who did this to you?" she asks, rifling through the bandages.

I scowl at Dillon.

"Just a misunderstanding," he says. I silently thank him.

Mum slathers Savlon all over Dillon's face. I will her to say something about how skinny he is. Surely she must notice that his cheeks are hollow. She must feel how tiny he is when she holds his face. If she notices, then she can be the one to help him.

"Why don't you lie down, Mum? You look tired," Dillon says. He wants her away.

"I want to look after you," she says. "I want to look after both of my babies. You're growing up too fast."

"Why don't you both go and lie on the sofa and I'll bring you some lunch?" I say.

"Elsie, my darling girl. My sweet children, who want to look after me when their father has gone and deserted us. Look! Look how beautiful it is outside. How can I go to bed on a day like this?"

She grabs her handbag. "I'm just popping out to get us some ice creams."

"Chocolate for me," I call.

When she's gone, I shove the first-aid kit out the way and sit on the table with my feet on Dillon's lap so he can't move.

"Does it hurt, poor Dilbil?" I ask nastily.

"You should see the other guy."

I grab his face and for a split second he looks frightened, but then he starts laughing. I let him go.

"I have seen the 'other guy', and you've probably broken his nose."

"Good," Dillon says. "He deserved it."

"Why? I don't understand. Did you really mean to do that? For God's sake, we were just talking."

Dillon stares at me, like he can't believe what I'm saying.

"He's the one who got you into all the diving."

"So?"

"Can't you see how dangerous it is? It's messing with your head, making you think you're remembering things that aren't true."

"What is it you're so afraid of, Dil? What do you think I might remember?"

"Nothing. There's nothing to remember."

"Yes, there is. I need to remember where Dad went, and I think you already know and you're covering for him. I remembered that you were looking for someone that day. Not Eddie. Some girl. Who was it?"

Dillon shakes his head. "You're crazy. You've turned into a fish. And I'm going to tell Dad everything. He's asked me to keep an eye on you – one word from me and he'll be straight down that harbour putting a stop to all this."

It takes all my effort not to grab him by the throat. Instead I grit my teeth.

"You tell Dad anything, and I will tell him all about you starving yourself to death, about the laxatives. He'll drive you to the nearest hospital and they will lock you up and force-feed you."

"That's not allowed these days," Dillon says. "Force-feeding is torture."

"It is allowed. It happened to someone in my year."

Dillon starts to cry. "Please don't tell Dad. I'll start eating again."

"If you eat the sandwich I'm about to make you, and keep your mouth shut about the diving, then I'll keep quiet."

"Okay," he says, defeated.

He whimpers quietly as I sit next to him, watching him break up the sandwich into tiny bits and push them into his mouth as though they were pieces of poison. I think Dillon's bluffing about Dad. The phone hasn't rung in ages, and Mum says he doesn't pick up when she rings. But what if he's not?

"What did you do with my pills?" he asks. "I need them – I get all blocked up when I eat."

"I threw them away," I say. "They're dangerous."

He chucks a bit of sandwich on the floor, like a toddler having a tantrum.

"Why were you at the bar last night, Dil? I thought you were too sick to come out."

"I'm not sick, and I don't need to eat. I came to make sure you were okay. Lara told me where you were going and I was worried about you. You don't like going to the city."

"I was fine. I was doing you a favour by keeping her away from you."

"No more diving, Elsie. I don't want to lose you."

"Eat the sandwich," I say. "Please, just eat."

Later, after Mum and I have eaten two ice creams each,

I remove Dillon's laxatives from under my bed, along with my Superdrug stash, and hide them in my cupboard in the boathouse.

Twelve

A WEEK AFTER TAY'S RETURN, we shore-dive from Rosemarkie beach. Tay follows me along the seabed as I twist and turn and run my fingers through the parsley seaweed. I put on a show for him and he laps it up. Bubbles trail from his open mouth as he laughs, and the minutes we spend under the surface feel like hours. And when our bodies collide against each other, our wetsuits feel invisible and we are just two creatures writhing around in our natural habitats. Dillon is wrong, though, I have not turned into a fish. I am turning into water, fluid and ever-changing. I am not a visitor to the ocean, I am part of it.

Tay and I play Rock Paper Scissors, and the loser has to

remove an item of clothing. Tay loses. When he has removed both fins, his booties, his mask and the top half of his wetsuit, and secured them under a rock, I start to feel sorry for him. He keeps blinking as the salt stings his eyes and he has goosebumps all over his arms but he still smiles.

He arches his back and reaches over his head to grab his feet. He is almost a perfect circle. I glide through him and then back underneath him, then he breaks and swoops down on me, engulfing me with arms, legs, body. We rise together, tangled. The sun beats down on our heads as we get our breath back.

"I need a rest," Tay gasps. "I can't keep up with you."

"Liar," I say. I know that he's holding back.

"I've got to save my energy," he says. "Mick's got me working hard at the diving club."

Tay thinks Danny needs a bit of time so I haven't been there since Tay's been back, even though Danny still owes me a couple of lessons. Not having the lessons is okay because I've got Tay, but I miss hanging out at The Black Fin, and I miss Mick and the boat boys.

As we bask in the sun on the pink grainy sand while our wetsuits hang over a rock, I tell Tay that I want to go back to the drop-off. He turns his head away from me.

"Are you listening to me?"

"I'm not listening because it's a crazy idea."

He tells me it's impossible. That I'll need extra weights,

that it's too deep, too technical, too cold. The tides aren't right, the current is too strong. He says it doesn't matter how long I can hold my breath for, it's the coming back up that's risky. He lists a hundred reasons why it's a crazy idea. Then I tell him that I'm going with or without his help.

He remains lying still with his eyes closed. I want him to open them and look at me just for a second so he can see how important this is to me.

"It's his resting place. I just want to see it. I was so close before."

Tay rolls over and kisses me. He's gentle but his weight presses down on me.

"Rest here with me," he groans. "We're not otters. We're humans. We're meant to do other things with our time."

Finally, I bargain with him.

"If you come with me, I'll get naked for you."

He opens one eye lazily.

"When will you get naked?"

"Soon," I say.

"I'll think about it," he says, and then covers my mouth with his.

We roll around in the sand until some kids climb over the rocks that were shielding us, sniggering. As I gather our wetsuits, Tay stares at something in the water.

"Do you see that?" He's beaming. I have never seen him look so beautiful, with his stubble and his new long hair.

The salt in it catches the light so it looks like he is covered in glitter. I look towards the spot that he's peering at but I can't see anything.

"Look closely. Can you see that reddish stone? You can see the light coming through it."

"What is it?" I ask, even though everything looks red to me.

"It's called jasper," he whispers. "Actually, it's a mineral not a stone."

I wrinkle my nose at him. "I had a toy frog called Jasper. It had red eyes."

He walks across the beach to the water, his soles stained pink from the sand. He crouches down and scrabbles around for a bit, lifting some of the rocks and throwing them back so they make a *clonk* sound when they land. Then he walks back, grinning.

"For you. Jasper quartz. I hope it's better than a frog."

I take the mineral and inspect it. It nearly fills my whole palm and it's beautiful – marbled red, pink and orange, covered in crystals. It's smooth on one side and rough on the other and looks like a cross between a Turkish delight and a pink pear drop. I want to put it in my mouth.

"Can I keep it?"

"Of course, it's yours." Tay sits back down beside me, looking pleased.

"We could always take it to the Grotto and add it to the

collection of stones," he says. "Did the boys show you all the rocks we've collected? We take one in with us each time we dive there. For luck."

His face colours.

I remember seeing something red when I was in there with the boat boys but I can't remember what kind of rock or stone it was.

"I saw the stones. You don't have to be embarrassed, I thought it was cool. Is there one of these in there?" I hold the stone up to the sun and my hand glows red.

"We definitely don't have a jasper quartz in there. But it's yours to do what you want with."

I curl my fingers around the quartz and something else comes to me.

"What are you smiling at?" Tay asks.

"Just happy," I reply. I have thought of another part of my plan.

Thirteen

NOT LONG AFTER MINE AND Eddie's ninth birthday, I came home from school one day to find my parents running up and down the stairs with boxes and plastic bags. Eddie was sitting in the hallway, inside a large cardboard box, pretending to be in an aeroplane.

"Brace, brace, emergency," he was saying.

My father, carrying a black bin liner under one arm and a small box in his hands, majestically stepped over him.

"The seat belt sign is on," he said to Eddie in his announcement voice.

"Are we moving?" I asked, dropping my school bag by

the door and kicking off my shoes. My parents were always talking about moving.

"We're having a rearrange," my father explained and nodded for me to go upstairs. All my toys were gone from my bedroom and in their place were Dillon's muddy trainers and smelly swimming shorts.

"Where's Jasper?" I asked, wanting to cry. I couldn't sleep without Jasper the frog and his lovely velvety fur.

"He's in your new room!" Mum suddenly appeared behind me with an armful of Dillon's clothes. She dumped the clothes on my bed and danced off across the hallway to Dillon's room.

Dillon was sitting on his bed, arms folded, looking cross.

I turned to Mum, confused, and she sat next to Dillon and pulled me onto her lap. Dillon said I was too old to be sitting on Mum's lap but I let her wrap her arms around me, making the most of Eddie not being around.

"We think you're old enough to have your own room now. It's better if the boys share."

Dillon huffed.

"It's not fair," he whined. "I'm the oldest and I should have my own room."

"It's not for long, Dil, just a year or so until we can afford a bigger place."

"But Eddie is so messy. He'll ruin all of my stuff and I won't have anywhere to do my homework."

My father appeared in the doorway and smiled at us all sat on the bed. His long legs made angular shapes against the frame.

"We'll make sure that Eddie doesn't disturb you," he says. "You can do your homework in here after school and we'll keep him downstairs."

"But what if I want to listen to my music at night? It's not fair!"

"Can I paint my walls green and silver?" I asked.

My father laughed and Dillon stormed past him, kicking the skirting board as he went.

"I'm serious, Dad."

"No. You can't paint your walls green and silver, Elsie. But you can help me give it a new lick of white." My father was always painting things white. He came into the room and kissed Mum on the forehead.

"You two are gross," I said.

After I'd moved all my clothes, I climbed into my new bed and pulled the covers up to my neck. It was cold and draughty in my new room but I liked it. Jasper's red eyes rattled next to me as I tried to get comfortable. I nearly didn't get to sleep with Jasper because Eddie wanted to have him in his bed. Mum prised him from his hands and said that he had his own toys. I still felt guilty, though. As I snuggled down, I saw a movement under the door and heard a small scratchy sound.

"Eddie the ghost, is that you?"

"Brace," I heard him say softly. "Emergency, emergency, crash landing," then something clattered down the stairs and I heard Dillon yell at him to get back into bed. A door slammed.

"This is illegal!" Dillon shouted. But nobody responded.

Fourteen

I PLUG MY MEMORY STICK into my father's old laptop and sit on my bed, scrolling through the PDFs I've downloaded from freediving websites. Eventually, I find what I'm looking for: weighting for deep dives. I write down the information on the back of a leaflet about adopting a porpoise. *If diving over forty metres, you should have neutral buoyancy at ten metres. Check by taking extra weights down to ten metres and gradually offload until you hover.*

I feel the jasper quartz in my hand and try to work out how heavy it is. Probably not even a kilo. I'm going to need quite a few weights.

I scroll to the bottom of the PDF and read the paragraph

about deep-diving ascents. The last few metres of the ascent are the most dangerous, it says. *With risk of blackout.* But I'm not worried about this – if I get my weighting right, everything will be okay. I note down a few reminders for myself: keep vertical; don't tilt head; relax.

I feel a wave of determination as I think about how good I will feel when I'm down there, how soft the sand at the bottom will be. I don't think about how the depth might mess with my mind. I don't think about the cold and dark.

That night, I dream of rocks and seaweed and Eddie, and I wake up at midnight gasping for air.

I'm coming for you, Eddie. I'll be there soon.

Fifteen

THE NEXT DAY, I GO to the pool alone and practise. I duck dive to the bottom and then dolphin kick back to the surface and I do this over and over again, using all my power to resurface in one kick, until my fingers go wrinkly. My legs feel strong now, thanks to Danny and his incessant squat routine that I've been doing every day. I will thank him, one day.

When the pool closes, I'm alone in the changing room and take advantage of the huge mirrors. I look at my naked self and notice that my body looks different. I still have large hips. But my stomach is flatter and tighter and my breasts are slightly smaller. They are still not as round and as perfect as Lara's but they look nicer, less wobbly, and my hair is so long now that it rests on top of them, just above my nipples. I stare at myself for a long time, seeing what I look like from all angles, what I look like when I hold my breath. When I raise my arms above my head as though I were ascending from the bottom of the ocean, my body side on to the mirror, I almost look like Scotland's deepest girl. I'm still in this position when Ailsa Fitzgerald and Lara burst out of one of the cubicles, giggling. So Ailsa wasn't up north for long. They wear matching gold bikinis to show off their slim figures, and tiny waists. They must have been in the other pool, or in the Jacuzzi. I wrap my towel around me and turn my back to them but it's too late.

"Urgh, she's so disgusting," Ailsa whispers to Lara. I cling onto the towel with one hand, ready to fight them off if they come near me. Ailsa parades around me, circling like a hyena. Lara watches, her lips tight. When she catches me looking at her, she hangs her head and pushes water into the drain with her foot.

"Are you anorexic like your brother?" Ailsa asks. She runs a bony finger down my cheek. "Have you been starving yourself in a desperate attempt to be *pretty?* Hmm. Not quite skinny enough, yet. Still got flabby thighs. It's a shame about your brother though. He used to be quite fit. I saw for myself, you know. And now he's an ugly mess of skin and bone."

I pretend I'm not hurt by her comments, and hold my head high.

"That's odd," I say. "I wonder why you still follow him around."

"Hey, you said nothing happened between you and Dillon," Lara says to Ailsa, her tone bitter.

"Relax, dopey. I'm just winding her up," Ailsa replies. But from the look on both their faces, I'm not sure that she is just winding me up. I'm disappointed in Dillon. But he's still my brother, and he doesn't deserve this. These girls are not worth my time and effort. Especially Lara right now. What a bitch. I can't believe I wasted my blue mascara on her. I start to gather my clothes but it's difficult with one hand.

"As if I'd touch him with a bargepole. He's pathetic," Ailsa continues. "They both are. Lara, I can't believe you hung out with either of them. They're so crazy they should both be locked up."

Ailsa swings for my face but misses and grabs my towel instead. She could let go, and we could all go home but in a split second, everything changes. She yanks the towel out of my hand. It falls to the floor and she kicks it away. I am naked, exposed, and livid. I go for her. I push her against the lockers and she slips to the floor, taking me with her.

"Lara, grab the towel," she yells, as I reach for it.

Lara, like a little lapdog, hops over me and snatches the towel, then runs to a cubicle with it. She stands in the doorway of the cubicle, chewing her hair, watching.

"Do you need a towel?" Ailsa teases. "You should cover up. You look like someone's roast dinner. All lumpy and fatty." She gets to her knees and looks me up and down. I try to cover myself with my hands.

I will someone to come in and help me, but the changing room is quiet. I look towards the door. I could make a run for it. I'd be naked and everyone would see me but at least I'd be safe.

Ailsa sees me planning my exit and then she pounces. She pins my arms above my head and straddles me. Her long blonde hair hangs in my face and tickles my nose. I grab it with my teeth and tug but she pulls away. I spit the stray hairs from my mouth.

"Lara, help me!" Ailsa cries. "She's such a lump, it'll take two of us."

Lara doesn't move.

"Lara, what's wrong with you? Grab her arms. Now."

"Let's just go," Lara whispers.

"If you don't help me, I'll tell everyone about your laxative habit."

Lara moves then. I see her stick legs running across the wet floor, and then she sits on my arms. Ailsa grabs my breasts. She pinches them really hard, both of them at the same time. Lara gasps and Ailsa laughs with glee as I cry out.

"Get off me," I cry. "Help!"

I manage to lift my head up enough to bite Ailsa's arm.

"You little bitch." She gobs into my hair and then shoves her knee between my legs so hard it sends shooting pains right up to my neck.

"What have I ever done to you?" I gasp.

"You were born. You've been in my way ever since I met you, making my life difficult."

"You made life difficult for yourself," I say.

Finally, Lara shifts her weight and I break free. My head connects with Ailsa's nose and she flies back and slides over a drain. The metal catches her gold bikini and I hear it snag. When I stand up I look down to see blood streaming from her face. While Lara fusses over her I pull my trousers and T-shirt on over my damp skin and thrust my underwear into my bag.

"You little slut," Ailsa calls. "I'll get you suspended for this."

"See if I care."

I look at Lara one last time and give her a chance to explain. She looks torn, her eyes dancing back and forth between the blood and my wet T-shirt. Eventually, she moves closer to Ailsa.

"Funny how there's always a fight when you're about,"

I say. "And isn't it annoying how you're always the one left mopping up the blood."

"Elsie, wait," Lara calls. "It wasn't me who told everyone about Dillon. Everyone's been saying how sick he is. He needs help."

"I thought we were friends," I say to her, even though I knew the truth all along. She was using me to try to get Dillon back.

"We are," Lara says to the floor.

"*Were* friends," Ailsa says. "Tell her, Lar. You don't want anything to do with her, do you?"

Lara glances down at Ailsa and bites her lip.

"You'll just have to make do with your weird bully boyfriend," Lara finally says. But when I look into her eyes I see that she is crying.

Ailsa heaves herself off the floor, still holding her bleeding nose.

"As if that ugly bitch could ever have a boyfriend," she mutters.

"At least I can get a boyfriend without following someone around."

But that's not really true. I went to look for Tay in the boathouse night after night, and he still left me. And even though he left me, I still went off with him after he punched Dillon. The memory of me leaving Dillon in the road bleeding makes me feel sick. But the thought of

Tay leaving me again makes me feel worse.

Without my underwear on, I feel exposed. My breasts are stinging but I don't dare touch them. I don't look in the mirror again. I don't need to see how ugly I've become when I can feel it seeping out of me every day.

Later, Lara calls the house phone. I sit on the step by the back door so the reception on the phone goes fuzzy. She wants to know how Dillon is. She says she's sorry.

"Ailsa made me say those things."

She still wants to be friends but only in private. She says she loves Dillon and she wants to help him.

"Sorry, the line's gone a bit bad," I yell, as though I'm trying hard to make out her words. "I'll have to call you back."

I listen to the fuzz for a while and then I make out the odd squeak of a cross-wire conversation. I end the call and pluck up the courage to dial another number.

My father answers his mobile immediately but I stay silent. "Dillon, is that you?" he whispers down the line. "Is it Elsie? What's she been up to? Hello? Look, now's not a good time, pal. I'll call you back tomorrow, eh?"

Sixteen

THE BABY OTTER IS NOT moving. Its paws lie on the dry rocks and its fur has dried in clumps. There are flies hovering around its head. I'm at Rosemarkie beach with Frankie because Tay has to help out at The Black Fin, and I can't bear to sit in the house all day with Dillon, especially now I know he's been talking to Dad.

Frankie reaches out with his foot and nudges it gently. The otter's body indents where his foot makes contact and then springs back again.

"It's still warm," Frankie says. "Not much we can do." He pushes his glasses up his nose and squints at me. "Come on."

I'm on a slant and feel my shoes slipping down the rock I'm on.

"What will happen to it?" I ask.

"Not a l'otter," says Frankie, sniffing.

"Frankie!" I cry.

He looks at me, confused. "Well what do you want to do? Take it home?"

The storm clouds are rolling over the water towards us. Frankie looks in his bucket and starts counting his collection. A wave of deep sadness passes over me as I look at the small animal lying helplessly half in and half out of the water. I wonder where its mother is, then I see a small splash a few metres out in the smooth, clear water.

"We have to do something," I say. "We can't just leave it here."

"We could roll it back in," Frankie suggests.

I suggest that we bury it but Frankie says he doesn't want to touch it and then points out that the only place to bury it would be in one of the rock pools.

"How can you be into science and not want to touch a dead animal?"

"I'm more of a numbers scientist than a biologist," he says.

I don't bring up the fact that he plays with dead crabs and other shellfish all the time.

"Do you think it drowned?" I ask.

"Unlikely," Frankie says. "It's not even in the water."

I think that it is possible, but I can't reason with Frankie today.

In the end, we walk back to town and tell the police, who phone the wildlife centre, who say that they'll send someone down to collect it.

"Collect it?" I ask.

"So it can be incinerated," the policeman says.

Outside the police station, Frankie puts his arm around me, which is really awkward because I'm a head taller than him. I get a waft of his weird smell and then his lips are suddenly on mine and as I pull away his teeth catch my lip.

"What are you doing?" I yell, moving my hand to my lip to see if I'm bleeding.

Frankie steps back. The crabs rotate in his bucket.

"I thought you liked me," he says sulkily. "I thought maybe you asked Lara not to come because you wanted to be alone with me."

"Why would you think that?" I cry. Instead of trying to make him feel better about it, I just keep yelling at him.

"Lara is not my friend any more, and neither are you, so leave me alone."

"But I love you," he says.

I want to cry. I don't want him to love me.

He trundles off with his bucket. I should go after him, but all I can think about is the dead baby otter. It feels as though everything around me is decaying. My life is completely out of control, like a heavy stone plummeting to the bottom of the sea.

Seventeen

I WAKE IN THE EARLY hours the next day, thanks to a dream that the dead baby otter was in my bed. After double-checking it's not there, I watch the sun roll up at four thirty from the living room window. Its glare coats the underside of the clouds in a magnificent orange. It's the longest day of the year and the sun won't set again until 10.30. When Mum has gone to work to run the emergency clinic at the surgery, Dillon appears next to me with his duvet wrapped around his shoulders.

"Let's have a duvet day and watch DVDs," he suggests.

"But it's really sunny," I say. "I want to be outside."

I want to be with Tay on his day off.

"Just watch one with me," Dillon pleads. He is already on his stomach on the floor, pushing a DVD into the player. I agree because I want him on my side and because I miss him. I feel bad that I've neglected him. We sit on the sofa together and Dillon arranges the duvet over us but I kick it off because it's so warm. When I touch Dillon's arm it is icy cold and makes me shiver. I sit with my hands holding my breasts, trying to make the pain go away. Luckily Dillon doesn't notice I'm in pain. How could I tell him what happened? I make a promise to myself that I won't be involved in any more fights.

Halfway through *Die Hard 2*, Dillon falls asleep and I turn the TV off. He stirs when I move.

"Stay a bit longer," he murmurs. "Don't leave."

I leave him on the sofa and go to the kitchen. The fridge and the cupboards are almost empty. I boil the kettle and slice up the last lemon.

"Please, just drink it," I plead when I've woken him up again. "It'll do you good."

He stares at the cup and asks what it is.

"Hot water with lemon. Lemon is good for your digestion." I read this in one of Mum's health magazines.

He sits up and takes the cup. I sit with him while he drinks it. It takes ages for him to bring the cup to his mouth each time.

"You don't have to feel guilty, because I'm making you

drink it," I say, quoting a piece of advice I saw on a forum for anorexics. It doesn't make sense to me, but Dillon takes a sip.

When he's finished the drink he starts to cry and I'm shocked. I try to imagine feeling so guilty about having a few drops of lemon juice that it would make me cry and then before I know it I'm choked up too and fighting the tears.

"You're killing yourself, Dil," I say, my voice wavering.

"I don't want to feel like this any more." His voice is thick with phlegm. "What do I do?"

"I don't know," I whisper. "But I'll help you."

I cry properly then, relieved that he wants my help but not sure how to give it, and still angry that he's been hiding something from me all these years. I hug his fragile body.

"I'll bring some of those nutritional shakes home later. The ones that some kids at school have instead of lunch."

Dillon continues to cry. "Are you sure you can't stay?" he splutters, as I get up to go. "You're not going in the water, are you?"

"I just have to meet a friend."

"Don't go in the water. Just stay here."

Part of me wants to. I want to play-fight with him and play rude hangman and pretend that we're a normal family. But Tay is waiting for me and so is Eddie and so is my four-minute goal.

"Rest up. I won't be long. Maybe we can watch another film together later?"

He nods but I know he thinks I'm deserting him. *Just hang on a few more days, Dilbil,* I think to myself as I leave him. I'm sure that getting to the bottom of the drop-off is going to give me all the answers: to remember what happened, to get closure. It just has to. And then I'll be able to focus on Dillon.

Inside the boathouse after our dive, I feel elated. Three minutes, forty-five seconds – my longest dive. And now I'm confident I can do this. Tay passes me a towel and I stand and watch him for a moment, as he peels his wetsuit down to his waist and rubs his hair. He seems happy, relaxed. I hope it's because of me. I think of Dillon and get a sudden pang of guilt for leaving him. I pray that he's eaten something.

"I should go back and see if Dillon is okay," I say to Tay as I dry my hair, trying not to look at his bare chest. And then he comes over to where I'm standing and kisses me on the lips. It goes on for ever and he holds me tighter and tighter, as I lean closer. And then his fingers are on the zip at the back of my wetsuit.

"Wait," I say. We are both breathless.

"What's wrong?" he whispers. "Please don't make me stop. I can't bear to let go of you."

"I need to get home," I say again. "I can't leave Dillon any longer." It's a strain to say it because I don't want to go. The boathouse is my home now, not McKellen Drive.

"He'll be okay for a bit," Tay says. He gently brushes my neck, making me shiver. I really shouldn't leave Dillon too long.

"Trust me, he'll be okay."

It's five o' clock. I've already been gone for hours. Perhaps if I make sure I'm back for six it'll be okay, and Mum should be home by now anyway.

"Okay, I'll stay just a bit longer."

He kisses me again and it's like being underwater. Clear but distorted at the same time. Everything is bigger underwater. I trail my fingers down his spine and he murmurs.

"Are you sure you want to do this? I mean, are you sure you like me?" I lean back so I can see his face. It's not that I don't trust him, it's just that I want to be certain.

"Can't you tell?" He nods downwards but I can't bring myself to look at his crotch.

"I…you're not going to leave again, are you?"

"I'm not going anywhere."

He moves his hand back to my zip. I feel fuzzy all over, and a bit faint.

A thought. I'm pretty sure that Tay will agree to anything right now, so it's my chance to get what I want. "Will you come with me? Tomorrow, will you come with me to say goodbye to Eddie?" I say it quickly before I change my mind. I press my face into his clavicle. I hear him breathe in deeply through his nose.

"Please come with me," I say again. "I need you there."

"Okay, I'll come with you," he murmurs into my ear, and then kisses my neck. "Why does it have to be tomorrow?"

"Because…because I'm ready." It's the only answer I have, even if I'm not a hundred per cent sure it's the truth.

As he pulls the zip down, I feel as though I'm being opened up after all this time spent inside a dark, suffocating box. I shiver as the air hits my exposed skin and he lays out our towels on the floor. My heart thumps erratically as he peels my wetsuit down from my shoulders, down to my waist and then I help him with the legs. Even though I'm wearing a swimming costume and Tay has seen me in it many times before, I feel almost naked. All the time Tay is quiet, looking at me. He passes me a blanket and I wrap it around me as I lie down on the floor. I watch him remove his suit. His foot gets caught in the leg hole and he stumbles, almost falling on top of me. I laugh and he smiles.

"Are you nervous?" he asks when he has recovered from the embarrassment and is standing in only his shorts.

I shake my head and focus on trying to not breathe so heavily. Tay reaches into my cupboard and produces a bottle of vodka.

Under the blanket together, we sip from the bottle. I only have two sips before I feel the heat in my stomach. Tay slides the straps of my swimming costume down my arms. When he puts his mouth on my breasts I groan, and his cold lips soothe the pain.

I reach around him and place my hands on his waist at the top of his shorts. I slip my hands under the elastic for a moment and then bring them back. When I do this he moans so I keep doing it until he reaches for my hand and moves it down further. I'm not sure what to do but I move my hand up and down and I feel him grow into my palm.

"Am I doing it right?" I ask, terrified. I raise myself slightly to work at a better angle.

He doesn't say anything at first and when I look at him I see his eyes rolled back in his head.

"Yes," he eventually mumbles. "Very right."

After a minute, he stops me and motions for me to lie back. I pull my swimming costume right down and have to wriggle to get it over my feet but Tay is too busy pulling his shorts down to notice my struggle. He lies next to me on his side and draws the blanket back over us. I run my fingers over his smooth chest and he runs his hands up and down my leg.

Then he stops again.

"We should use something," he says breathlessly, his lips glistening.

"What?" I'm trembling and don't know why he's moved away.

"For him." He nods downwards. "I don't think I have one, I mean, I wasn't expecting to…"

"Ah," I say, suppressing a giggle, and then I remember about my Superdrug stash.

Tay fumbles in the cupboard until he finds what he's looking for. I want to explain that I wasn't expecting to either, but I'm too embarrassed to even watch him put it on, let alone speak.

When he's finally ready, he rolls on top of me and tries to push inside me.

"Wait," I say. "I don't think you're in the right place."

Tay blushes and moves around a bit, then tries again. This time it's right, and after a couple more attempts, he slides inside me. It hurts a bit, but it feels good. I pull him closer and closer again.

Afterwards, we lie side by side, dozing, touching each other and occasionally lifting our heads to sip more vodka. I feel different. I wonder if anyone will notice.

"Is this real?" I ask him, wishing that we could stay like this for ever.

"This is real," he replies, stroking my hair.

"Tell me a secret," I whisper.

"Okay. Promise you won't tell?"

His breath feels cool from the vodka.

"Who would I tell?"

"I cried when I got kicked out of school."

"Liar." I want this to be true but I know it's not.

"Your turn," he says.

I don't hesitate.

"There are over ten thousand different types of seaweed," I say.

"That's not a secret."

"Did you know about it? No. So it's a secret."

"Cheat."

"Tay, can I ask you a serious question?"

"All your questions are serious."

I sit up a bit so I can see his face. "Why don't you like talking about yourself?"

He sits up and spills the vodka in the process. It leaks all over the blanket.

"I've just told you my biggest secret," he says, feigning annoyance.

"No, you didn't. And that's the point."

He smiles and tries to mop up the vodka. We both smell like alcoholics.

"I'm just not that interesting," he says eventually. "I'm socially awkward, like you. And a bit of a twat sometimes." He throws the vodka blanket at me and then pulls me back down to the floor and kisses me. Everywhere.

I can tell it's twilight when I wake up because it's almost

dark inside the boathouse, and I feel a chill coming in through the gap at the top of the doors. We've been asleep for hours. I shake Tay awake to tell him that I need to go. He murmurs, sleepily.

"Tomorrow is the day," I remind him.

Tomorrow is the day I finally get to see Eddie again.

Eighteen

THE HALLWAY IS QUIET AND dark when I get in. The kitchen too. There's a draught and I feel uneasy. The back door swings on its hinges. Slowly, I step outside back into the violet night. Dillon's obstacle course takes up most of the garden – orange cones for running around, Mum's aerobics step and gym ball. Then I see Dillon. Illuminated in the security light, he lies on his side under the apple tree, not moving, a dumb-bell by his head.

I run to him and roll him over.

"Wake up," I cry. "Get up, Dil."

His skin is cool and clammy. His trainers look enormous on the ends of his pale stick-legs and his white T-shirt is covered in grass stains. I put my ear to his face and just make out his breath. A gust of wind whips over the garden, and the back gate that leads to the cemetery flies open, slamming into the fence. I walk over to it and look out into the cemetery but it's empty.

My head is fuzzy from the vodka but I run to the phone and my hands tremble as I dial the emergency number.

When I come back Dillon's eyes are half open so I can see the whites of them and the thick red blood vessels at the bottom. At first I think he's dead but then he moans.

"Where is she?" His voice is barely a whisper.

"Mum? I don't know. She's not back yet. Hang on for me, okay? An ambulance is coming."

"I was going to find her."

"Don't worry, I'll find her."

Dillon lets out a long raspy breath.

"No," he croaks. "That day. That's who I was looking for. I saw her from the water when I was swimming. She was on the beach."

I can't make sense of what he's saying. I ask him if he's taken something. I ask him if he smoked weed or if he took pills but he shakes his head. I sound like Dad.

"She wasn't there that day, Dil. She was at home, remember? She came later, after the police arrived."

His head becomes heavy in my arms, his blond hair greasy and sticking to my skin.

As the ambulance crew come into the garden, he murmurs again.

"She was," he says. "Mum was there that day. She was having an affair."

The images flash through my mind again, the pebbles, the blue haze – her coat, Eddie splashing about, Mum arriving in the car. I can't make sense of it all. The memories are too cloudy.

As the crew load Dillon on a stretcher into the ambulance, Mum appears at the end of the road. She stops short and then throws her hand over her mouth and starts to run, stumbling over the cracked pavement. I try to take her in. I don't even know who she is.

"Dillon," she gasps when she reaches us. She lifts the oxygen mask from his face. A paramedic pulls her back and then she looks at me with bloodshot eyes.

"What happened to him?" she wails, her voice high and squeaky. I can smell the booze on her breath but then I wonder if it's me. I clamp my lips shut, too afraid to speak.

A paramedic turns to us. "We're taking him to Inverness A&E. You can follow us in your car."

Mum launches herself at him. "I'm his mother!" she cries. "I need to be with him."

The paramedic holds her at arm's length and looks at me. He tells us that there's only room for one of us. Mum breaks free from him and clambers up into the ambulance.

She throws me her handbag and it lands on the road with a great clunk.

"Get a taxi, Elsie, there's money in my purse."

I am too stunned to move. The other paramedic whispers in my mum's ear and looks at me but Mum pushes her away.

"Call your father and tell him to come quick," she yells as the doors are closing. I stand alone on our street, my hair still slightly damp. Even though it's gone ten, the light hasn't completely faded yet. The sky is now a rich indigo and the midsummer air is balmy.

In the taxi on the way to Inverness, I search through my mother's bag looking for her mobile. I find a whole load of pictures of me, Eddie and Dillon that I didn't even know existed – us on the beach, at Fairy Glen, on a farm. Most of them are creased and faded. I find three bottles of sleeping pills and an unopened box of condoms. I feel sick and I hate her even more than my father. I hate Tay for making me forget that my brother needed me but most of all I hate myself. I'm still covered in salt from the sea and when I lick my lips it makes me heave. The taxi slams on its brakes and the driver helps me out to be sick at the side of the road.

"Do you think my brother will die?" I ask him when I finish throwing up.

"I'll sure he'll be fine," he says, rubbing my back in small circles. I can hear the meter ticking.

I call my father from Mum's mobile but he doesn't answer. I keep pressing redial. Eventually, I withhold the number and he picks up. When I tell him about Dillon he makes a noise that sounds like he's being strangled. I know that when we all crash into each other at the hospital, there's going to be one almighty eruption.

Part Four

EDDIE: *Just* **one** *more, then I'll go to sleep.*

DILLON: *I can't think of any more.*

EDDIE: **Pleeeeeease.**

DILLON: *Eddie, I'm all out.*

One

THE DOCTORS ARE VERY WORRIED about Dillon. I stand between my parents outside the door that leads to intensive care, as two doctors with masks around their necks tell us that he is severely malnourished and there is a chance he will go into organ failure. They say he is dehydrated, that he needs nutrients immediately.

We stare at him through the small window. He is either asleep or unconscious but he doesn't seem bothered by the flurry of people in scrubs fussing around him, sticking needles in his arms, squeezing fluid into his veins. Clear tubes snake across his face and up his nose, and his face is almost the same colour as the sheet covering him.

"Can we go in?" my father asks.

"No, we need to stabilize him first."

My mother holds onto my arm and digs her fingernails into my skin. My mind swings wildly between worrying that Dillon will die and imagining my mum having an affair.

We are shown to the relatives' room.

A series of people in different coloured scrubs enter the room one by one to ask us questions. The same questions over and over again.

Has he collapsed before?

Does he have any medical conditions?

How much does he weigh?

What has he eaten in the last few days?

What about fluids?

Is he depressed?

Are there any problems at school? At home?

How long has he been restricting for?

"What do you mean *restricting*?" my father asks the first time this question is fired.

"I mean limiting his intake of food or fluids."

My parents cannot answer these questions and I don't want to, so I stay silent. It comes easy, just like it did five years ago.

Hours pass. I sit by the door so I am the first to see any visitors coming down the corridor. My parents sit against the back wall, a single frayed brown chair between them.

My father pulls the stuffing from the middle chair. My mother yawns. They both have their eyes on the floor.

When the corridor is empty, I slip out and wander down the hallways, peering into all the rooms until I am stopped by a lady doctor wearing a white coat and clickety heels. She was in our waiting room earlier.

"Are you looking for the toilets?"

I shake my head.

"The coffee machine?"

I nod, only now realizing how thirsty I am. She points down the corridor.

"I'm just going to check on your brother," she says, smiling. Then she turns and clicks off in the direction I've just come from.

"Wait," I call.

"Yes? It's Elsie, isn't it?" She walks back towards me, adjusting her stethoscope.

"Yes." I suddenly feel afraid of what I have to say but the doctor keeps smiling. She is listening.

"He...I mean Dillon...Dillon has been ill for a long time. He makes himself sick and he pretends to eat. I don't think he's eaten for days."

I swallow what feels like a golf ball and wait for her to yell at me, but she speaks softly.

"You found him, didn't you? Well done for ringing an ambulance."

I want to tell her that it was my fault, that I didn't stop him, that I let him do this to himself because I was too busy trying to sort my own life out, but then I tell her about the lemon water. On her badge it says Dr S Shaw. I wonder if her first name is Sarah. Or Sally. Or Serena, like the tennis player my dad fancies.

"Thank you," Dr Shaw says. "That's very helpful."

When I get back to the relatives' room with two coffees, I notice the room smells of alcohol. I hand my parents the cups and take my seat again by the door.

"Where have you been?" my father asks.

I frown. "To get you drinks."

My father looks down at the cup in his hand, perplexed. He gulps the coffee back in one go and then grimaces at the taste.

"Look at the state of you, Elsie. What have you been doing?"

My hair is all straggly and salty. I smell of rubber and sweat, and Tay.

"I went for a run."

He throws the cup on the floor and the plastic crackles.

"For Christ's sake, I leave you all for a few weeks and look what happens."

"Not now, Colin. Can we focus on Dillon?"

"Oh, now you want to focus on Dillon?" My father turns his whole body to her so she can't avoid looking at him. "Now you care about your son? You didn't seem to care about him earlier when you were AT THE PUB."

"And where were you?" she screams back at him.

Her whole body is trembling. My father storms out.

At three a.m. Dr Shaw tells us to go home. We have no choice but to stay at my father's flat in Inverness.

I don't hold my breath as I lie on the sofa. Instead I take big deep breaths and count them and count them. Mum is on the other, smaller, sofa, whimpering. I don't go to her. I don't even ask if she's okay. I just stare at her silhouette and try to make sense of everything Dillon said. It can't be true. Dillon's brain must have shrunk so much he's got confused between his own parents. My father was the one missing that day. Not Mum. She arrived in the car later. I know this. I was there.

When everything is quiet, I get up and wander around the flat. There aren't many places to wander to – the bathroom, the kitchen, and back to the living room. I prop myself against the kitchen cupboards and the cold tiles beneath my feet keep me awake. There are twenty-six large tiles on the kitchen floor. Above the oven there are twelve small ones, grey and white and black. I follow the patterns with my eyes, left to right, right to left, top to bottom, zigzag.

At seven thirty a.m. the phone rings. We need to come in straight away.

Dr Shaw greets us in the corridor as we approach the ward. I'm guessing she hasn't been home to sleep but she looks as though she has. She tells us that they need to get a tube down Dillon so that they can get nutrients and calories into him. His heart rate is too low and oxygen isn't getting to his major organs. They can't wait any longer. He could die.

"Give him some orange juice," my mum suggests in a wobbly voice.

My father moves me out of the way and grabs her by the shoulders. "It's not a fucking cold, Celia." His teeth are bared and he snarls through them, spit spraying into the air. "How could you not notice how thin he is?"

"You're the one who walked out on us."

"I thought that you might actually get out of bed and start looking after your children. Instead you just shoved your head inside a bottle. And what's wrong with Elsie? You've been letting her drink again."

"He needs his *father*," my mother hisses. She doesn't look at me.

Dad clenches his fists and draws in a very long, slow breath. Mum stares at him, her eyes glistening. Their eyes remain locked until the doctor steps in.

"Excuse me, your son—"

"For God's sake, do what you have to," my father says to Dr Shaw. "Sort out the tube."

"Okay, the problem is we'll need to restrain him to do this. We managed to get some fluids in him last night via a drip but he's pulled all the tubes out and now we can't get near him. He's very upset," she says. "We need your permission to restrain him."

"Restrain? There's no way you're touching my son. Let me speak to him. I'll talk some sense into him," Mum says.

"I'm afraid he's asked not to see you. If you're not able to give permission, we may have to section him."

In the end my father gives permission.

Dr Shaw explains that they will insert a feeding tube which goes up his nose and down his throat into his stomach, then they will pump liquid food into him.

"You'll be gentle, won't you?" I ask. Dr Shaw nods.

The three of us stand in the corridor outside Dillon's room and listen to Dillon scream and thrash about. Something metallic falls to the floor and then I hear Dr Shaw say, "Swallow, swallow. Keep swallowing."

Two

AFTER THREE DAYS WE'RE FINALLY allowed to see Dillon. He has his own room away from the younger children so that he doesn't upset them with his screaming. This means that I can talk to him without anyone listening. I need to know if he was telling the truth. I leave Mum in the hospital gift shop and run upstairs so I can get to Dillon first.

Dr Shaw waves at me as I come up the stairs and takes me into Dillon's room.

"I went down there," he slurs. "And it was goooood. Come w'me… And we can eat spaghettiiiii…"

I look at Dr Shaw, confused.

"He's been sedated so he's a bit woozy. It should be

wearing off now, though. He pulled out his feeding tube and kicked a nurse in the groin as she tried to restrain him."

"He's never been violent, Dr Shaw." I feel like a mother defending her naughty child to the headmaster. But it's not even true – Dillon did some serious damage to Tay's face. It's like he's had a personality transplant. Guilt trips me up mid-thought. I should have noticed something was wrong. I should have realized after that party on the Point when he grabbed my arm so hard it left a bruise. I was so engrossed in Tay that I barely even noticed how out of character it was.

"Where's your mother? Is she coming?" Dr Shaw asks.

"She's gone to the shop."

Dr Shaw hesitates and pulls me outside into the corridor.

"How are things at home? Are your parents separated?"

She studies my face. I know she's looking for clues, just like the doctors did when Dillon and I stopped talking. She wants to know if Dillon stopped eating because of my parents. She won't find anything in my face or in my voice. I keep my jaw clenched shut.

Before I have a chance to speak to Dillon alone, Mum walks up the corridor with a white carrier bag full of sweets and magazines.

"Mrs Main, I'm sorry to say that we've had to sedate Dillon. I have to let you know that the CAMHS team will send him to a more secure unit if his behaviour continues to be unmanageable without medication."

"The *what* team? Can you speak English, please?"

"Child and Adolescent Mental Health Services."

"Dr Shaw," my mother says loudly. "You're part of this *team*, are you?"

"I am," Dr Shaw replies. "Look, spend some time with Dillon and then perhaps before you leave, we can have a chat?"

"Fine," Mum says, but I can already tell she has no intention of staying for a chat. She heads into Dillon's room and starts talking non-stop about completely pointless stuff, like how warm it is, what a nice day for a walk in the glen it would be, how the birds have taken over the cathedral ruins.

Dillon barely looks at her. He lies in the bed measuring his arms with his fingers and sighing. Eventually, he interrupts her to ask me how school is.

"It's holidays," I say.

"Oh yeah, I forgot," he replies. "Happy holidays."

Later that night, I sneak out of my father's flat and get a taxi to the hospital. I have to hide in the toilets for half an hour but eventually I get into Dillon's room and shake him awake. He smells of vanilla and stomach acid. The skin around his nose is red from where he ripped the feeding tube out.

"You've got to get better," I whisper. "They're going to lock you up."

Dillon looks at me wearily. The blue light of the moon shimmers through the window, making everything look dusty grey.

"I'm already locked up," he replies, rolling away from me. I walk around to the other side of the trolley bed.

"What you said before about Mum, is it true? Did you just make it up? Do you mean Dad was having an affair?"

Dillon's eyes focus for a few seconds.

"Forget I said anything. I think I was a bit delirious."

"You think? So you remember what you said?"

"It doesn't matter."

I want to grab hold of him and beg him to come home, but I'm too afraid of breaking him, too afraid of everything that will happen after now.

"It matters," I hiss. "It matters for Eddie."

"I saw Eddie," he croaks. "I saw him in the water."

"I see him all the time. In the street, in my bed, in the sky."

"In the water," he says again.

He splutters and his breathing gets heavy. I watch him for a couple of minutes, wondering what to say.

"What happened to you, Dillon? What made you break?"

But he's no longer awake.

"Dillon," I say softly, "Dr Shaw says you're unmanageable."

In his sleep, he smiles.

Three

AS JUNE TURNS INTO JULY, the weather remains hot and sticky, and the only respite is the cool water around Sandwich Cove. I see Tay as much as possible but he's being difficult. He and Danny don't seem to be talking and he's taking it out on me, snapping at me when I ask him what's wrong and holding his breath for so long underwater that I keep thinking he's not coming back up. He ignores me, then gets stroppy when I leave him to visit Dillon, saying he misses me.

I don't mention the drop-off to him, but I still think about it every day. As soon as Dillon is well again, I'm going down – I just hope Eddie waits for me. He's been quiet since Dillon's been in hospital, and he's started ignoring me when I call for him. Deep down, I suspect his silence has more to do with what I did with Tay than with Dillon being ill. Eddie will never get to have sex, or even have a girlfriend. I've never felt so far apart from him as I do now. Guilt creeps over me every time I think of what I was doing while Dillon was lying unconscious in the garden, but when I'm at the hospital with Dillon I feel guilty about leaving Tay, especially when Dillon is being nasty.

The tube is working – Dillon has gained some weight but it's put him in a foul mood.

"How can you do this to me?" he yells. "You're just trying to make my life difficult."

"We're trying to help you," I say. I can't keep the annoyance from my voice. It's not really fair that I'm spending my summer holiday visiting him in hospital, trying to cheer him up, and he's so ungrateful. How dare he blame me for this when he's the one keeping secrets all the time?

I'm sent home to pick up some more of his clothes, under instruction from Dr Shaw to bring loose-fitting stuff – nothing that Dillon wore when he was at his lowest weight. She says it like that, "lowest weight", rather than "skinny as fuck" or "at death's door". I'm used to all the hospital-speak now. I can read between the lines of everything they say and everything they mean.

Dillon's bedroom still smells vomity, even though I squirted air freshener all over it. I peer down into the garden and look at the spot where I found him. The orange cones are still there, rolling gently on their sides in the breeze.

I grab a bag and start shoving old T-shirts into it. Trousers are harder to select. I can't choose the baggiest ones because they won't stay up and the hospital doesn't allow belts. In the end I put in tracksuit bottoms that have an elastic waist and some shorts that might fit.

The sock drawer sticks and when I yank it the whole chest of drawers wobbles, sending Dillon's collection of swimming trophies and science awards crashing to the floor. Exasperated, I kick one of them and it breaks. I don't even care. I flick the socks out of the drawer into the bag. A small piece of folded-up paper flies out. It's probably a love letter from Lara. I put it in my pocket to read later. Then I'll tear it into tiny pieces and post them through her letter box.

Dillon is in an even worse mood when I get back with his clothes. I guess that my parents have been winding him up about something; Dad going on about the impending exam results and Dillon's future, Mum fussing with his tube and pillows.

"Go away," he growls as we crowd around his bed.

"I think you could be a bit nicer to us," I say.

"Don't be rude, Elsie. He's sick," my mother responds.

Yet again, one of my brothers is being a nuisance and I'm the one who gets pushed aside.

"Well, thanks but no thanks. No visitors today, please," Dillon says and rolls away from us.

I'm suddenly fed up with his disgusting smell, his arrogance, the fact that he keeps saying weird things and then denying them. I'm totally fed up with him.

"Why are you such a knob? Don't you care that you're killing yourself?"

Mum gasps and starts crying. Dillon's face bunches up and I think he's going to cry but then he bursts out laughing, spitting as he does. We watch him uneasily.

"Calm down, Dillon. Let's all start again," Dad says.

My father seems to think that the past can be erased. My throat itches.

Dillon straightens his face and then he looks at me and cocks his head to the side.

"Elsie can stay. Everyone else, leave."

My parents start arguing but Dillon presses the alarm by his bed and a nurse comes and escorts them away.

"You've got ten minutes," the nurse says to Dillon and me.

When the door is shut, Dillon pulls my head towards his. I try to keep my nose away from his mouth, which smells of vile vanilla meal replacement.

"I need your help," he whispers. "I need you to do something for me, but you can't tell anyone."

"I *am* trying to help," I hiss.

"No, I need you to do something for me."

His eyes dart about as though he's worried someone's watching.

"You need to ask that boyfriend of yours about Eddie's T-shirt."

I sigh. This sounds like more delirious nonsense. I tell him to rest and that I'll be back tomorrow, but his grip around my neck is firm.

"Listen to me. Eddie's T-shirt is out there somewhere. Tay thought I had it – he wanted to know if I'd destroyed it but I never found it. I looked everywhere, for months after, but it was gone. You need to talk to Tay and find out what happened to it. And if he knows where it is now, you need to find it and burn it."

It must be the drugs he's on. Or he is dying. People say crazy things when they are about to die. Why would Eddie's T-shirt be anywhere and why would Dillon want to burn it? I hold back tears. My brother has gone mad.

"Dil, do you know where you are?"

He stares at me vacantly. I panic. What are the other questions to ask to find out if someone is okay or not?

He refocuses. "I'm serious. Tay has it, ask him about it. The red T-shirt Eddie was wearing that day."

"Red? No, you're wrong. Eddie was wearing a blue T-shirt that day. Don't you remember? He had a tantrum about it. And recently I was starting to think that Dad was holding it and then he dropped it on me when I collapsed. I kept seeing this blue material in my dreams and flashbacks. But now I know it wasn't the T-shirt. It was Mum's coat. And that's another weird thing, because why was he holding her coat? It was freezing, why wasn't she wearing it?"

Dillon pulls me even closer.

"No," he cries. "You've got to believe me on this. Eddie wasn't wearing blue. Don't you remember? He changed right before we left the house. The phone rang as we were about to leave and he ran upstairs and changed. He put the red one back on, the one that had the rip in it."

Colours whiz through my mind. The blue haze before I passed out, the grey pebbles, the white froth, Eddie's red T-shirt with the yellowy-gold lion logo on it, Eddie wearing it, splashing in the water.

The red against the misty grey water.

I remember him wearing it.

Dillon is shaking me.

"Elsie, will you find out where he hid it?"

I tear myself from Dillon's grip.

A flash of red. I think of the jasper quartz, and the other stones – the ones the boat boys take to the Grotto for luck, and then I know where Eddie's T-shirt is.

"I don't understand," I stammer. "Why has Tay got Eddie's T-shirt? And how did you know?"

"He wrote me a note. For five years I've been waiting for someone to find out what we did. And now it's all going to come out."

"What did you do?" I whisper and my words feel as though they are thousands of miles away.

"It's my fault. I could have saved him but I didn't."

"What did you do?" I repeat. "Who's we?"

Dillon starts tugging at his tube. The thick vanilla liquid squirts all over the bed as he wrenches it from his nose.

"No visitors today, please," he shouts.

"What else do you remember?" I plead. I can hear the nurse coming.

"Nothing."

"What else?" I shout.

"Dad found Mum's coat on the beach when he was asking everyone if they'd seen anything. I told you. She was there."

A nurse comes in and leads me out of his room.

Four

THE REVOLVING DOORS TAKE YEARS to get me out of the hospital. I take two steps and sit on the wall, the note from Dillon's sock drawer in my hands. My whole body shakes as I unfold it.

> *D*
> *I need to talk to you about what happened that day.*
> *I'll be at the Point tomorrow at 6. Please come.*

I turn the note over.

> *PS Destroy this letter. Tay*

The words scream at me.

D
I need to talk to you about what happened that day.
Tay

I tell myself that there is another Tay, that this is all a misunderstanding. But I recognize the writing. The note is written in the same loopy writing that's on all of Tay's notes to me. It doesn't make any sense. I have to go and find Eddie's T-shirt, right now. I've got to get all the way to Sandwich Cove and go down into the cave, and it's almost dark already.

I get a taxi home using money I've stolen from Mum's purse and get my head torch and my watch. There's no time to fetch my wetsuit from the boathouse. I run the whole two miles to Sandwich Cove without stopping once. When I get there I'm exhausted but I don't wait to recover. I strip down to my top and underwear and brace myself for the pain of the freezing water. The rocks spike into my hands and feet as I crawl over the rock pools. The sky is clear and there's a chill in the air, even though it was so warm before the sun went down. I comfort myself by reciting Eddie's jokes. I remember one about angelfish – it keeps me motivated and helps ease the pain.

Finally I'm underwater. I can't feel a thing. My head torch flickers, lighting up the molluscs on the archway into the cave for a second before plunging me into darkness. Damn. The battery is dying. I wiggle the torch and the light comes on again. I just need it to last a few more minutes. My brain is telling me to swim fast and get the T-shirt but I go carefully so I don't bump into anything. My heartbeats slow as I count them. Navigating my way in is easy. I know that once I get around the corner I have to force myself down another metre and then kick hard to get to the top. When my ears pop, I know it's time to kick. One, two, three, four, five – and I'm bursting through the surface.

I suck the stale air in as fast as I can and then pull myself out of the water onto the rock. My head torch shines down on my feet. They're covered in blood from brushing against the jagged rocks.

Oxygen gradually flows back through me as I climb the steps and edge my way across the narrow ledge to the throne. My feet leave a slippery trail of blood and I nearly slide over the edge several times. When I get to the throne, I reach in and feel the cool stones against my fingers. At first, I pick them up slowly, feeling the weight of each one before dropping it into the water below. Then I grab the stones by the handful and fling them down, the popping echoing all around the cavern. There are so many stones, way more than I remember, and I have to balance on the side of the wall to reach into the bottom of the bowl. Finally I feel material in my fingers.

The T-shirt is hard and damp. In the darkness, even under my torchlight, it looks grey and for a second I think I've got it wrong and I'm relieved. But then I notice the lion. There's no mistaking that this is Eddie's T-shirt. I feel sick to think that I touched it back in June, and thought it was a piece of sea rubbish. I shudder, as I remember Danny's face the last time I was here in the cave. White, like he'd seen a ghost, right at the moment when I was up here looking at the stones. He must have something to do with this. Now I get why Danny was behaving so oddly that day: not wanting to go in the cave at the last minute, telling me to stay close to him. I was right, he was afraid – but not of the cave, of me finding something.

The words of Tay's note roll around in my head. *D, I need to talk to you about what happened that day. Tay.*

D. D for Danny? Was this note meant for Danny and not Dillon? Perhaps Dillon got it by mistake. No, that doesn't make sense. I can't think straight – I just know I have to get out of here.

With a spinning head and a pounding heart, I clutch the T-shirt and pencil-jump off the ledge, praying that I don't get lost on the way out.

The water crashes around my head, and *whomph*, I'm back there again, the day Eddie disappeared.

The wheels spin as Mum's car screeches to a halt at the beach car park, sending stones and grit into the air. I run to the driver's door and open it and hug her before she even has her seat belt off. She smells of salt and seaweed. Her white top is covered in chocolate cake mix.

"I came as soon as I got the call. Where is he?" she asks. "Have they found him?"

She fumbles with the seat belt and as she swings her legs round a piece of dried seaweed flies from her shoe and lands on the policeman behind me. He shakes his leg to get rid of it and then offers his hand to help her out of the car.

"Mrs Main?" he asks. "We're still searching for your son."

She sounds like a dying cat in a distant alleyway. The policeman leads her down to the beach. Her bare arms are pale and goosebumpy and I want to run to her and throw my coat around her. I follow them silently, wondering if they see me or if I am missing too.

We stand on the tip of the Point, watching the coastguard launch the lifeboat. My father wanders along the beach behind the lighthouse, asking everyone who's there if they saw anything. Then he stops and picks something up, a piece of clothing, or perhaps it's just a bit of rubbish. He holds it up and inspects it. What is he doing? Why isn't he in the water looking for Eddie? I point again in the direction of where Eddie was paddling, but no one is paying any attention. People are wading in the white froth, looking down, looking for little lost Eddie.

"Over there," I say. Still no one listens. I make my way to the edge of the water but fall down onto the pebbles. Shaking, murmuring, I try to work out if I'm looking at the sea or the sky. There's a loud crack of thunder and it keeps on going, vibrating through my head, and then I see my father's feet moving across the pebbles towards me. In his hand he has my mother's blue coat. He throws it over me.

"Help, someone! I need help," he cries. "She's fainted."

There's the overhang. My legs, strong and powerful, propel me through the arch and out into the open water. Then I follow the moon's reflection to get back to the surface. When I break through I'm further out than I thought, at least a hundred metres from the rocks, and the water out here is choppy. Rain stings my face as I swim back to shore, Eddie's T-shirt clenched tightly in my fist.

Mum wasn't wearing her coat when she arrived at the beach. And yet my father had it in his hands. Dillon was right. She must have been there on the beach earlier that day, and she'd left her coat behind.

Five

THE WET GROUND SOOTHES THE cuts on my feet as I walk through the deserted high street towards the harbour. It's nearly nine p.m. when I get there.

Inside the boathouse, I find Tay leaning against the wall, his head shrouded in smoke.

"Shit, what happened?" His eyes are wide and he holds out a blanket towards me. It's like he's moving in slow motion. Or maybe it's me moving slowly.

I hold up Eddie's T-shirt. It takes a few seconds and then Tay groans.

"Where did you get this?" he asks, reaching out to touch it.

I don't answer because it's a rhetorical question.

"I found your note," I say instead. "Who is *D*? Dillon? Danny?"

"Your brother. I'm so sorry, El. I wanted to tell you."

"Tell me what?" My voice is deep and shaky. "Please, I'm so confused."

Tay grabs my hand, possibly to stop me reaching out and smacking him. He's trembling.

"I wanted to tell you everything, but I couldn't because I made a pact," he whispers. "I promised Danny."

Danny, Dillon, Tay. They all know something and I'm completely in the dark. I wrench out of Tay's grip and slide back towards the corner by the loose panel. I can't bear to be near him, yet I need to hear the truth. I lay Eddie's T-shirt over my knees and run my fingers across the lion logo. It's frayed and bobbled from its years spent in the cave under all those stones.

"Just talk," I say. "Tell me what happened to Eddie."

Tay's eyes are pink, from the weed, from the lies.

"It was an accident," he starts. "I'd only gone down to the beach to get Danny's bike, because he'd left it there earlier in the day."

"What happened earlier?"

"We followed Uncle Mick down to the Point on our bikes because Danny thought he was up to something. We saw Mick arguing with this woman down by the lighthouse. Then there was all this commotion, people yelling, and

Mick and the woman raced to the car and drove off. Danny went crazy about his dad being with someone else, and kicked his bike to pieces. He had to run home because he was already grounded and wasn't supposed to be out. I couldn't carry his bike back while I was riding so I went back for it later."

I picture the scene. "What was the commotion?"

Tay screws up his face so tight I can't even see where his eyes are.

"I didn't know anything bad had happened. I swear. I would've stayed to help. I thought it was just excitement over the dolphins."

"You thought that people screaming was excitement over the dolphins? Are you insane?"

"No! It wasn't like that. I wasn't close enough to see what was going on." Tay pauses but I keep quiet, waiting for him to tell me what happened.

"It was dark when I went back," he continues. "As I was trying to put the chain back on the bike, I saw Danny on the beach. I was pissed off with him for not telling me he was coming because it was freezing and I would have just stayed in and finished my computer game if I'd known. I crept up and wrestled him down onto the pebbles. But it wasn't Danny, just someone who looked like him. It was Dillon. Then he shouted that there was something in the water. We both waded in up to our waists and there was definitely something there…"

Tay's voice cracks. I brace myself for what's coming next. Blood pulses loudly in my ears. I picture Tay and Dillon on the beach. Tay would've been twelve, and Dillon thirteen. Two boys, who didn't know each other, alone in the dark, about to…

"I didn't know it was a body," Tay whispers.

"Stop!" I shout. "I don't want to hear any more."

Images flash through my mind of Eddie's drowned body, covered in seaweed and scum, all floppy and grey and blue and swollen. As much as I want the truth, I can't bear it. I'll never be ready.

Tay crawls across the floor of the boathouse to me. His eyes look glazed in the dim light. Suddenly he launches himself on top of me.

"I've got him," he says, grabbing my hair.

"You're hurting me!" I cry. I put my hands on Tay's to try to ease him off me, but he grips tighter, his eyes still unfocused.

"You're scaring me, Tay. You need to let go."

"I've got you," he whimpers, his breath hot in my face. "Just hold on. I'm not letting go this time."

God – he's having some kind of out-of-body experience and thinks I'm Eddie. What if he kills me?

"Tay, it's me, it's Elsie," I say calmly. "Let me go and tell me what happened."

He slides an arm underneath my back and lifts me towards him, but then presses our bodies against the wall.

"Please, Tay. Stop. I can't breathe."

He turns and shouts to the corner of the boathouse.

"I've got him. Help me. No, not the police! They'll think we did it. They'll think we killed him."

"Tay, let me go."

Tay's arms go floppy, and I fall back on the floor. I lie still, breathing as lightly as I can, even though my lungs feel like peas and I can't get enough oxygen circulating. Tay stumbles around the boathouse, shouting incoherently, running into the walls as though he were blind.

"Danny, wait," he cries. "I found your bike."

The kayak is Tay's downfall. He trips and lies half on it, cowering and sobbing.

After a minute, I go to him.

"Tay, it's Elsie," I say, touching his shoulder lightly. His T-shirt is drenched in sweat but he feels cold. I expect him to grab me again, but he looks up and asks if he hurt me.

"I'm okay," I say, rubbing my arm where he held me so tightly.

"His eyes were just like yours. Sea green."

I let out a sob, and sit down next to Tay on the cold concrete floor, leaning back on the kayak.

"My dad was a cop. The police had my fingerprints from the moped incident, and I'd heard stories about people being in prison for things they hadn't done because the police had found their DNA. I know it sounds stupid, but I believed the stories. I was holding a dead body and my hands were covered in what I thought was his blood. I was terrified."

"He was bleeding?" I ask, feeling tears forming.

Tay wipes sweat from his forehead. "I thought it was blood. I only realized later it was oil from Danny's bike."

There is some comfort in the fact that he wasn't bleeding. But it's short-lived.

"I let him go," Tay says, his voice barely audible. "I don't think I meant to but he was heavy and my shoulder felt like it was going to pop out. After he'd slipped from my arms it was a relief. It was like the clock had just gone back."

"Tell me that's not true," I whisper. "Tell me you didn't let go."

"I wish I could turn back the clock again and this time bring him home to you."

My head throbs as my sinuses become more blocked. I take some deep breaths to help compose myself.

"What did Dillon do?" I ask. "Wasn't he helping you?"

"He was there, right behind me, but he was trembling too much, and the rocks made us unsteady on our feet. When Eddie slipped, he threw himself into the water, but it was too late. I think he hit his head. He staggered about a bit and I tried to help him, but he just ran off.

I can't believe what I'm hearing. So many thoughts are running through my head. Dillon. Tay. Eddie.

"Didn't you go after Dillon?"

"I wanted to, but Danny stopped me. He was standing in the long grass behind the beach, just watching us. He came back for his bike after all, and saw me with Eddie's body. He wouldn't let me go after Dillon – he made me go home."

"None of this makes sense! You, Danny and Dillon all saw Eddie in the water and none of you said anything. I've spent the last five years wondering where Eddie ended up, what happened to him, and you knew all along. You have destroyed my life, Tay. All three of you. Destroyed it."

Tay wraps his arms around himself and rocks back and forth. "You've got to believe how sorry I am."

"Why didn't you say anything?" I ask again, barely able to speak. "Even later, the next day, the next week."

"Danny made me promise."

"Why?"

"I don't know. He was older, I trusted him."

"You're lying, Tay. What aren't you telling me? Are you protecting him?"

"No, I swear."

I close my eyes and feel the room spin. I want to lie down and fade away but I force my eyes back open and keep going.

"Did you make a pact with Dillon, too?"

"No. I never saw him again. Not until a few months ago."

"Then why didn't he say anything?"

"I don't know. Danny was supposed to find Dillon and persuade him not to go to the police. He told me he'd sorted it – that he and Dillon had burned the T-shirt, that Dillon wasn't going to say anything. But he lied, Elsie. Danny never spoke to him, because he's a coward. I swear I didn't know that he'd hidden the T-shirt in the cave until a few days ago. When I told him about Dillon being in hospital, he went crazy – saying what had happened was our fault and he'd warned me all along not to get involved with you. That's when he told me where the T-shirt was. I didn't think you'd find it – I was trying to work out what to do."

I walk back to the top of the boathouse where the T-shirt is and Tay follows.

"How did you even end up with it?"

I hold Eddie's T-shirt up for Tay to see, like a criminal investigator on *CSI*, only this is real, and the evidence belongs to my twin brother. I feel hollow and heavy at the same time.

"It all happened so fast," he cries. "My hands were slippery. As I let him go, my finger somehow got caught, there must have been a tear, but I heard a rip, and the next thing I knew he was gone and I had his T-shirt in my hands."

It all comes flooding back. My father telling Eddie that

he couldn't wear the red one because it had a hole in it. The phone ringing, Eddie disappearing upstairs. Then we were in the car and Eddie was grinning, wearing his favourite red T-shirt with the lion logo on it.

My throat tightens.

"So when did you write the note to Dillon?"

"After the party on the Point. I knew straight away he was the boy from the beach, and then he said you were his sister. I felt sick. He came to meet me but didn't even give me a chance to talk. He asked me for the T-shirt and when I said I didn't have it, he smashed his fist straight into my nose, and told me to stay away from you. When I talked to Danny about it, he said if I stayed around, the truth would eventually come out and we'd all be in serious trouble."

I piece it all together. Dillon's bloody knuckles that I thought were the result of dehydration. Tay's bruised and bloody nose that he claimed had happened in his sleep, the argument between Tay and Danny, Tay disappearing. There were so many signs that I just didn't see.

"Maybe you just weren't looking," Danny had said the day I jumped off the harbour wall.

He was right. I did *see* the signs. I just didn't read them properly.

I think about that day at the party on the Point and how badly I'd wanted to kiss Tay. How embarrassed I felt when he ran off, how angry I was with Dillon for ruining our moment. And all that time, all three of them were hiding the most awful secret from me.

"You let him go," I say.

This is where Dillon's nightmares come from.

The boy I love was the one who let Eddie go. I can never forgive Tay. Never.

"Take your things," I whisper. "And don't come back."

"No, please," he begs. "I want to make it up to you. I love you."

"Go. Now."

Snot bubbles from Tay's nose as he forces his diving gear into a rucksack. He stumbles through the panel and I listen to his footsteps on the pebbles fade away. Every part of me feels broken. The only thing that's left is a tiny part of Eddie.

"Eddie," I whisper into the darkness. "Are you there?"

"Down here," Eddie says. But I can't see him anywhere.

Six

A MEMORY. A VERY OLD one. Eddie and me lying on the sofa together after one of his hospital visits. He has a bandage on his arm where they took blood.

"They put magic cream on it," he says, holding his arm out for me to kiss it.

I kiss it.

I'm jealous that I didn't have magic cream, or any blood taken.

Dillon lies on the floor by our feet.

"Do you want to watch a DVD?" he asks.

We say yes. Eddie wants *Ice Princess*.

"Mum," Dillon shouts, "the twins want to watch a DVD.

Can I put one on?"

Mum brings us hot chocolate and a blanket. She covers us.

"Yes. Then it's an early night for all of you."

Dillon joins us on the sofa and Eddie snuggles into me.

"Ellie, if they take more of my blood, will I die?"

"I don't think so. If they take more, you can have some of mine because we're the same."

"Ellie, if I die, will you come with me?"

"Okay. And Dillon. You'll come with us, won't you?"

"Okay," Dillon says. "Shhh, it's starting."

Seven

THE DAY AFTER TAY'S REVELATIONS, I decide to go ahead with my drop-off plan, and then leave the Black Isle for good. I have nothing to stay for. I wait until it's dark so there's less chance of me being seen.

Dillon's asleep when I go to say goodbye at the hospital. I tuck a note under his pillow saying *Sorry*, and leave my parents in the relatives' room, arguing about how often my mum stays at my father's flat.

There's no money for a taxi, so I have to take the bus back home. It's gone midnight when I finally get back to the harbour. My legs ache from all the running around, but at least I have Eddie's wooden memorial cross, which I've brought from the Point. Another ribbon has disappeared, but I remove a shoelace from one of my trainers and tie it on tight. I have everything I need, except my torch because the battery has gone. Instead, I found an old one in the kitchen drawer. I just hope it's okay in the water.

The Black Fin is closed but I want to take one last look at Mick and Danny. I peer through the window. My heart jumps.

My mother is sitting on a bar stool drinking a glass of wine.

My thoughts race. Is she looking for me? Does she know everything?

Then it all becomes clear.

She slides off the bar stool and walks to the end of the bar. Her curly hair is sprayed and set, and she's wearing my Ruby Red. Mick reaches out, she reaches out, and then they are in each other's arms. He bends his neck.

Uncle Mick. Affair. My father picking up a piece of clothing from the beach. Mum arriving without her jacket.

Mum *was* there that day. Before we called her, before Eddie went missing. Dillon knew, and so did my father.

I run down the steps, across the pebbles, along the jetty.

I loop the slimy rope around my arm as I unmoor *The Half Way*.

The motor starts first time.

* * *

The boat swings out in a sharp right when I move the throttle, pitching me to the floor. I scramble back up and adjust the tiller, keeping the boat steady until I'm clear out of the harbour. Then it's full speed ahead with the lights off. My destination awaits. I don't dare look back.

At the end of the Point I slow down so I can find the spot. I turn on the front headlights and see the buoy immediately, fluorescent in the lights, white foam spraying up around it. I sit for a moment, taking in my surroundings, soaking up the Black Isle horizon for the last time. There are streaky clouds high up in the indigo sky. Guillemots cluster around the top of the lighthouse, crying out for mates. In the distance an oil tanker chugs slowly out to the North Sea, into the darkness.

It takes me ages to tug on my wetsuit. The rubber feels tougher than usual, my hands clumsier, and I'm not able to grip it hard enough to pull the excess material up my thighs. The weight belt feels lighter than it should. I count the weights. There are three but I can't remember whether there should be four – my brain is foggy, but I'm sure I worked out that I needed seven kilos in total. I add an extra weight and fasten it around my waist.

The zip on the wetsuit jacket gets caught halfway up. I yank it but it's stuck fast. Everything feels wrong, lopsided, unbalanced. I shove Eddie's T-shirt into the jacket pocket, then loop the torch around my wrist and turn it on. It flickers then stabilizes. The light slices straight through the surface and makes the water underneath look green. It looks serene down there. Finally, I grab the wooden cross and Jasper the frog and tuck them into my weight belt, then lower myself into the water.

My body temperature instantly drops. I kick towards the buoy, aware that I'm using energy just to get to the starting point. I take three deep breaths, and on the fourth, I suck in as much air as I can hold, making sure it gets into every part of me, and then I go down.

The torch lights up all the tiny particles that you don't usually see; translucent blobs that could be plankton and all the disturbed sand from burrowing rays. The water swishes about my body as I guide myself down the wire head first – against Danny's advice, but it's the quickest way. The current tries to sweep me away. I keep going, feeling the water pass around me as I fall deeper and deeper.

I stop for a rest and to check the time, and my stomach lurches. I have forgotten to put my diving watch on. It doesn't matter. All I have to do is get to the bottom.

Something rumbles above and the wire shudders. Boat waves must have knocked it. My jacket billows out where water has seeped inside. Cold water swills around my middle, chilling my core. I slip further down, pointing the torch towards the bottom.

My chest starts to spasm. I can't have been underwater two minutes already.

The dust cloud is beneath me – all I have to do is get through it and Eddie will be waiting. As I descend, I reach for the T-shirt in my jacket pocket. The torch keeps getting in the way. I remove the loop from my wrist and tuck the torch into my weight belt so I can grasp the T-shirt. The red looks colourless down here.

My chest has stopped pulsing. Damn. I have let out some of my breath by mistake and now I need oxygen. I'll have to surface for air and try again. I'm not leaving the Black Isle without saying goodbye to Eddie. I summon the energy to frog kick back up…

As I push my legs down, there's a loud fizz and a pop. I'm back there, on that day.

"Where are the fins? Where's Mischief? Where's Sundance?" Eddie asks, still sitting in the water as the waves break around him.

"Come on. We need to get you dry."

"No. I want Dillon."

"Dillon's over there. He's probably with all the dolphins because he's not splashing about making a racket. Get up."

Eddie doesn't move. I reach down and take his hand. His hands are colder than mine.

"I want fins!" he shouts at me.

"Fine, go on. Go and find Dillon. That's where they are.

Go on, go and swim out to the dolphins."

"I don't want to go on my own."

"It's about time you started doing things on your own. I won't always be here to look after you."

I shove Eddie's hand away from me and turn around to look for Dad again. He's still not there. Eddie clambers to his feet, then throws himself into the water and starts to swim.

"Eddie, no!" I cry. I wade after him and grab his arm. "Eddie! Come back!"

Something knocks me off my feet. My head goes under, just for a second, as a wave washes over us, and when I pull myself up Eddie is gone.

"Eddie," I gasp. I look down my arm to my hand because I can't feel anything. Eddie's hand isn't there. In its place, a thick, slimy piece of kelp has wrapped itself around my wrist.

Finally, the last gap in my memory. It was my fault all along. It doesn't matter where Mum and Dad were, or Dillon. It doesn't matter that Tay could have pulled his body out of the water. It doesn't matter, because I'm the one who sent him into the sea.

I make my decision. I'm not going back up.

My body fights my decision.

Go up, you need air. You can escape, go up north, start a new life.

Not so fast, stay down, you have nothing to go back for.

I let go of the wire and kick towards Eddie. I remember Jasper the frog tucked into my weight belt and pull him free. I look down just as the torch slips away. I watch the beam tumble into the murkiness and fade. This is it. This is my time.

Sorry it took me so long to find you, Eddie.

The light comes back at me, blinding me. The angelfish are not in the sky, they're here… Then everything goes dark.

Part Five

CELIA: *Which fish go to heaven when they die?*

EDDIE: *Angelfish! But I don't **believe** in angels.*

CELIA: *Angelfish are not angels. They are more beautiful and they are brighter than anything in the sky.*

EDDIE: *Brighter than the **brightest** star?*

CELIA: *Brighter than all the brightest stars put together. You'll never get lost if you follow an **angelfish**.*

One

RAIN FALLS ON MY FACE in sharp splinters, stinging my cheeks. I sit up. Danny has tied *The Half Way* to the side of another fishing boat and we are moving slowly back to the harbour. The mist clings to the rocks around Chanonry Point and even in the purple night I can see the swell of the ocean rolling back out from the shore.

"You followed me." My voice is groggy and muffled.

"You stole a boat."

I feel like I'm weighed down with sandbags. I reach down to unbuckle the weight belt but it's not there. Neither is Eddie's cross. My wetsuit has been rolled down to my waist and I'm wearing the hoody I had on earlier.

"The ribbons!" I shout. "Where are they? You've got to stop the boat, I need to get them."

I scramble towards the outboard motor and reach for the cord, but a firm hand on my shoulder pulls me back.

"Joey!"

He drags me between his legs and wraps his arms around me. I wrestle out of his grip and grab his collar.

"You've ruined everything!"

"You could have died!"

"I wanted to die," I sob.

Joey shakes me. "No!"

I punch him in the arm until I run out of energy.

I turn away and hang my head over the rudder. A white frothy line snakes away from the back of the boat, like a giant foam ribbon.

Two

AT THE HARBOUR, MICK AND Rex are waiting with Mick's car.

"She should go to hospital," Joey says. "She was out of it."

"I'm fine," I say, taking a towel from Rex and wrapping it around my shoulders.

"She's fine," Danny says. "I'll drive her home."

No one moves for a while. Eventually I get in the back of the car because I need to sit down. When Mick climbs into the passenger seat, I lean forward and whisper to him.

"I saw you with my mum."

Mick gulps. "She...I... We were just talking. She thought you were at the hospital – she's gone to find you. She left

347

right before Danny discovered the boat was gone."

Danny gets in the driver's seat and I lean back again. I shouldn't be here; I shouldn't even be alive.

As we pull up to the front of my house, the gate swings open and my dad runs to the car and yanks me out.

"Where have you been?"

There's desperation in his voice. He shakes me and runs his eyes all over me, taking in my wet hair, my exhaustion. Before I can respond, Mick opens the passenger door and tells my father to let go of me.

I watch my father's face morph from anger into the beginnings of rage.

"You!" he bellows at Mick. He moves his face so close to Mick's that I think he's going to nut him. "How dare you come to my house after everything you've done?"

Mick steps back and holds his hands out to my father the way you would to an angry, barking dog.

"Trust me, the last thing I wanted to do was come here, but your daughter nearly drowned and I wanted to make sure there was someone here to look after her."

"You mean you hoped that my wife would be here. You sick, sick man."

"Dad, don't…"

My father ignores me and carries on shouting at Mick. Danny is still in the car, hands fixed on the steering wheel like he might just drive away.

"Please, Colin. This isn't about Celia. That's been over for a long time. This is about Elsie and what's best for her."

"I don't need you to tell me what's best for my daughter. You have no idea about my family."

"Oh, really? So, I have no idea that Elsie spends most of her days down at The Black Fin because she can't bear to be at home?"

"Let's go inside, Dad," I say, trying to drag him through the gate before Mick can divulge any more of my secrets.

"You go," he replies. "I'll be in."

But I don't move.

"It's not enough that you tried to steal my wife – now you want my daughter too?"

"You are a poor excuse for a father, and a poor excuse for a man! God knows why Celia chose you."

"Don't talk to him like that!" I scream at Mick. "Don't you get that my family is only this messed up because of you? If you hadn't been at the Point with my mum that day, Eddie might still be here. And if Danny hadn't trashed his bike then things might have been different – Tay wouldn't have gone and I would have found out what happened to Eddie back then. This is your fault. And his fault."

I point to Danny and he looks at me through the car window, his face all shadowy through the glass. He shakes his head as if to warn me not to say anything else, but it's too late. Mick bangs on the car door and asks him to get out.

"What is this about, Danny? I thought your bike was stolen that day? I thought Tay stole your bike."

So many lies have been told.

"Tell them, Danny," I say. "You might as well tell the truth now because I'm going straight to the police."

"I'm done talking about it," Danny says.

"How can you be done talking when you've never said a single word?"

"I do talk about it. I talk to myself about it every single day. Don't you think I wish I'd never followed my dad to the Point that day? That I hadn't wrecked my bike?"

"Danny, what do you mean?" Mick says. "Tay's dad found your bike in his garage. When did you follow me?"

Danny crumples, and then lets it all out.

"Tay didn't steal my bike," Danny says. "I smashed it up after I followed you to the Point and saw you with that woman. I blackmailed Tay, I told him that he had to take the blame for stealing it or I'd tell everyone what he did."

"Who's Tay?" my dad asks. "What's this got to do with anything?"

"What did Tay do?" Mick asks, his face pale, his jaw quivering.

Danny splutters. "Tay didn't do anything," he says. "He was trying to help."

"You got Tay sent away!" I yell. Mick holds me back from launching into Danny. "I knew he was protecting you.

350

We could have found out what happened if it wasn't for you and your lies. You're scum and I hope you rot in hell."

My father explodes. "Will someone please tell me what happened?"

He stands completely still with his hand over his mouth while Danny talks. When Danny gets to the bit about Dillon running off alone, my dad's whole body shudders.

"Why didn't you tell anyone what actually happened?" Mick asks.

"Because I was a stupid kid," he says. "I didn't want you to know that I'd followed you. I thought you'd stop me coming to stay if you found out. Because I felt guilty about breaking my new bike when I knew it was expensive. Because I didn't want to believe any of it. The little boy. You and that woman."

That woman. My mother. A gust of wind blows over us and I long to get inside and dry. I want to lie down and never get up. In the distance, there's a siren. We all hear it.

"Don't call the police, Elsie. They were just kids," Mick says.

But I already know that I'm not going to. Tay and Danny are not to blame. I'm the reason Eddie died. Blood rushes to my head and I stagger into my dad as I faint.

Three

IT'S DARK OUTSIDE WHEN I wake up. A lamp glows in the corner of the room and the clock on the TV tells me it's eleven p.m. I have no idea what day it is or how long it's been since I went to find Eddie. I'm lying on the sofa covered with my own duvet and with my head propped up awkwardly on about four of the sofa cushions. My mouth is dry and my throat is on fire. When I breathe, it hurts. I can't feel my legs. I reach down to check my legs are there. They're cold to touch.

"Hello?" I cry hoarsely.

My father enters the living room wearing his brown woollen jumper. I get a waft of his smoky smell.

"Hey, kid," he says softly and it makes me want to cry. "How are you feeling?"

He walks over and perches on the sofa arm above my head. He doesn't touch me but this is the closest we've been in a long, long time.

"Cold," I say. "Have you spoken to Mum?"

"She knows I'm here with you. I haven't told her what happened yet. She's been very worried."

I wait for him to start yelling but he continues to whisper.

"Your brother is in a bad way."

"I know." I turn my head to the back of the sofa. The fibres smell musty.

"Want some dinner? I made pasta."

The thought of food in my mouth makes me heave. I cough and sound like an old man.

My father reaches out and touches my forehead.

"You're hot," he says.

"I feel cold."

"I'll get you another blanket," he says but he doesn't move. "That boy came by. He wanted to see if you were okay."

My stomach leaps. Tay. The boy who lied to me. The boy who left my brother in the water. I feel myself blush as I remember our naked bodies in the boathouse. I hate him for still being able to make me long for him.

"What did you say?"

"I thanked him for saving your life last night."

He means Danny. The one who ruined all of my plans. The one who hid Eddie's T-shirt for five years inside a damp, mouldy cave.

"I didn't want to be saved," I say quietly.

My father snaps. "That's enough, Elsie. Have you any idea what it was like for me to have that man turn up on my doorstep with his son and tell me that they'd just saved you from drowning? What were you even doing in the water in the middle of the night?"

"I was trying to find Eddie."

"Damn it, Elsie. Don't you think it's enough that we've already lost Eddie?"

"I just wanted to see where he went!"

"He's not down there! He's not anywhere." My father leans on the window sill and presses his head into the glass. "He's gone."

"If he's gone, then so am I."

"No. You're here."

"Am I? Really? I didn't think anyone had noticed."

My father leaves the room. I wonder if I really meant what I said about not wanting to be saved. The plan was to escape, to run away and never be found. But I only made my decision not to come back up while I was down there. The depth may have messed with my mind.

*   *   *

When I wake up again, I'm in my own bed. I search for Jasper and remember that he's gone. The phone rings and I hear the deep rumble of my father's voice. If I had the energy, I would drag myself to the phone in the hall and listen. Pain sears all the way down my throat when I swallow.

My father knocks on my door and waits. I don't move. Eventually he peers in.

"Can I come in?"

He has changed and had a shower.

He comes in and places a cup of tea by my bed and rubs his face. He tells me I've been out of it for three days, that a doctor came by and gave me antibiotics for a lung infection.

"Was that Mum on the phone? Is Dillon okay?"

My father looks tortured.

"They've sectioned him."

"So they're making him eat?"

My father rubs his face again. "I don't know what they're doing to him. They've locked him up. They've locked up my boy."

I pause to take this in. Dillon, sectioned. Because of what happened that day.

"Can we see him?"

"Yes, come on, get dressed." He opens my wardrobe. "This?" He holds out a navy blue jumper. I take it and slip it over my head. It used to be tight and now it hangs off me. I must be really sick.

"Do you still wish it was me who died instead of Eddie?"

My father freezes and slowly moves closer to me.

"What? Of course not. Why on earth do you think that?" He holds my head in both hands, so I can't move.

"But I heard you. The day after he went missing, in the bedroom, you said, 'Why did it have to be him?'"

Dad looks puzzled, and then sobs into my hair. "No, sweetheart. I wasn't talking about Eddie."

"Who then?"

But I realize I already know.

"Mick? You saw them together, didn't you? On the Point that day."

My father's eyes widen.

"I've worked it all out," I say. "You saw her with someone, and you went after her but she drove off. And then you found her coat on the beach when you were looking for Eddie."

He nods, gravely. "Mick was your mum's boyfriend before I came along. She dumped him for me, but then somewhere along the line I think she realized her mistake. Something happened again between them when you and Eddie were about nine or ten – she nearly left me but I begged her to stay. She promised she'd never see him again. I guess she could never keep that promise, and I punished her for it. I should have let her go."

"I'm sorry, Dad," I say.

"Don't be sorry. I walked away from you kids. And I have to live with that." His face looks as though it's melting. I want to catch it and stop it falling away. We are united in our guilt.

It was never me he hated, it was himself.

Four

I'M ALLOWED TO SEE DILLON for a few minutes on my own first, at his request. He's propped up in bed doing a crossword puzzle. There are no tubes attached to him. No vanilla. He's still scrawny as a rake, though.

He sits upright when he sees me and thrusts his arms out.

"I hear you went for a swim," he says, hugging me tight. I feel like we connect and for the first time since my "swim" I'm glad to be alive. All the anger I felt at him a few days ago has dissipated. Seeing him here, I already know that the secrets have ruined him too.

"Diving, actually," I tell him.

"Jesus, Elsie. I didn't know it could be so dangerous."

He shuffles up so I can sit next to him.

"Are you eating, Dilbil? No more tubes?"

"A bit. I'm on half portions. They said they'd keep me sectioned if I didn't eat. I don't want to be locked up."

His blue eyes seem too large for his face. I can't help but stare into them, like I'm still looking for answers.

"Are you okay, though?" he asks.

"Bit of an infection. I had a blackout and swallowed some water but I'm okay."

Dillon leans in suddenly and lowers his voice.

"Look, we've only got a few minutes before Mum and Dad come in for 'family' therapy. Did you find the T-shirt?"

I nod. I haven't got the energy to explain everything that's happened over the last few days.

"I found it. Danny had hidden it. God, you don't even know who Danny is, do you?"

He shakes his head.

"He's Tay's cousin. He was down on the Point that night too. He saw everything. Listen, Tay told me what happened. Everyone knows now, and it wasn't your fault."

Dillon starts to cry. I feel myself float up again and then I float down and take control.

"Why didn't you go and get help? Why didn't you tell anyone what happened?" I whisper. I still don't understand how three people could keep quiet for so long.

Dillon wipes tears from his eyes.

"For ages I thought I imagined the whole thing, or that it was a dream. Then I started to have really vivid nightmares and when I finally realized that it might have been real, I thought it was too late. I knew he was gone, and I didn't want Mum or Dad to know that I found him but didn't pull him out. I was so ashamed. I thought it would destroy our family. And my blood was on Eddie's T-shirt."

"What! Why?"

"I hit my head on a rock when I was looking for Eddie. Tay tried to help by pressing Eddie's T-shirt on it. It's a bit hazy – I think I might have had concussion."

I picture Tay trying to help Dillon. It doesn't fit with the image of Tay letting Eddie go back into the water, and the relief that he felt after.

I tell Dillon again that none of this was his fault.

"Why did you let me fall for Tay?" I say. "You knew all along."

"You falling for him had nothing to do with me. Even when I nearly broke his nose you still went back to him."

I nod, defeated.

"It doesn't matter," Dillon says, taking my hand. "The truth is out. Now we deal with it."

I don't yet tell him that Eddie would never have gone if it wasn't for me.

"I gave Eddie his T-shirt back," I say softly.

We hear footsteps coming down the corridor.

"Everything will be okay, Dil. Make me one promise?"

"What?"

"Just eat."

Dillon places a scrawny hand on his stomach and exhales loudly. "I'll try. And you promise me that you'll breathe."

"I'll try," I say.

Five

FAMILY THERAPY DOESN'T HAVE TO involve the whole family. It doesn't even have to involve Dillon. He has sessions with different people once a week. I have therapy with my parents. Sometimes with Dillon, sometimes without.

We talk about blame and secrets and we talk about truth. Sometimes my Laryngitis comes back and I say nothing at all and other times I scream or walk out. Eventually, everyone tells their story.

Everyone saw Mum and Mick together that day. Dad, Dillon, Tay, Danny.

Mum tells us over and over again that she only went to the Point the day Eddie drowned to end it with Mick.

I respond by telling her that I saw her in The Black Fin with Mick the day I went to find Eddie.

"I was so lonely," she says. "I was scared I was losing you all. I just went for some company."

"Did anything happen?" my dad asks.

"They kissed," I say.

"Just once," Mum says. "It was a goodbye kiss. He was so kind. He told me he'd been keeping an eye on you, Elsie. To make sure you stayed safe. I promise you nothing had been going on. It was just a couple of times before Eddie died, and nothing since. I swear."

I guess she doesn't know that Dad told me about when she nearly left him. But for some reason I believe her that she was ending it that day. I don't know what this means for her and Dad now. Maybe they'll work it out.

The person who's suffered the most is Dillon.

"I had to keep all your secrets!" he screams one day. "Mum's affair, Dad running off, Tay being on the beach, Elsie's diving."

"How did you feel about this, Dillon?" the therapist asks gently.

"Angry."

"With everyone?"

"No." Dillon sniffs. "I wasn't angry with Dad."

Dad hangs his head and Mum asks for another tissue, which she shreds on the beige carpet.

"Why weren't you angry with your father?"

"Because it wasn't his fault."

"No, Dil," Dad interrupts. "It *was* my fault. I was the one who should've been watching you all."

We're all silent for a bit. The therapist looks at his feet, and occasionally at me. I think he wants me to say something.

"I think I know why you're not angry at Dad."

"Yes, Elsie?" the therapist prompts.

I turn to Dillon. He looks afraid.

"I think it's because, that day, Dad was only doing what you were planning to do – running off to confront Mum."

"No! That's not true," Dillon shouts. "That's not why. I felt sorry for him. Mum was the one having the affair. She's the one who betrayed us all."

The therapist runs out of tissues.

Dillon tells me later, when no one is listening, that I'm right. He also says that he failed Eddie by not swimming back earlier, by not listening to my calls for help.

The sessions go on.

Six

BY SOME SMALL MIRACLE, I pass all my exams. A handful of Cs and two As – Biology and Technology. I keep quiet about my A in biology to Dillon. It was just as much a shock as his No Award. Dillon is allowed to do his retakes at the hospital, as long as he follows his care plan. When I return to school at the end of August it's the same as ever, but this year we must all work harder. This year is even more important than last year. This year, we must focus; we must drive ourselves forward and emerge as young men and women, not girls and boys. I might be sick. The school says I have to take on more subjects this year. I opt for photography and hope that the first project is about changing light.

Frankie is pleased to see me. We sit and have lunch together and he tells me how many crabs he caught over the summer. He doesn't get why I find that so funny. I tell him that I spent most of my summer at the hospital with Dillon, and that's why I couldn't see him.

"I came to your house to see you but your dad said you weren't up to visitors."

"I know. Sorry. Thanks for coming."

"Did you really try to kill yourself? That's what everyone said but I told them it wasn't true."

I hug him. He doesn't even smell that bad.

"It wasn't a suicide attempt," I say. "It was just a stupid thing to do."

That's what I tell myself. In truth, when I was down there I really thought I had nothing to come back for. That was the stupid part.

The rest of the kids are quiet around me. Lots of people ask after Dillon and ask if they can do anything to help. Even the teachers. Someone gives me a leaflet on coping with grief which I throw in the bin, but later retrieve. Inside the leaflet is another one – from the Dolphin and Seal Centre about adopting animals. I slip them both in my pocket – an idea forming.

Ailsa and some of her sidekicks still glare at me and make snide comments about Dillon, but there are no compasses and I make sure Ailsa's not around when I change for PE. She can't get to me any more.

When I finally head out of the gate on Friday after my long first week back, there is a familiar and uncertain face waiting for me. He's got a nerve.

"Can we talk?" Danny asks.

I have nothing to say to him. "No."

"Please. Just for a minute. Hear me out."

"You lied to me. You *manipulated* me and you blackmailed Tay."

When I say Tay's name, my chest closes in around my heart. As I turn away from him so he can't see the water forming in my eyes or the flush of heat in my face, my bag catches his arm.

"Yes, I lied." He tugs the strap of my bag and I jerk back into him, my elbow colliding with the top of his hip. "And I'm sorry."

Sorry. He's *sorry.*

"Just let me get on with my life," I say. I blink back a tear but another one immediately forms and trickles down my cheek.

"And I'll just get on with mine, shall I?" His voice is deep and foggy. He lets go of my bag and I stumble back.

"I don't know," I mouth. "I don't know what your life is." I want to get as far away from him as possible. I could run, right now. But I don't. Can't. He scrunches up his face in his hand and when he pulls his arm down, his face and neck are blotchy with stress marks.

"My life," he says, looking at my feet, "is waking up every day, wishing that I had jumped in the water that day and found your brother so you could've said goodbye."

A gasp escapes from my throat. I thought he was going to say he wished he'd stopped his dad and my mum from having an affair, or stopped Eddie from drowning. But then, as I process his words, I realize that preventing those things were never options. It was already too late. Danny looks up, and I finally see it, written all over his face. It wasn't pity I was seeing in his eyes, it was regret, guilt, fear, sadness. It's about time I open my eyes to what's really around me.

"I'm sorry too," I whisper.

Danny stands up straight and I have to tilt my head back to see his face.

"I should have tried harder to keep you and Tay apart. I knew you'd get hurt and I let it happen."

We're apart now and I hurt more than ever, but there's no point saying this.

"Did he go back to Dornie to live with his mum?" I ask.

"Aye. He's not in great shape either."

I want to ask what he means but the words are stuck in my throat. Instead I ask about Mick.

"My dad's gone to St Lucia for a dive season. He's running some instructor classes out there."

"Will he be back?" I ask.

"He'd better be. I'm not running this dive school on my own for ever. I guess it's good for him to get away."

I nod. I think my mum wishes she could speak to him. I miss him too.

"We're going to check out that wreck off Lossiemouth next week," Danny says. "Do you want to come?"

I haven't been in the water since my "suicide" dive.

"I'm not sure I'd be up to it," I stammer. "I can't go that deep."

"You don't have to go that deep. Sure, the bottom is at forty-three metres, but it's a big boat. In my opinion, it's better to look at these things from slightly further away, anyway."

Maybe he's right. Or maybe that's the easy way.

"I didn't even say thanks for saving my life."

Danny frowns. "I didn't really."

"Was it Joey then? Either way, you were both there."

"You mostly saved yourself. We just pulled you out of the water and took you home. It's good that you ditched the weights, but they're expensive. You owe me."

Danny grins while I try desperately to remember ditching the weights. I remember that one half of me was fighting to stay alive, and the other was giving up – saying goodbye – but I don't remember ditching the weights. Perhaps there was a third half of me.

"So, think about Lossiemouth. The water down there is out of this world."

"I will," I say, suddenly longing to be back in the water – to feel the open space around me, to feel the power in my legs and the pressure in my lungs as I kick for the surface.

I think about all the people who travelled on that doomed boat – where they went, what they looked like. How they felt when it was sinking. Where they are now.

Seven

THE WORST FAMILY THERAPY SESSION is the one when I finally tell everyone that I told Eddie to swim. By the end of that session I'm in the room alone. Mum stays longer than everyone else but eventually she goes off to find Dillon. I wonder if our relationship is permanently damaged.

I talk about this in my own individual therapy sessions. I've talked so much recently that I think my voice might wear out. My personal therapist, who is called Dr Jones, and who looks a lot like Mr Jones my technology teacher, tells me that these things take time. He is also the only one to tell me that the rip tide might have taken us both if I hadn't let go.

"In the past you had a difficult relationship with your father because you felt he let you down."

"Yes."

"And now perhaps, with new truths that you've learned, you feel your mother has let you down."

I nod. But I am not ready to agree out loud. I like Dr Jones. He talks a bit and then he lets me make my own mind up.

"Do you think we'll ever be a normal family?" I ask.

"What do you think normal means?" he replies.

I don't answer because I don't know. For us, normal is keeping secrets, and feeling guilty about Eddie. I think this is the first time that any of us ever thought about each other.

Eight

ON NEW YEAR'S DAY, I take the sailing boat I made from the top shelf of my wardrobe. It's covered in a soft layer of dust. With a duster, I carefully wipe down the decking. The model of me has faded and come slightly unstuck. Dad finds some glue and presses it back down.

"I think that's probably it, Dad."

"I think it probably is." He gives the model a wiggle to make sure. It's nice having him back in the house again, even if he's only visiting.

Dillon writes big swirly letters in blue ink on the side. *Eddie*. He does a couple of loops on the final "e" and also adds the outline of a dolphin. It looks brilliant.

The four of us stand around the boat. Anyone looking in through our kitchen window might think we're performing some kind of strange ritual. In a way we are.

"Right, now for the finale!" Dillon says, springing forward. He's been waiting for this.

The motor slips over the bow easily and makes a whirring sound when Dillon presses the remote control. He giggles to himself, pleased that it works.

Mum and Dillon don't come on the boat that Dad's hired – from Danny. Dillon says he'd rather swim out. Mum is too scared, and won't let Dillon swim, so they stay on the shore together.

"Someone needs to be on the shore," she explains. "Just in case anything happens and we need to get the coastguard."

She says it like she's joking but deep down I know she's still afraid.

Instead of leaving from the harbour, Dad trails the boat down to the Point, and we set off from the beach where Eddie went missing.

Dillon hands me the remote and tells me not to drop it.

And then it's just me and Dad and the water. Dad rows us all the way out to the buoy. He huffs and puffs with every pull – he must be getting old – and I sit there thinking that I could do it without even breathing. In the ten minutes it takes us to get there I only breathe in twice. I can do over four minutes easily now.

We sit back for a moment and look to shore. I can just about make out Mum's blue coat. I can't understand why she still wears it. Perhaps she's not ready to let go yet. She and Dillon stand side by side. The lighthouse looks small from out here, with its black turret like a tiny rain cloud hovering above Chanonry Point. I take the small red stone from my coat pocket and place it on the model boat, on top of the bed of fresh pine needles Mum collected.

"What's that?" my dad asks, pointing to the stone.

"It's jasper quartz," I tell him. "It's very rare."

I kiss the boat and then I place it on the water. It wobbles and then steadies itself.

Dillon said the range was about two hundred metres, so I keep my finger on the button until we can no longer see it.

The clouds roll in and the rain makes tiny wet dots on my jacket. Dad pulls out a packet of cigarettes.

"What are you doing?" I ask, a strange air of authority in my voice.

He looks at me sheepishly as he puts one in his mouth. "Don't tell Mum," he says.

When he's finished smoking, he lets me row back.

* * *

Later, I take Tay's sixth letter from under my pillow. I haven't replied to any of his letters yet. I've tried, but every time I start with a blank piece of paper it just ends up covered in doodles of ocean waves and ripples, and storms. My whole body aches when I think about him. It's an ache that's so deep inside me, I wonder if it will ever work its way out. I open the envelope.

There's one more thing I have to tell you...here goes.

I read the letter over and over again until my eyes are so blurred that the words just quiver before me. When I fold it up again, it has my tears inside and I slip the damp piece of paper back under the pillow along with all the others.

I wipe my face and wander into Dillon's room. He closes his biochemistry book.

"Happy New Year, Els."

His beautiful blond hair has grown long again.

I show him the picture of the dolphin I've just adopted.

"Meet Mischief," I say. The picture shows Mischief jumping high out of the water, the light reflecting from his shiny skin, and a backdrop of the North Sea. "I used my Christmas money."

"That's very cool, Els. Eddie would have loved that."

I rub my finger across Mischief's nose, and hear Eddie laughing somewhere in the distance. I can't believe I didn't think of this years ago.

"I'm spending the day with Dad tomorrow. Do you want to join us?" He looks hopeful.

"I'll come," I say. "But only if we can go into town and get burritos."

"It's a deal," he says and goes back to his book. He looks nervous, and out of the corner of my eye I see him push his stomach in. If he eats half of one, I'll be happy.

Outside the sky is completely black. It's a new moon. The only colour out there is the silver handle of our back gate. And then I know what I have to do.

Nine

THE HANDLE IS COLD IN my palm. I twist it and step out into the cemetery. It's not as eerie as I imagined it would be. Even in the dark I can make out the flowers surrounding the headstones. The frosty grass crunches beneath my feet. The air is still and so quiet I wonder if I've gone deaf. Leaning against Eddie's headstone with my diving torch around my head, I write my letter.

Tay,
In response to your first five letters: I'm applying to Inverness College to study marine biology, photography and maybe sports fitness for my Advanced Highers.

I'll be starting in August as long as I get through S5 without messing up. I've also signed up to do my AIDA level 1 course at the dive centre there. Obviously, I could go straight to level 4 but they wouldn't let me without having the certificates. I'll soon show them! My parents weren't very happy about it but they couldn't really stop me. My dad said he'd go to the Bahamas to watch me compete in the world championships! I hope that happens one day. I'm glad you've finally got your instructor exam booked. Good luck, and let me know how it goes.

In response to your sixth letter: thank you. Thank you for finally being honest with me. Here's the thing. Deep down, I think I always knew, I just couldn't admit it to myself. I was in my own safe bubble and I didn't want to see the things that were right in front of me. I was too busy seeing things that I didn't want to see, but my subconscious must have been driving me to find the truth. An accidental detective. Or something. Ha!

I think about you all the time. I miss you, but I'm glad you're not here. I hate you and yet imagine your arms around me. I smile when I remember us in the water but cry when I think about you and Eddie. The crying is a recent thing – before I'd just fill up with rage, so I guess it's progress. I wake up every day feeling horrible about those few moments before Eddie disappeared. But you

379

were at least brave – you tried to bring Eddie out of the water and look after Dillon. I suppose what I'm trying to say is, despite the awful truth and the black ache that rolls around my chest when I think about us, I forgive you.

I'm coming to Loch Duich in the spring for the West Coast Big Dive! Will you be there? I haven't told my mum yet but I will. She's doing okay. I don't think my dad will be coming home anytime soon, but things are better between us. Dillon's okay too. He gets weekend leave now and he should be able to come home for good next month – but I think he's got a long road ahead. He still hides food sometimes and does stomach crunches when he thinks no one is looking, but I think he is trying. And as for me? I'm just Elsie.

Elsie Main (The Black Isle's deepest girl)

I haven't got any pockets so I slip the letter inside my bra, and stretch out on the ground so that Eddie's headstone is behind me. I glance over at the house and see a silhouette in Dillon's bedroom window. My brother waves from the window and I wave back.

Despite the frost, I feel warm. I empty the air from my lungs, from every cavity in my body, and look up at the angelfish in the sky.

Dear El,

I'm not expecting you to reply to any of my letters. Although I hope you will one day.

Once again, I'm sorry I didn't tell you the truth, and even sorrier that you found out the way you did. There's one more thing I have to tell you...here goes.

Danny never told me who you were. I'm sorry I let you think that. And it wasn't the day of that party that I realized either. The moment I met you I knew you were cool. You were my kind of girl – hiding out in the (my!) boathouse eating sweets and smoking cigarettes, but there was something familiar about you. Something that disturbed me a bit. I told myself that I was imagining it, but then you jumped off the harbour wall, and when I dragged you in, it hit me. I knew you were that boy's twin sister. It was like I was reliving that horrible moment again, five years on. It felt like a punishment, but one that I deserved. I despised myself when I was with you, but I couldn't stay away. I saw your loneliness and how alive you became in the water. I'd failed you once and, selfishly, I wanted to put that right. No one wanted me around – not my dad, not Danny. Mick was too busy to give me lessons. But, you were there and you didn't seem to mind that I was socially awkward, or that I'd done lots of things I wasn't proud of. When I came back and ran into you at that bar, I realized something. I wasn't saving you from yourself or fixing my mistakes – it was the other way around. I needed you to keep me from loneliness. I should have told you everything then – I wanted to, but I knew it would be the end of us and I wasn't ready to let go.

I don't expect you to ever forgive me but you should know that I love you and I never meant to cause you this much pain. Please forgive Dillon. He needs you.

T x

PS Let me leave you with a few interesting facts about the River Tay. You probably already know this, but the River Tay is the longest river in Scotland. It flows east, did you know that?

Acknowledgements

I OWE HUGE AMOUNTS OF GRATITUDE to the following folks for being utterly awesome:

Becky Walker, my wonderful, committed editor at Usborne – for totally getting it, for your amazing insight, and for being a voice of calm in response to my panicked emails; Anne Finnis, Sarah Stewart and Rebecca Hill (it's wonderful to have so many editors) – for your ideas, wisdom and editorial rigour; Connie Gabbert in the US – for creating the beautiful cover design and Sarah Cronin for coming up with the incredible inside design; Elizabeth Bewley at HMH in the US – for your detailed revision notes, brilliant suggestions, and for being a champion of Elsie from day one; Hellie Ogden, agent extraordinaire – for seeking me out, for your unrelenting enthusiasm, for making me do endless revisions and for finding this book a home – simply put, you've changed my life.

Thanks also to: the Janklow & Nesbit crew on both sides of the Atlantic, in particular Kirsty Gordon in the UK, and Stefanie Lieberman for finding this book a home in the US; my fellow Birkbeckers who read and encouraged during the first draft – your comments about it being a bit morbid were noted, honestly; my Birkbeck tutor, Julia Bell – for noticing the story's potential and giving me the confidence to write it; the apneists – for your world records and breathtaking YouTube videos; all friends and family whose special occasions I missed because I was in writing lockdown – thank you for understanding; my mum – for being my best book friend and for hoarding so many books; my dad – for allowing her to hoard and secretly enjoying it. Thanks to both of you for everything (not just the book stuff). And finally, Peter – for being my number one reader, encourager and supporter, and for never doubting. I couldn't have written this book without you.

Discussion Questions

* *"The thing I hate most about my father is that he hates me. And he has good reason to. It's something we don't talk about."* The first line of the book is quite shocking. Consider Elsie and her father's relationship throughout the book. How does it change?

* The author has included a quotation from e e cummings's "maggie and milly and molly and may" at the beginning:
  "For whatever we lose (like a you or a me), It's always ourselves we find in the sea."

What do you think this means? How is this reflected in the book?

* *"He shouldn't have. He should have learned not to listen to me, and then I wouldn't have to feel so guilty."*
  The narrative continually returns to the ideas of guilt and blame. Discuss the way in which this focus affects the characters' actions in the book.

* *"To me, he's not gone. My twin lives inside my head and is part of me."* At the beginning, Elsie seems to act as if Eddie is still there, and is a part of her. Why do you think she's acting in this way? Do you think Elsie really believes that Eddie isn't gone?

* The author's use of flashbacks means that the narration jumps in and out of chronology. How did this affect your overall reading experience?

* Elsie's flashbacks also rely on us trusting her memory. Did you trust all of these flashbacks? Why do you think Elsie had buried those memories?

* Consider the title based on your reading of the novel. Do you think it reflects the story?

* *"Sometimes it feels as though we're on the edge of the world."* How has the setting of the Black Isle shaped the narrative?

* Do you think Elsie believes she killed her brother? Why do you think it's so important for her to get down to the drop-off?

* Look back at the depiction of girl-on-girl violence in the novel. Did it surprise you? Why do you think Aisla is driven to these lengths to torment Elsie?

* *"The boathouse is my home, not McKellen Drive with my crazy family."* Using this quotation as a starting point, discuss why you think Elsie feels more at home at the boathouse than she does at McKellen Drive.

* Elsie finds herself increasingly drawn to Danny as they

work together on her diving. But she thinks he pities her, not fancies her. How did you read this situation? How does the first person narration affect the way in which certain situations are revealed to you?

* How much did you know about freediving before you read this book? Did the story change your perception of it?

About the Author

Sarah Alexander works as an editor and lives in London with her husband and two chickens. *The Art of Not Breathing* is her first novel.

 @SarahRAlexander

Q&A with Sarah Alexander

What inspired you to write The Art of Not Breathing?

I wanted to write about the aftermath of a tragedy, more specifically the long term effects – how time isn't always a healer and how a tragedy affects the people involved in different ways. Grief and the way we cope has always fascinated me, and I wanted to explore the fragile relationship between the dark days and those glimpses of light and hope.

What got you into writing?

I didn't talk at all during my first year of school – I had things to say, I just couldn't bring myself to say them. Writing became my way of communicating. When I was seven, I had an operation, and while I was recovering I wrote a story about "someone else's" experiences. My teacher made me read it to the class, and a fellow classmate awarded me ten house points for my efforts. It was the first time I felt proud of something I'd created, and that was the turning point. After that, I just couldn't stop!

Were there any scenes in The Art of Not Breathing *you found particularly difficult to write?*

Emotionally, the hardest scene to write was Tay's confession in the boathouse. He has a violent flashback and physically hurts Elsie. It felt horrible to write because Elsie wouldn't normally stand for this – she'd fight back – but Tay was out of control, leaving her very vulnerable. But, it was an important scene that showed how Eddie's death had affected another person. Elsie feels betrayed, frightened, but also worried about Tay. Those are hard emotions to understand all at once – she is completely overwhelmed by them.

Which books inspired you growing up?

All of them. I think it helped that Sarah was a really popular name in eighties children's literature. I felt like all the books were written for me! I was a huge fan of adventure stories. *The Magic Faraway Tree* was my favourite book – and I still look at trees and wonder if there might be a secret land at the top. Judy Blume was hugely influential, in life as well as writing – something I only realized recently when re-reading some of my favourites last year.

What drew you to the Scottish setting?

Scotland was a huge part of my childhood – I spent many holidays there with family being whipped by the icy wind and rain, as I searched for pebbles on the beach, or sprinted across the Forth Road Bridge. Despite the weather, we had a good time. Even through the fog, it's a beautiful place. It's also a tribute to my grandfather. Among the interrogations about whether I was "courting", he provided some interesting perspectives on life and death – mostly, he told me not to worry about stuff.

With the character of Dillon, you explore the issue of eating disorders from a male perspective. Can you tell us a bit about why you chose this point of view?

An eating disorder is a truly devastating illness that affects both genders. I had little idea of the complexity and severity of these disorders until I worked in an adolescent psychiatric hospital as a support worker. There I saw, first-hand, the extreme battles that patients and their families go through on a daily basis, not just with food, but with all aspects of their lives, including family relationships, friendships and the pressure to do well at school. The hospital supported males and females, but the number of male patients was incredibly low. A misperception that eating disorders only affect women means that it's difficult for men to get appropriate treatment and support. Thankfully, this misperception is changing, but we still have a way to go when it comes to mental health and gender stereotypes. I hope that writing about it will contribute to the growing awareness.

Your descriptions of the ocean, and of the feeling of being underwater are exquisite, Sarah. Do you have any personal experience of freediving?

Oh, I just love the water! In my past life I was definitely a mermaid, or a manta ray. But it hasn't always been that way – after a swimming pool incident I spent most of my childhood and teen years being afraid to put my head under. But my curiosity about what "lies beneath" won in the end. I'm more of a scuba diver than a freediver (because I like breathing) but I have dabbled in freediving – mostly in warmer waters, though! I spent time working for a diving school where the ocean was my office. I've always been intrigued by the conflicting emotions of going into the sea – fear and euphoria. There's something quite magical about the underwater world. Time slows down, sounds are far away, and there are beautiful things to watch. It's the best kind of mindfulness.

Important note on freediving:

Freediving is a discipline – and one which
requires years of training and supervised practice.
The characters in this book are amateurs, even if they
don't think they are. They don't always follow the
safety rules, and some of the things they do are
exceptional. Freediving should never be done alone,
and requires certification through a professional
organisation such as AIDA.

And for more thought-provoking Usborne YA reads, news and competitions, head to usborneyashelfies.tumblr.com

For PJER

First published in the UK in 2016 by Usborne Publishing Ltd., Usborne House, 83-85 Saffron Hill, London EC1N 8RT, England. www.usborne.com

Text © Sarah Alexander, 2016

Photo of Sarah Alexander © Melissa Valente

Front cover design © Connie Gabbert

Hawaii, Oahu, Waimea Bay, Girl jumping into water © Carles Soler / Getty Images

Bubbles © PlanctonVideo / Thinkstock

Hand-lettering on back cover by Patrick Knowles © Usborne Publishing

Extract from "maggie and milly and molly and may". Copyright © 1956, 1984, 1991 by the Trustees for the E. E. Cummings Trust, from COMPLETE POEMS: 1904-1962 by E. E. Cummings, edited by George J. Firmage. Used by permission of Liveright Publishing Corporation.

A CIP catalogue record for this book is available from the British Library.

ISBN 9781474903066 03901/04 JFMAMJ ASOND/16

Printed in the UK.